THE GHOST

AN ASSASSIN'S STORY

A.E. SAWAN

WILDBLUE
PRESS

WildBluePress.com

The Ghost: An Assassin's Story published by:
WILDBLUE PRESS
P.O. Box 102440
Denver, Colorado 80250

WILDBLUE PRESS is registered at the U.S. Patent and Trademark Offices.

ISBN 978-1-947290-79-2 Trade Paperback
ISBN 978-1-947290-78-5 eBook

Interior Formatting/Book Cover Design by Elijah Toten
www.totencreative.com

AUTHOR'S NOTE

The Ghost is fiction, not a memoir, but my characters are based on composites of real people, and the major events described in these pages are historically accurate. I should know, because I lived them.

A.E. SAWAN

PROLOGUE

I've become the kind of man I hate. Without knowing why, perhaps just the scent of death that surrounds me, women pull their young ones closer to them when I walk by. Nobody sits beside me on a crowded bus, or asks to share my table in a busy food court. In fact, I am the kind of man people would spit on behind his back. Out of fear. Out of loathing. They don't actually do it, but I feel and sense it. And I understand.

I do the dirty work, the kind that people would rather ignore and pretend it has nothing to do with them and their lives. Yet they hope that somebody is out there to do it for them, to keep them safe from the wolves so they can go back to their TVs and ready-cooked dinners, and take their kids on vacations. I do what most governments are not willing to do, worried about the polls, or the blood-soaked trails leading back to them.

You see, I kill bad people. I am a freelancer, an independent assassin. I did not choose to be a killer. It just happened. But I don't work for any government or agency. I pick my targets and only take on the assignment after careful consideration.

I am selective. I don't kill rapists, serial killers, gangsters, or politicians, even if they deserve it. I don't even murder lawyers. Maybe I should kill a few, but I don't. I only kill terrorists, and I never play politics. If you are thinking that is too small of a niche market, and that business is slow, you will be wrong.

Who am I? That is a good question.

My given name is Paul. I was born in a small town in the Bekaa Valley of Lebanon. The son of a mechanic, a real mechanic, unlike me. But that is about all I can tell you. And it was many years ago, a different life than the one that was thrust upon me when I was just ten.

Now I go by many names. Whatever suits my purpose at the moment. But those I hunt call me by an Arabic name *Al Shabah*. The ghost.

PART ONE

1

PAUL—LIFE DEFINED

1975 Bekaa Valley, Lebanon

I learned at a very early age that all of us have one defining moment in our lives, a moment when all things change and will never be the same again. But when it happens, only a few of us recognize it for what it is.

My childhood hometown on the outskirts of Zahle was quiet and generally harmonious. Christian boys and Muslim boys played together on the same soccer team, and Christian parents and Muslim parents stood shoulder-to-shoulder, cheering us on. We came together for volleyball in the courtyard of a small school between the church and the mosque, and we were in the same Boy Scouts of Lebanon troop. Everybody knew each other.

I was the third of five children. When I was two, my second oldest sister died from a mysterious illness. I don't remember her. I adored my other two sisters. My older sister, Zeina, was very beautiful and took care of me every day at home and at school. We were both sent to a private French school; it was a long way off, and I enjoyed the bus rides. My younger sister, Leila was also beautiful. She was always the thinker of the family. My younger brother is Jean; we called him Hanna. He and I were very different. I was fire and he was ice.

I was the sparkplug in the neighborhood, the instigator of most trouble and the mastermind of dubious plans. The other kids' parents hated me, and the kids loved me. Back then nobody knew about ADHD; I was simply diagnosed as a "bad boy." By age ten, I was so famous for getting into mischief that I was called the *El Shaytan Alahmar,* The Red Devil by both kids and grownups—*alahmar* for the color of my hair and *shaytan* you can figure out for yourself.

When I was seven years old, I was sent to a private monastery school deep in the Chouf Mountains, in the small town of Deir el-Qamar (the Convent of the Moon). How ironic. On the first day of school, when my parents were helping me with my suitcase, I noticed most of the women on our street standing in our driveway, watching. I was touched and told my mother, "Look, see, they are coming to say goodbye and good luck! You always said they didn't like me." My parents exchanged their secret look. You know the look that long-married couples have, right? After we were on our way, my mom said, "I don't want to hurt your feelings, but they were there to make sure you were leaving." After a moment of silence, the three of us burst out laughing.

I also had freckles, which weren't very common in the Middle East. The other kids tried to tease me, without any success; I thought it was cool to be different,: olive skin with dark brown or black eyes was the norm, but my eyes are naturally light brown. I did not know back then my light complexion would serve me well later. As a child I was often mistaken for an Italian or a Spaniard, though as an adult I often pass for French, Greek, or Portuguese.

My adult life would be different. As different as the calm blue waters of the Mediterranean Sea at night and a tsunami in the Pacific. But I had a normal idyllic childhood full of laughter, mostly harmless adventures, fun and love. Then, on an otherwise pleasant if breezy day in 1975, my defining moment arrived, and my life turned upside down with the sound of gunfire and the metallic smell of blood.

If I close my eyes and think back, I can still hear the sweet voice of my big sister, Zeina, calling for me. I could tell she was worried. The neighborhood, usually bustling with activity, was deserted because almost everyone had gone to a family wedding on the other side of Zahle, and she was supposed to be keeping an eye on me.

I was up on the roof of our uncle's house with my BB gun, keeping birds away from the unripe grapes that dangled from a trellis over the rooftop gardens like ornaments on a Christmas tree lying on its side. Thanks to my older cousin Joseph's coaching, I could hit the cap of a pop bottle at a distance of thirty feet every time.

"Paul? Where are you? Paul!"

At first I didn't answer her. I was concentrating. My rifle was loaded with wheat kernels, not real BBs. Wheat kernels were free, and we had a fifty-kilo bag of it in the *mouneh*, that's the storage room. I saved the real BBs for when I was really hunting. I aimed at a vine on which a small black and yellow finch was perched. I took a deep breath and exhaled slowly, the way Joseph taught me, and I squeezed the trigger. I wasn't really aiming at the bird, just the vine it was sitting on. The bird and his friends scattered, squawking in protest.

My sister called again. Zeina knew where I was, but for me staying quiet for this long was unusual. I yelled, "I'm up here!" just to ease her mind.

She was playing hopscotch on the concrete patio in front of the house. Our home was right next door, separated from this one by a narrow alley. Holding my gun by the barrel, I scrambled to the edge of the roof and peered over.

Zeina was staring up at me with her hands on her

hips and a grownup look on her face. She was four years older than me but acted like she was my mother. I winked at her and waved, before pulling back from the edge. I took up my position again, lying full-length on the roof, guarding the grapes. I could hear the soles of her shoes hitting the concrete in a hopscotch rhythm: hop, hop, pause, hop, turn, hop...

The bravest birds were already coming back to the grapes. Sand blown by the *khamsin,* the hot southeasterly wind that blew in every spring from Egypt, was getting in my eyes. I reloaded my BB gun and brought it back up to my shoulder, but the wind set the leaves to rustling so fiercely that the birds took off on their own.

From the minaret less than 200 meters to the east, the Mouazzin started his call to the midday prayer. I looked up at the sun overhead.

Allahu akbar!

Though my family was Christian, I could recite the Muslim call to prayer by heart. I'd heard the call five times a day all my life. I liked the melody and the Mouazzin's high-pitched voice. I started to sing along.

Ash-hadu an-lā ilāha illā allāh!...

No sooner had the last echoes of the Mouazzin's voice died away than I heard a man laughing not too far away. On my belly, still holding on to my BB gun, I scooted back to the edge of the roof.

Two young men were walking down the long driveway toward the house. I knew them both: they were brothers, and they lived in the same town. Ghassan, the short and stocky one on the left, was the elder of the two. The younger, Bassam, was taller; he was handsome, with a perfect smile and hazel eyes so light they seemed almost yellow. Although Muslim, they were friends of my older cousins and had been regular visitors to the house until this past winter, when they had been recruited into one of the many Palestinian Liberation Organization, or PLO, camps that were springing up all over the Bekaa Valley. I hadn't seen either of them since.

I had passed near some of the camps several times while tearing around the area on my bike, and I had heard the adults talking about the Palestine Liberation Organization.

To me it was all a meaningless stew of names and leaders: Fatah, Saika, Popular Front, Black September, and many more. But those PLO jeeps and pickups did look cool as they roared around town raising clouds of dust, and the Muslim teenagers, clinging for dear life to whatever they could while holding onto their Russian-made Dotchkas and the American 12.7 mm machine guns, looked powerful and daring.

The two young men had stopped halfway down the driveway. They were gazing at the front of the house. Yellow-eyed Bassam grinned and jutted his chin forward, as to say, "Let's go!" Ghassan hesitated then quickly caught up. Zeina, trim in her tight red shorts and white top, was watching them too. With both hands she pulled her long brown hair back from her face and let it fall down her back. Did I say that my sister Zeina was very beautiful? She was.

Ghassan whispered to Bassam. Bassam smiled and nodded. Ghassan crossed over to the narrow alley between the two houses. He was blocking Zeina's way in case she tried to run home. My heart was racing; I could hear it thumping in my ears. I remembered how, whenever Bassam came to hang out with my older cousins, he would come on to Zeina, making suggestive remarks about her eyes, her hair, her shapely figure. She would leave the room and sometimes even the house to get away from him.

As Bassam drew closer, Zeina backed up till she was flat against the wall and couldn't move. Bassam walked slowly up to her and put his hands against the wall on either side of her face; she tried to push him away, but he didn't budge. He said something that I couldn't hear then bent his head close to hers, trying to kiss her. Over in the alley Ghassan was doubled over laughing.

I raised the BB gun to my shoulder and aimed it at Zeina's face, which was inches from Bassam's. I had to compensate for the wind, which was blowing as hard as ever, but I knew I wouldn't miss. If only I had real BBs with me. I took a deep breath, focused my mind, and squeezed the trigger.

Bassam howled in pain and surprise and began jumping around in circles and swearing, one hand pressed to his neck. It was comical to watch, but I didn't laugh. I was already reloading.

Ghassan was still laughing. Probably he hadn't heard the first shot and just thought that Zeina had bitten his brother in the neck. Then the second shot hit him in the cheek right under his right eye.

I slung the gun over my shoulder, jumped on one of the round steel poles supporting the trellis, and slid down like a fireman. I'd done it many times before, but this time I landed wrong and my ankle twisted. There I was, right between Zeina and Bassam, with pain shooting up my leg and my ankle trying to collapse under me. "Run! Run!" I yelled. Zeina ran, heading toward the house of some neighbors who hadn't gone to the wedding.

However, I was in big, big trouble. Ghassan was coming from one side, Bassam from the other, his yellow eyes flashing like a wildcat's. He grinned then grabbed me by the neck and squeezed hard. As I started to choke, Bassam's smile got bigger and bigger. I clawed at his hands, but he was much bigger than me and stronger; I couldn't move them. I thought I was going to die.

Then Bassam smacked me backhand across the face and dropped me on the concrete patio. I was barely conscious, but I can remember that I landed on the number nine square of the hopscotch board.

Bassam rummaged in my pockets for BBs, but of course didn't find any. Dimly I saw the butt of my gun coming down toward my face and hitting me hard on the nose. I heard the bone crack and felt blood flowing down both sides of my face. Now Ghassan had the gun. He lifted it as high as he could, like he was chopping wood with an axe, and smashed it down on my forehead.

My left eye wouldn't open and I thought I was blind. I could feel the hot sticky blood flowing over my face.

The next thing I knew, I was hanging upside-down. I remember thinking, *like the grapes hanging from the trellis,* then my head was scraping along the concrete as they dragged me over to the round garden pond. I felt cool water as they dunked me into the pond headfirst. I involuntarily took a breath and swallowed a lungful of water. I tasted blood and panicked. I was drowning. I tried to cough up the water but could not; when I tried to swallow it, I just inhaled more water. Darkness enveloped me. It was okay. I had saved my sister.

Then from what seemed like very far away I heard shouting. Bassam hissed in my ear, "I am coming back to kill you, *Shaytan Alahmar*—RED DEVIL. You are already dead." He dropped me, and I fell full-length into the little pond.

I could hear Zeina screaming. "They've hurt Paul! You have to help my brother!" Then strong hands lifted me from the water.

Later I learned that two of my rescuers had given chase, but Bassam and Ghassan got away, jumping over the fence behind the house and running toward the PLO camp.

The incident was the start of the defining moment on which my life would change, but it was only a taste of what was to come. The full meal would be served two days later.

On that day, I was riding my bike in the driverway, my face bandaged with a swollen nose, two black eyes and sporting a dozen stiches on my forehead. I had the only bike on the block, a blue Velamos model that was the envy of every kid on the street. But I was bored because I was not allowed to leave the property as my mother wanted to keep an eye on me. I was anxiously waiting for 5 p.m. when the two local television stations would start broadcasting. It was a Sunday, Tarzan, king of the jungle, started at 5 p.m. followed by six million dollar man Steve Austin at 6 p.m. Usually, all the neighbrhood kids came over, and we sat on the carpet while my mom made us popcorn, the old-fashioned way. Microwaves did not exist. We had one of two TV sets on the street, a black-and-white that took almost five minutes to warm up the old bulbs. It was built into a credenza with two sliding doors that my mom would lock when time was up, or when I was bad. I always tried hard to be good on Sundays.

My mother was hanging our laundry in front of the house. I remember she was wearing one of her flowery dresses—it was yellow and light blue—she always wore light colors to maximize the contrast with her dark skin and hair. But after this day, she would only wear black.

It was sunny outside, as it always was in Lebanon during spring and summer. The breeze ruffled the hanging clothes and quickened the drying process. Just another peaceful, pleasant Sunday in the Bekaa Valley.

Then I noticed a white, dust-covered Peugeot sedan driving back and forth on our street. On the second pass, I recognized the driver. It was Ghassan with a bandage under his right eye. Another teen I didn't recognize was sitting in the front passenger seat, and Bassam was sitting in the back.

At the same time, my attention was drawn to three university students walking on the dusty shoulder of the road in front of our driveway. These boys were also local, three cousins from my neighborhood, and I knew them all very well. They waved to us and we waved back. My mother stopped pinning clothes on the line and asked one of them, "Elias, where is your mother? I did not see her this morning at church."

"I don't know," he answered as he and his cousins continued to walk.

The two groups of teenagers—those walking and those in the car—no doubt had known each other since early childhood. There was no difference between them, except that the teens in the car were Muslims and those on foot were Christians. At the time, that difference—Christian, Muslim—meant next to nothing to me. But little did I know it meant everything to some. It was the reason some of them would kill, the reason some would die.

The car made a last pass, and then made a sharp U-turn. Ghassan had a twisted grin on his face. Dust flew and the tires left rubber marks on the old asphalt as he accelerated down the street. As the car came alongside the three teens on the road, it slowed. That's when Bassam and the other teen stuck their Kalashnikovs out the windows.

The AK-47s roared, unleashing sixty rounds from their combined magazines in seconds. It was the loudest sound I had ever heard in my life, besides the Israeli jets flying over our house as they broke the sound barrier.

I don't know how they missed me: I was still at the end of my driveway holding onto my bike. The three boys went down in a heap of tangled body parts mere feet from me. I was frozen in place. Their blood ran into the street, but it was the only part of them that moved.

I looked up as the car slid past me and saw Bassam staring back with a menacing grin. I averted my eyes, hands and knees shaking. He had promised to kill me. I hoped he wouldn't shoot me now.

Then the car stopped and I saw the white reverse lights come on as Ghassan backed up until it was five meters from me. Bassam gave me his patented perfect smile and aimed his AK47 right at my face. I did not move a muscle or flinch, but not from bravery, I was frozen by fear. I saw one of his yellow eyes behind the rifle's cross hairs as he sighted on me; smoke was still coming out of the barrel. His finger was on the trigger: he pulled.

However, nothing happened. No bullet sped toward me. My life did not end. He had emptied his magazine and apparently had no more bullets.

I know Ghassan was shouting, I could see his lips moving. But my ears were still ringing from the sound of the guns just moments before, and I couldn't make out the words. He stepped on the gas, and the car took off down the road. I could see Bassan still looking back at me as the car rounded a corner and disappeared.

My mother ran to the fallen teenagers. She knelt down on her hands and knees as if in prayer, trying desperately to help them. In shock, she scooped brains from the dusty road and stuffed them back into the skull cavity of one of the teens, trying to save him by rewinding the clock.

That image of my mother is etched in my memory along with those other moments that changed my life forever. By the time I reached twenty years old, I had seen more body bags than most people in the civilized world have seen garbage bags.

BASSAM--

PLO Camp

The Peugeot 504 sped through the opening gates of the terrorist camp at breakneck speed. Then Ghassan did his favorite manoeuvre: he put all his weight on the gas pedal, cranked the steering wheel, hard, then yanked the hand brake, which caused the car to spin 180 degrees before coming to a full stop.

The vehicle disappeared from view for a few moments, engulfed in dust. The debris took almost a full minute to settle. Then the three teenagers emerged from the car with their rifles held high, as if they'd just accomplished some great feat of daring. After all, they had just slain three infidels.

Others in the camp acknowledged their deed. Applause, shouts of "*Allahu akbar, Al-maout li-Israeel,* Death to Israel," and backslaps accompanied them as they strutted to the camp headquarters office to report. The teenagers deflated a bit when they were told to wait outside. The council was meeting, and they would have to postpone the accolades they were sure would be forthcoming from Abou Al Ghadab.

The camp belonged to the Saika, a Syrian-backed group of Palestinians who did the dirty work a sovereign nation like Syria would not do in the open. Two of the boys had no problem with waiting, not too anxious to meet the scary and fearless-looking leader. But Bassam, the maverick, did not like waiting for anybody. He hated taking orders even more.

Inside, the big, dark-bearded revolutionary called Abu Al-Ghadab (this was, of course, his *nom de guerre*; they were all Abu something—it meant "father of") was meeting with his inner group. They had given the order to kill earlier and now they wanted to assess the situation and the reaction of the town.

Most important, over the next few days they had to capitalise on the results and not let the town get organised.

These men prized the long, dark-bearded look that frightened women and children. But they were warrior wannabes, mostly Palestinian Liberation Organization veterans who had never fired a shot against their real enemy, Israel. King Hussein had kicked them out of Jordan because they attempted to take over his kingdom. Motivated by the disaster of the Black September in Jordan, the PLO moved its resistance movement to Lebanon.

Since its independence in 1943, Lebanon has been governed by a confessional political system in which parliamentary seats and governmental and civil service positions are distributed among religious sects in accordance with their population ratio. The rise of Arab nationalism exacerbated the sectarian tensions in Lebanon. Sunni Muslims were supportive of the anti-Western policies of Egyptian president Gamal Abdel Nasser, while the Christians adamantly refused to allow Lebanon to join the pro-Nasser camp. Lebanon was on the brink of civil war in 1958 when the Christians' president asked for help from the United States. The landing of the U.S. Marines in Beirut quelled the violence that same year.

You see, in 1948 the ethnic structure of Lebanon was transformed with an influx of nearly 120,000 Palestinians taking refuge from the Arab-Israel War. A second large influx of mostly Muslims Palestinian refugees entered Lebanon after the 1967 Arab-Israeli war. At the time the Lebanese civil war broke out in 1975, there were nearly 500,000 Palestinian refugees in Lebanon. This unbalance in the demographics, encouraged the Muslims to seek more power.

Syria has never recognized Lebanon as an independent nation: this was the time for Hafez El Assad and the Syrian regime to take advantage of the fragmented political scene of Lebanon, it gave them the excuse they needed to finally annex Lebanon to Syria and declare the Greater Syria. The PLO also had supporters in Lebanon that were sympathetic to the Palestinian cause. Financed, equipped and supported by Syria the PLO started recruiting and training Muslim men to start a civil religious war.

"*Shoo, ya shabab*," said Abu al-Ghadab. "What are we going to do to escalate this little episode into a massacre and take control of the town?"

"Don't you mean control of the Christians?" asked Abu Khaled. A Lebanese man in his forties, he had joined the PLO because it was better than unemployment or jail, his only other options.

"No, I mean everyone who is against us. We will scare the Muslim population into silence, to force them to look the other way while we recruit their sons. The Christians, on the other hand—we will drive them to Mount Lebanon, for a start, and then into the sea if they won't leave for Europe or Canada."

"We should send the Muslim teenagers from the town out again tonight or tomorrow night, after we see the reaction," Abu Khaled suggested. "Maybe get them to kill a few more."

"Oh, yes, I agree," replied Abu al-Ghadab. "We wait until tomorrow to see what we should do. Maybe we will send them to kill more people inside their homes. This will teach them that not only are the streets unsafe, so are their little locked houses. They don't call me Abu al-Ghadab because I am gentle. I am the father of anger and I will prove it soon."

Now Abu Seif, the third member of the council, spoke up. "This way the town's people will think it's the beginning of a religious conflict," he said. "Not the PLO against the Lebanese." Abu Seif was responsible for propaganda.

The decision was made: over the next few days and weeks, they would select a few soft targets, escalate the violence, and slowly enlarge their theater of operations into the surrounding towns.

Abu al-Ghadab looked at his recruiting officer, Abu Khaled. "I want you to concentrate," he said, "on young, single Muslim men without much education. They make the best soldiers. They do not ask questions. They will be the next graduating class of our terrorist university. Now bring in the guys waiting outside, and pay special attention to the crazy one with the yellow eyes."

The three young men came in and sat down in the office. The leaders praised their courage. Each boy got a few hundred liras as a bonus and a small ball of hashish; this black hash, proudly made in Lebanon, was known as the finest. They were informed that single-handedly they had terrorized a whole town full of the wimpy infidels. Those tiny Christian men sometimes wore pink shirts, shaved their faces smooth, played volleyball wearing tight shorts in the central court near the church, and even socialized with different girls, not their sisters or mothers.

"Can you imagine how scared they are? A few more attacks and we would cleanse this whole area and have total control," said Bassam.

"Bassam," said Abu al-Ghadab, "don't do anything stupid. Wait for my orders. We are coordinating this with our comrades in the four corners of this country. Stay put and I will let you know what to do."

But Bassam had other plans.

2

A NIGHT TO REMEMBER

PAUL:

Our street was a collection of small houses, if you can call a lane that's only one car wide a street. It was named for a type of tree that is no longer there—I tried unsuccessfully to find it many times. The houses were lined up on both the north and the south side of the road. They were of the exact same design, designed by the same man, my father's uncle. The property was subdivided for members of the family, and all the residents were related. The kids were my cousins or second cousins, and the next cluster of homes south of us belonged to more distant relatives.

On the night the PLO leaders decided to serve us a cold dish of terror, the day after the drive by shooting, they sent the local Muslim boys out to parade their weapons and uniforms around the Christian neighborhoods. I was looking at them with conflicting emotions, jealousy mixed with a larger dose of fear. They looked cool and super macho. Just like a regular army, in the same dark green uniforms and black high-top boots. Until yesterday, the day of the drive-by shooting, I had never seen an AK-47, which we later called Kalash (short for Kalashnikov). They also had some Slavias, the AK-47's Czechoslovakian cousin, and one of them had an RPG B7 (a grenade launcher) on his shoulder; most had more ammunition magazines and hand grenades on their belts. I was standing on the couch in order to see over the windowsill. My mother yelled at me to get down. She was still in shock and terrified from the events of the previous day. I ignored her. A single thought was going through my mind: *How can I take possession of the weapons and shoot these bastards down?* I was ten years old, a skinny kid. There were at least twenty men and older teens on parade. The odds were pretty bad even for a suicidal person.

And right in the middle of the pack was Yellow Eyes. I ducked under the windowsill to avoid making eye contact with him. At that moment, I vowed either I would kill him or he would kill me.

Till death do us part.

After the parade was over and the fighters went back to their base, the residents gathered at our home to discuss defense strategy. My father was a smart and well-respected man. He had worked overseas and had invented many machines for the local winery. He owned a few tractors and trucks and the most modern machine shop in the whole area. The townspeople decided they should buy a few weapons themselves and guard the neighborhood from the rooftops. I was excited, thinking I might get to handle a machine gun and do my part. This, of course, never happened.

Meanwhile, the professional killers of the PLO and the new recruits were casing a soft target for the night. Not a hundred meters from our street lived a family of five. The two girls were fourteen and ten, and the boy was twelve. The fourteen-year-old was blonde with green eyes. This was not totally unusual, since Lebanon had been occupied by many peoples over thousands of years, including the Greeks, the Crusaders, and the Turks; until 1943, it was under the French Mandate for Syria and Lebanon. Blonde kids with blue or green eyes were not that rare. In this case, however, being pretty was a curse, not an advantage.

I woke up the next morning to screams and the wailing of women. People were running down the streets and in and out of the neighboring house. I got the impression the whole town was there. My mother told my older sister to make sure my younger sister, younger brother, and I stayed inside the house.

I snuck into the chaos behind one of my older cousins, when no one was paying attention. I still wish I had stayed home that morning.

In the middle of the family room lay four mangled bodies. They had not been shot. Their throats had been slashed. The man's hands were tied behind his back, while the wife and the twelve-year-old boy and the ten-year-old girl were on top of each other like a pile of dirty laundry. They looked as if they were playing Twister, but they were not. The house was small, so I could easily see through the open door to the next room, where a blood-stained blanket was covering another body. Before I saw any more, my cousin Joseph took me by the hand and led me back home.

I protested to save face, but deep down I was relieved. I later learned an unknown number of attackers had taken turns raping the pretty fourteen-year-old blonde girl before they cut her throat. This poor family was directly related to two of the young men who had been shot on the street.

The police didn't come, there was no investigation; everybody knew who had done it and nobody could do anything about it. The next day, they held a funeral where the men smoked cigarettes under the large tree outside the church and the women wailed and cried themselves into a frenzy.

I hated funerals—not that anybody really loved them, besides funeral home owners. But in Lebanon at that time, we did not have funeral homes. The corpse would be arranged in a bed, in his or her home, and if the home was not large enough for visitors, then the body would be moved to the church hall.

People came to this funeral from all over the Bekaa Valley, so the wake was held at the church.

I listened to the men and talked to my cousins and friends. Nobody was making sense. They were planning a counter-attack, knowing full well they would never go through with it. They lacked training, funds, weapons, and, most of all, courage. These were peaceful, hardworking blue-collar workers—no match for the well-funded and well-trained PLO fighters.

I was sitting on top of the church fence watching the few Muslim residents who showed up to pay their respects and offer condolences. We knew these people: they were friends and clients of my father. I had visited their homes and eaten at their tables; I had even slept over during the holy month of Ramadan fasting ritual. It was fun waking up at dawn to have a breakfast that was equal to a feast. How could the sons of these people do this? The PLO leadership wanted to ignite a religious civil war, and they were succeeding. We assumed the boys from the parade had committed this horrible act.

How could I be feeling alone when I was surrounded by a few hundred people? I did not share my thoughts with anybody. How could I? I wanted to track down and kill the murderers, but I was ten-years-old and I was scared. The killers were not far away, nor did they hide. They were parked in a white Peugeot a couple of hundred meters from the church, watching us. Again I looked the other way, fearing the young man with the magnetic yellow eyes. I was scared of him. I felt that if I looked into his eyes for too long, I would be sucked into a bottomless abyss.

I decided to pray to defeat Yellow Eyes, knowing I needed to get bigger, stronger, and much smarter to make that prayer come true. I also had to get rid of my fear and become courageous. I did not know anything about mastering fear and living with it, controlling it. I needed to learn how to accept that fear, and understand that it was good and could keep me alive—and that courage did not mean being reckless and stupid. I needed to fight to live, not to die. All this I learned much later.

BASSAM:

The good looking Jihadist, the one named Bassam, and his older brother Ghassan and their cousin Mohamed, had no idea what the PLO council leaders had planned. They felt something scary was in the works, something to drive the wimpy Christians quickly out of town. However, the PLO did not trust the youths with the details.

Bassam wished they had picked the house of the little Red Devil as a target. The boy, named Paul had shot Bassam with a BB gun in the neck; luckily for Bassam, it was not loaded with a lead pellet. The girl always gave him looks of disdain, and Bassam hated the sight of the *Shaytan Alahmar* and obsessed about the sister.

"One day I am going to kill that creepy bastard. I should have saved a few bullets for him when I shot the stuck-up cousins on the road," he said to his brother.

The jihadist had a crush on the pretty sister. She wore tight shorts when she played volleyball. And it drove him crazy. Most girls loved hanging out with him due to his good looks and unusual hazel eyes—until they found out he was Muslim. Bassam saw the sister showing off her long, bare legs and knew her for a tease and that she was asking for it. He would whistle or try to talk to her, but she acted like he doesn't exist. The more she ignored him, the more obsessed with her he became. He wished his parents weren't such good friends with the family.

He wished he was in charge; their house would be shot to hell. He hated taking orders from anyone, including the PLO leaders. This was his town and he knew it better than the PLO imports. He knew that these assholes did not trust him and his gang. He kept saying to his brother over and over, "The day will come soon when I set up my own group and run it with rules based on no mercy for the infidels, the way I choose. I hear those wannabees speaking of a start-up Terrorist University. I will be the one that makes it happen. If they want to be true warriors, let them attack Israel. I asked and they would not let me kill the Red Devil, rape his sister, and burn his house. What kind of terror is that?"

3

FOUR BEDS IN THE COURTYARD

PAUL:

Each family usually bought a hundred or more kilos of wheat during the summer; they ground it into flour to make their own bread, for the whole year. Most people did not have pre-made pita, like you would think. Pita was a luxury we bought only if my mother was sick or busy and we ran out of homemade bread. Yeah, I know you might think all Lebs eat pita and hummus daily, but this is a stereotype.

Salim was our neighbor and a good friend. He was not directly related to us, but his mother and my grandmother were cousins; this is as distant a relation as you can get in our small town. He was a big man, a nice honest guy who owned the only gristmill, called a *tahouni*, in town. He had a monopoly and so thrived. To expand and modernize his business, he bought an empty lot on the south side of town, out of the way, and there he built a modern, bigger gristmill. This was a mostly Muslim area, but he had no enemies. Nobody back then paid any attention to the demographic and religious differences.

He had four sons. The youngest was Joseph, and we called him Zouzou, which is a common nickname for Joseph. We have many such nicknames that don't make any sense. "Like Nicolas is called Hajj, Jean is called Hanna and Elias is called Lallous or Lillo, and so on; you get my drift". The other three were older—all big, strong, honest, and friendly. They helped in the mill, including my friend Joe, whenever possible.

Joe and I were good buddies. We made and flew paper kites together and played with marbles; he rode my bike—remember, the only bike around. We ate together at either his house or mine, depending on whose mom had the better meal ready.

The PLO had their eye on the mill. It was on the outskirts of town, providing privacy and good storage. They could train new recruits outside, in the surrounding fields, and hide the weapons inside, protecting them from the weather and the Israeli jets. They started harassing Salim and his sons on a regular basis, thinking they could intimidate them into relocating and abandoning their only source of livelihood. I wish it had worked, but just like his kin in town, Salim thought he could defend his property and protect his assets. He bought a few 12-gauge hunting rifles and one pump-action shotgun. This would soon prove the biggest mistake of his life.

The details of what happened remain vague to this day. We know the PLO attacked, and Salim and three of his sons defended. One of the older boys was out of town. Ten-year-old Joe happened to be there, delivering dinner. They were all killed, and during the fight the mill was torched and burned to the ground.

Once the shooting stopped, the rumors started. We heard many things: Salim and his sons killed the attackers and drove some of them away, or nothing happened; it was just shooting practice.

Everybody was scared that night. This was the first brazen attack on property, and we felt like targets. My mother took us inside and locked the doors while my father and his ragtag army positioned themselves on the roofs, ready to defend their homes and families. It was the honorable thing to do, right? I thought they were courageous while I was a coward, hiding with my mom and sisters and younger brother in the living room. Not one of those guys on the roofs could shoot straight or had any experience in warfare. They were sitting ducks for the professional PLO fighters.

With good luck, not skill, we got to see morning again. I was itching to go and find out what exactly had happened. I snuck out the back door while my sister was busy, and headed to Joe's house. As I approached, I could hear the screams and the crying of women from inside the courtyard. The house was a typical old Arab home, designed like a big square with an open yard in the middle where women did the laundry and prepared the meals before taking them to the kitchen. There was no laundry to do on this day or food to prepare; the neighbors brought food and coffee, a Lebanese tradition when attending funerals.

This was not your typical funeral. It was a mass burial. In the center of the courtyard, surrounded by women, were four beds draped in white sheets. The bodies of Salim and his three sons were laid out and on display. The place was packed, and I was too short to see through the mourners. I had to make sure my mother would not spot me. She had made it clear to my sister I was not allowed out. I knew this home's layout like it was mine. I had spent years playing in the courtyard and on the roof. Joe and I had designed and made our paper kites from bamboo sticks, glued them with flour mixed with water, as they had no shortage of flour, and flew them from the roof. I headed to the back of the house and climbed up the heavy wooden ladder that had been there since before I was born.

From the roof, I sought an angle where I could see the center of the yard without being spotted. The men had erected a huge canvas to shield the mourners from the sun; however, I found a spot with a perfect view. I crouched down on my hands and knees to stay below the knee-high wall bordering the flat roof, and I peeked over. The scene was not nearly as scary as I was expecting, I had braced myself for a shock. Instead, it looked like a set in a play. Four beds were laid side by side, the four bodies were in black suits and white shirts. Salim was on the far right; his children were next to him from oldest to youngest. That put Joe on the extreme left of the courtyard and directly under my field of vision. This version of dead bodies looked nothing like the three young men on the street or the slain family I had seen just days before—maybe I was getting used to death. This group looked like they were sleeping peacefully. Of course, they had been cleaned and prepared.

To this day I have no idea how they did it. We had no funeral homes and no morticians. I guess maybe the old midwife that delivered half the town's children, including my brother, did this. I know she delivered my brother because I watched the whole thing from behind the window. My mother told me that due to anticipated complications I was the only one of the five children who was delivered by an actual doctor, joking that I was a troublemaker even before I was born.

I looked down at my friend, the smallest of the four. He was tiny to start with and the bed on which he was laid out looked almost empty. I had the impression he was smiling at me—I was hoping this was a sick joke and they would all just get up. No such luck. The more I looked him over, the more I saw small signs of wounds that were not perfectly hidden. He had a tiny fat lip, a couple of small abrasions on his face, I am assuming from when he fell, but I saw no other sign of injuries. Salim's only surviving son was beside his mother, holding her hand and trying to look strong and composed. He appeared to be in a trance.

The women were around her, helping her every time she fainted by putting rose water on her face. I stayed up on the roof for an hour, a long hour, thinking of what would happen to these two now that their lives had been destroyed. Would they be able to pick themselves up and rebuild some semblance of life? Would she ever manage to smile again? I doubted it.

Being an ADHD bad boy, I could not stay long in one place. I spotted some friends and climbed down to join them. Everybody had a theory and a completely different story. I listened and did not add anything. I did not know any details and I was sure none of my friends knew any either. I waited with them under the big old tree beside the church. Salim's house was right behind and closest to the church, so convenient.

In mid-afternoon, a group of the town's older Muslim residents arrived, and we perked up, thinking we might get to see a confrontation. Absolutely nothing happened. I felt a mix of disappointment and relief. The Muslim women outperformed their Christian friends in the crying art. My father and uncles embraced the men and sat down with them outside the courtyard, where they all drank coffee and tea. You could mostly tell, though without absolute certainty, that the Christians preferred coffee and the Muslims preferred tea. We kids resumed our vigil as we waited for the band to arrive.

It is called a mourning band—not like the black band you put around your arm, or a band that only plays in the morning. This is a professional funeral marching band, with a leader whose singing can draw tears from cold, hard stones. If any of the women have not already cried themselves to exhaustion, the arrival of the band will quickly take care of that. The drums and the beat always fascinated me, maybe because I was always marching to a much different drumbeat than the people around me.

The band came and unloaded its instruments a few hundred meters from the house. They started marching and playing that scary drum and trombone rhythm, a cross between a military march and a prayer tune. My friends and I followed at a respectful distance; after all, it was their show. The lead singer started his sad, high-pitched songs that made us cry; they stopped at the front of the house and continued playing their repertoire. My lower lip quivered, I felt a knot in my stomach, a pain in my throat; I kept trying to hide the tears running down my freckled cheeks, wiping them with my shirt sleeve until I had a wet spot from my elbow to my wrist. Macho is not an exclusively Latin trait: I am sure my ancestors took it with them to Andalusia. I did not want to show weakness. I was still naïve and thought that tough men didn't cry.

The time had come to bring in the four coffins and place the bodies inside them. This is when the family of the dead realises that this is the last time they will ever see their loved ones. Until that moment, they can look with love and sadness over the bodies and touch them. However, when the bodies are placed in the coffins and sealed, that is the point of no return. If wailing and crying were an Olympic sport, Lebanese women would win gold, silver, and bronze; they have it down pat. They started the high-pitched *zaraghit,* or "ululating"; they have one variety for weddings and a different set for funerals. When the *zaraghit* started, the men moved into the courtyard to place the bodies in the coffins and carry them into the church for the prayers. There were no limousines. Dead people were carried first to the church and after that to the cemetery on the shoulders of the men, all the men, whether they were bearers or not, since the distance was long and a constant rotation was needed. In this case, the church was next door and the four coffins were moved quickly into the center aisle.

Warde, meaning Rose, was the mother of three dead sons and one surviving one and the wife of Salim. She was helped into the church's front pew and was fussed over by a whole bunch of women, which almost made her faint. The service was quick; the tension in town was razor-sharp and the bodies needed to be put to rest before dark, when the PLO jeeps started roaming the streets like bats.

The Christian cemetery was located on the eastern side of town. To get there, we had to go through the Muslim neighborhood and pass beside what was the only mosque at that time; now there are five, maybe six. We followed the band and coffins toward the cemetery, passing under the mosque's minarets and between the houses. People were watching from the rooftops, and the thought was going through my head that if these people wanted to kill us, this was their best opportunity. All the Christians of the town, in one very narrow street, unarmed and so conveniently close to the cemetery. Nothing happened; in fact, they were throwing rice and rose water at the coffins, a sign of respect and shared sadness. Bassam and Ghassan's mother and father were there. We knew them and they knew us; they were helpless. As usual, the few extremists can silence the peaceful masses by terrifying them.

The bodies were laid inside the small room, like a mini mausoleum reserved for this family; each family had its own enclosure. The room's walls were designed like a western morgue, but without the drawer mechanism, instead containing twenty or so small openings with steel doors. The coffins were slid in, and the doors were sealed the next day by a mason.

This ritual happened fast, then we headed home on foot; a car took the immediate family back. And not far from the cemetery was the ever-present white Peugeot. My whole body tingled and my knees weakened at the sight of it.

I made my way home, confused, scared, and angry. In this sacred land where prophets walked on its soil and preached peace, God seemed to desert us. My anger was rising and I was absolutely helpless. Neighbors and friends were dying every day. I knew it in my heart that if we stayed at home, my own family would be touched by this evil. My uncle next door had seven children; one of them was a gorgeous girl in her teens, and the other six were big, scrappy boys, between the ages of seventeen and twenty-four. All prime targets. Even at my age, I knew this was not the time to fight. Now I had to survive and prepare better for another day. Voicing it out loud was another issue altogether. The macho mentality we were raised with prevented me.

BASSAM:

Bassam's new Jihadist gang was forming faster than he even had thought possible. Young men were recruiting their own brothers, cousins, and friends, and so on to join Bassam. He kept reinforcing the same message to them. "The Christians are like lambs to be slaughtered, a bunch of wimps. They are getting killed left, right, and center. They know who killed their families and friends, yet they walk quietly with their heads down, go to their churches, bury their dead while singing sad songs, come back to their little fucking homes and drink coffee."

Sitting in the car, watching the funeral, and not able to act made him resent the PLO even more. He fantasized about killing most of the Christians while they were bunched up together. One or two grenades would have done it. At the cemetery would have been ideal, no reason to move their miserable bodies, and the best part, it would have happened while his parents were watching. But those were the orders of the PLO.

If he only had some funding and training for his men, he could develop his own army of fearless warriors. The PLO bosses talked tough, but they followed the orders that came from Syria. This was not the way to win a war. He wanted to strike the enemy with so much terror that they keep running out of the country or into the sea, not just to the safe haven of the Christian mountain.

When he was younger, he used to like some of the Christians. His father took him to their homes on visits. They went before going to the mosque on Fridays and he played with the kids. The sheikh at their mosque had spoken about being the same as the Christians, saying, "They are our brothers, they need us and we need them. Together we can build a great country, just like our grandfathers and fathers before us. We existed with them for a thousand years, and we should build on that harmony and embrace it."

Bassam almost, almost believed him, but that was when he was young and stupid. Now he knew better. Thanks to a sheikh who he now revered, Bassam and the other young Muslim men in the area had their eyes opened to the fact that this was their land, and they should purify it of the infidels at all costs. According to the radical sheik, the prophet said, "Convert to Islam, pay the Jizya, or be killed." Bassam and his gang knew this to be the truth, a black or white truth. No room for compromise. These extreme beliefs felt right to Bassam, who planned on ruling over his land, and destroying those who would defy him.

4

MY LAST NIGHT AT HOME

PAUL:

The night after the mass funeral, the men went to the roofs with newly purchased weapons from a PLO black market dealer. They had four AK-47s and, their pride and joy, a .50 calibre machine gun. I was sure that if they fired it, they would hurt themselves. I begged my father to let me go to the roof with him. He laughed at me and told me to stay with the women to protect them. This I took with a grain of salt, but I saved face and stayed, the ten-year-old bodyguard—well, almost eleven.

Just after midnight, we heard a loud explosion. I thought the house was going to collapse on our heads. Somebody fired an RPG shot over the heads of the men guarding the rooftops, and it hit my uncle's house just behind us, opening a small hole in the concrete.

The house was targeted because it had a painted cedar tree on it, the logo of the *Kataeb,* the Phalange, the main Christian political party. My father's uncle had been the president of the town chapter, but he had died many years before. The logo had become part of the wall; nobody even noticed it. But the PLO did.

Luckily nobody was there. The house was empty because they were at our house, sleeping on foam mattresses in the middle of the living room. A stupid military tactic, right? Hiding your family and loved ones in the same house where you are making your stand? When you start drawing fire, the first house to be hit is the one where your family is hiding. Sun Tzu the Chinese military strategist was having nightmares and turning in his grave.

Our team of "commandos" fired back a few token shots in the general direction of the source; they probably missed the RPG shooter by a mile. We heard them shouting and felt them running on the cement roof, then calm descended—the calm was scarier than the noise, believe me. Nothing happened for the rest of the night. My nerves were raw from the waiting and the silence. I tried to go to sleep and I couldn't, images of my friend Joe kept invading my thoughts. However, first thing in the morning, my uncle and his wife packed up their kids and left. Their house was burned to the ground only days later.

The next night was the last time I saw our home for more than twenty years. I was zipping up and down the street on my bike, chatting with my friends about the explosion and checking out the damage. We had become instant military advisors: we were having a debate about the angle and the location of the shooter. Suddenly, my mother called and told me to get in the car.

I asked her, "Where are we going?"

"Just get off the bike and get in the car right now."

From her tone of voice, I knew better than to argue.

"Can I take my bike? I can put it in the trunk."

"No," she said. "I will be back with your father later this week, to collect some clothes and stuff, and I will bring your bike with me then. Leave it inside the house."

I got in the car with my parents, sisters, and brother, and we left. My mother packed pyjamas for each of us, took the stash of cash that she had in the house, and off we went. My parents, the optimists, thought this siege would end in a couple of weeks or so, and we would come back. I took one last look at our house and waved goodbye to my buddies. Some I never saw again for obvious reasons, others because they moved to other areas. I kept looking back and waving until first the friends and then the house disappeared from view. Then I turned around and looked forward. I was both anxious and excited. It felt like we were going on a road trip—a new adventure.

BASSAM:

The PLO plan worked. Many of the Christian families left almost immediately, and the Christian streets became deserted. The ones who stayed were scared and kept to themselves. They rarely ventured out and gave no resistance. Bassam, Ghassan, and the rest of the gang confiscated the empty houses and collected protection money. To identify the homes, they spray-painted the letter N in Arabic, pronounced *noon*, on the front wall. If these people did not convert to Islam, they had to pay a *jizya* (tax) or die. That is what is written in the holy book and everybody believed it. They rented or sold some homes to Muslim refugees who had relocated from the other areas. The gang quickly became an organization, and Bassam named it Jihad Base *Quaidat AlJihad*, or QJ, It was growing and making money.

No one challenged them, since Bassam's QJ gave a cut of the money to the Syrian intelligence officers. The PLO commanders looked the other way. QJ kept the biggest and nicest home as a command center. It motivated the troops, and they recruited even more friends. These guys just wanted cool weapons, a car to zip around town with, and hashish.

During a meeting of the QJ, Bassam told his inner circle, "We made some money selling the Caterpillar tractors and tools before we burned the machine shop. It gave me double pleasure: it was full of nice tools that the PLO bought for cash, and it belonged to the Red Devil's family. This is a bonus for me."

Ghassan asked, "I wonder where the PLO gets all that money they throw around?"

Bassam had already thought long and hard about this, and he answered. "Weapons and drugs, that's where the money is."

5

OUTRUNNING THE WAR

PAUL:

My sixth-grade school year was a blur. I went to five different schools that year and learned nothing. We left home, a town with a mixed population and many different religions. My parents took us just ten kilometers away, to another town that had the exact same demographics. I think about it now and chuckle. My father had many friends all over the area. He was well known as the top diesel mechanic. I thought he was a genius without any business sense. He used to complete a repair and tell the client, "Just go now, come back and pay me whenever you can."

This was the only thing my parents argued about. My mother would ask my father if the customer paid for repairing a tractor or a farm machine, and he would answer, "The poor man has a family to feed, he needs his machine to make money, and he will pay later, don't worry."

Her answer would be, "What about this family? Who is going to feed and dress them? Your impeccable honest reputation or your generosity?"

A month later, we had to run again. The conflict was following us, and the Christians were losing. We would stay with one family for a week, sleeping on the floor in their living room, on foam mattresses we rolled up and packed against the wall behind the curtains during the day. It was fun but a little embarrassing.

My mom would take us to the local school, give them some cash to enroll us. At this point, it was not about education as much as about keeping us off the streets and out of trouble. My father, who had just lost his home and his business, although he did not know it yet, would try to find us a home to rent. By the time he found us a vacant house, we would have to move again. He couldn't accept that the civil war would continue—how could he? He had lived in one town all his life and made friends with Muslims, Shia and Sunni, Druze and Kurds, and so on. We were lucky in Lebanon: we had seventeen—yes, seventeen—different faiths.

We ended up moving five times that year.

During one of the moves, we lived in a small one-bedroom apartment my father rented from one of his client friends. My mother and two sisters slept in the bedroom; the boys slept in the living room. The only issue was the washroom. My mother had a rule: the girls always had priority over the boys because apparently they can't hold it as long. So my brother and I had to wait. Remember, my brother was ice, so if he got in before me, I was in trouble.

That town was high up in the mountains; the population was mixed Christians and Druze. It was cold and the snow was heavy that year. We basically had a month's worth of snow days from school during the two months we were there, which suited me fine. I made two friends: Tony, a Christian, and Marwan, a Durzi. Don't be shocked. I never had any problems with anybody because of faith. I was ten—OK, maybe almost eleven—and religion meant nothing to me. I had no idea why this was happening. But I knew that if I had been born 200 meters south of my home, I would have been a Sunni, or 300 meters east and I would have been a Shia. I judged people by their actions and still do.

Tony, Marwan, and I found an abandoned old building that had once been a *tanour*, basically, a bakery specializing in flatbread. We tracked down the old owner, who was retired, and convinced him to let us clean up the building and reopen it for a small fee. He agreed to let us operate it in exchange for daily bread for his household. It was an instant huge success; we were never able to make enough bread.

We only stayed in that house for a few months, until the *coup d'état* of General Ahdab. That coup was unsuccessful, and it caused the split of the Lebanese army. Every high-ranking officer took his equipment and the soldiers from his faith and set up his own mini-army. Eventually, those from the same faith consolidated, and then the fun started. The weapons that belonged to the army, which was supposed to protect the nation, were now in the hands of extremists and separatists from every faith. The psychopaths joined up quickly, and killing and kidnapping became the national sport, based on faith. It was easy to figure out who belonged to what religion. Accents and dress could do it, and, if all else failed, every citizen's religion and faith was written on his or her identity card. Stop smiling and thinking, "What a stupid idea!" The politicians in Lebanon thought it was brilliant.

Each time we moved, it was only a few more kilometers away, getting into new schools and so on, until finally my parents accepted that this war was going to take longer than they originally thought. My mother and father made one final trip to our town, alone, in order to get some clothes and a few belongings. They found that a Muslim family who had escaped the war from another region occupied our home.

They would not let them into the house, of course. They were paying rent, and the house belonged to them now; the kids were playing with my bike and would not give it back. My father went to his shop and found it sacked and burned. His equipment and tools were gone. The tractors and other heavy machines now belonged to the PLO. It had taken him fifteen years of hard work, much of it away from his family in Saudi Arabia, Kuwait, and the UAE, to save enough to set up his business. In one day, he lost everything.

We became refugees in our own country. From being upper middle class, we became poor, broke, and homeless.

When my parents came back that night, I knew something was seriously wrong. My mother's face looked darker than usual, and by the way my father's shoulders slumped, I knew he was a defeated man. He never fully recovered. My mother did not complain about our living conditions or lack of money. Maybe because she was my mother and I am biased, but I can tell you with total honesty she was probably the most supportive woman I have ever met. Marriage was for better or for worse; right then, she was at the worst and you would never have known it.

BASSAM:

Finally, Bassam was getting a small measure of revenge on the Christians, who looked down on the Muslims. Oh, they tried to act like they didn't, but it was obvious in so many ways.

Bassam had dropped out of school and tried to get work. The only man who gave him a job fired him without giving him a chance: the Red Devil's father, a Christian. The condescending man phoned his father after only a few hours and asked him to take Bassam back home, saying he was not cut out to be a machinist.

The Christian girls never talked to him. They used to look at him and giggle, flirting with their eyes and body language until they found out he was a Muslim, at which time they would walk away without a second glance. The Christian boys never even made eye contact, or made faces of derision, like the Red Devil. It was insulting and demeaning.

Early one afternoon while at the QJ headquarters, the brothers saw the Red Devil's parents arrive and get out of their car and look at their old house with confusion. They found new residents moved in and claiming that the bike and furniture belonged to them now.

Bassam rubbed his palms together, staring at them with hatred. *Too bad they did not bring their little hottie with them*, Bassam thought. He would have made a deal for her and let them back in.

The money he made selling or renting out the Christian homes confiscated by his QJ men was peanuts. The big money was in drugs and weapons. Once he and the QJ moved into the drug business, setting up new, protected labs, the money started rolling in. Nobody was going to challenge them, not as long as the Syrian officers were getting a cut. There were a lot of buyers who were willing to take a risk, paying for large shipments. Bassam and his boys became mass producers.

Ghassan walked in one day and started shouting at his older brother: "Our father does not talk to us anymore; he said he is ashamed of us. I don't understand what his problem is. We are winning, and getting rich, and yet he is angry."

"Don't raise your voice in my face again, you understand?" Bassam stared him down. "Our father thinks it's immoral and against our religion to kill. I don't care about morals, and even less about religion. Power and money is the name of the game. Shouting Allah Akbar gives the ignorant the excuse they need to do our bidding blindly, asking no questions of themselves or me."

6

DIGGING FOR OIL

PAUL:

Maybe you'll find this funny or maybe not: it is up to you to decide. I personally found it hilarious. Before we left the town, at the start of the war, gasoline became hard to get. Anticipating an imminent shortage of gas, my father filled up a 200-litre steel barrel and asked my cousin Joseph to take one of the tractors, dig a hole beside our house, and bury the barrel for a rainy day—we had a large empty lot beside our home. Joseph dug the hole and buried the barrel. Then all the kids gathered and played a game in the resulting muddy patch. It was the most popular game we played.

On the day when my parents returned and found they had lost everything, my father wanted some kind of moral victory. My aunt's husband and my father dug out the barrel using shovels and picks; we had no tractors left. They filled their cars, plus five twenty-litre jerry cans, under the watchful and bewildered eyes of the new occupants of our home. To complete the joke, my father and uncle walked around the lot and placed small wooden sticks as markers, all the while pointing in different directions in an animated fashion.

Lebanese are worse than Italians with our hand gestures and excited conversation. An outsider would think we were fighting and arguing while we were really discussing serious philosophy—oh yeah, we are all philosophers. Socrates and Plato have nothing on us.

The occupiers thought they had hit pay dirt: barrels of gas! That night they set out to dig for oil.

The next morning, the lot looked like it had been hit by a meteor storm. More than twenty huge holes had been dug where the markers were placed. It must have taken them the entire night. Surely they found nothing because there was nothing there to find. My father had the last laugh. He would retell this story with a smile on his face many years later, whenever we asked him.

7

THE REFUGE

PAUL:

On the night of the failed coup of General Ahdab, my parents decided to make a run for it and reach the predominately Christian area in the middle of the night. We left the last house and my flatbread business behind, got in the car and were on the way to my aunt's home. We were stopped on a roadblock minutes after we left. My father and mother were asked for ID, though they did not bother with us in the back. They got my father to come out and open the trunk. While he was at the back of the car with two of the unknown soldiers, being searched, another lunatic with hard empty black eyes, stuck his gun in my mother's face, grinned at her. Without a word, he put his hand down her bra and took the last remaining money we had. He was not a brilliant detective; the bra hiding spot was like the central bank for all Lebanese women at the time.

The tendons on my mother's neck went taut as a guitar's strings. I was helpless. I kept my mouth shut. He stole our money, fondled my mother's breasts, and all I could do was watch. I was mesmerised by the barrel of the gun and hypnotized with fear. My father got back in the car, unaware of what had happened, and we were waved away. I remember my fingernails digging into my arm the entire way to my aunt's home. I rocked back and forth, silently repeating to myself, "Paul, you are the biggest coward."

Aunt Isabelle, my mother's older sister and my favorite aunt, was living out of town in the Maten area, where most of the people were Maronite Christians. That was the faith of my family, as well. Please don't confuse it with Mennonite, okay? Not that I have anything against them, but I am constantly having to explain the difference. As soon as I say, "Maronite," the first words out of a North American's mouth are, "Mennonite? Oh, you guys are good at woodworking, right?" And I answer, "No, we Maronites are good at defusing car bombs. When it becomes an Olympic sport, we will win the gold medal." Talking about car bombs and terrorists usually puts a quick end to the conversation.

We finally made it to my Aunt Isabelle's town, a safe haven from future moves. If we were forced to move from Aunt Isabelle's, it would mean the Christians had been eliminated from the entire country. I knew the town as well as the kids who lived there because I had spent countless months during my summer vacations living with my aunt. Her old house was small. But by the time my parents arrived, she was busy building the largest villa I had ever seen. She had four boys who were much older than me. The oldest was in med school in France, and the younger three, including a set of twins, were in the United States, also studying. Sometimes they would come home during summer vacation and spend a few weeks with their mother. I rarely interacted with them since they were so much older, but at that time my favorite was one of the twins. Many years later in Dubai, when I got to know the other twin, my choice became harder. The youngest was the joker, the funniest and the toughest of the four.

Thanks to the summer months I had spent with my aunt, I knew almost all the kids in that town. During those summers, I learned how to play music and make paper kites. I built a tree house and actually slept in it. I also learned how to hunt. Yeah, even at eight and nine years old, I would take an air rifle or sometimes sneak out with a small 12 mm and go hunting all day.

My elbows and legs were always a mess from falling while playing and running. My part-time nurse and full-time aunt had a small first aid kit, and she made it her duty to clean and dress my wounds every evening while lecturing me to be more careful. She was a smart woman, arguing with contractors and scheduling workers, while her husband was off working in some Arab Gulf country and making loads of money.

I loved my vacations there. I knew the people, and most of them knew me and accepted me as one of their own. Most of the adults and the kids knew me by my nickname, Boulous. I liked the way they pronounced it with their mountain accent.

The homes were built with thick stones. Most of them had red brick roofs. The town was built in the middle of a mountain, and just south of it, at the bottom of the valley, was a deserted hamlet with a dozen beautiful homes, locked up; the owners had emigrated years ago to the west. It was actually called the valley town. It had a small old church and an abandoned cemetery. Surrounded by an evergreen forest and multiple freshwater streams and in total solitude, I spent most of my days roaming around the ghostlike village. It was like my own kingdom, surrounded by nature, and I had it to myself. I did not need to act brave or macho back then. I was being me, a kid running and jumping without a care in the world.

Just before the war started, Jim, my aunt's husband, returned home with a fortune and they moved into the new villa. The youngest of their children moved back home. This home could sleep two dozen people comfortably, so they welcomed us with open arms. My mother relaxed, but my father was uncomfortable. Being homeless and broke and staying at his relative's home did not sit well with him. He was proud and did not want to be a burden. I felt safe for the first time in months and was having the time of my life.

My father set up a small shop and started working, and my mother was helping her sister set up the new house, which was no easy task. It was summer, we had no school, so I was let loose to roam and play. I would play all day but kept an eye out so I'd know when Jim got home. Being retired, he would leave the house every morning on some daily visits and meetings, probably to play *tawle* (Turkish backgammon) or chess, and he sure made it looked like he was busy. After lunch he had his daily nap, a ritual that he never, ever broke, then if he were free after the nap, we would go hunting. He was continually telling me there was no challenge in shooting birds while they were standing on a tree branch. A true hunter shoots while the birds are in full flight. We would take two hunting rifles from his collection and go to the top of the hills, wait, and practice. This was where I honed the shooting skills I would use the rest of my life, without realizing the importance at the time.

I looked up to him—everybody did. He was big and soft-spoken, with bold features and a full head of pure snow-white hair; he also had the thickest eyebrows and moustache you have ever seen. When he spoke, people listened. He was almost like a judge or a peacekeeper of his town. In the evenings, many people would come for help in resolving their differences. There were many important guests. The sectarian war had started and he was well connected, and rich. Endless planning sessions were done in that house, while I hovered around eavesdropping, trying to understand the situation.

As a matter of status and honor, the young men of this town were sent to the front lines separating the Christian forces from the Muslim and PLO forces. My aunt's youngest was among the first to volunteer. I watched the fighters go and come back while the parents stayed awake and worried. My aunt tried to send her youngest back to the U.S., but her husband used to tell her, "We have four boys, and at least one of them should participate in defending the Christian region. We can't hide our sons and let others go and fight for us."

I wanted to join, and asked every time they left if I could come. They would tell me no, that I was too young and inexperienced.

"I am almost eleven and three quarters," I would say. My uncle Jim would ruffle my hair and say, "Boulous, your turn will come soon. Be careful what you wish for, my son." His words did not make any sense to me then, since it was exactly what I wanted.

One morning, the fighters came back, and the old green car they drove was riddled with bullet holes on one side. My cousin had been driving when they came under fire. Not one of the four young men in the car was injured, and the people of the town thought that was a miracle. The fighters had elastic armbands on their biceps that allegedly contained a sliver of Jesus's wooden cross. I had one, too; almost every male at that time had one. If the tale is true, the cross must have been too huge to be carried by one person. Like all miracles, there was no logical explanation for it. No comment.

I was waiting for my chance to fight when one day Raymond, a friend of my father's, asked me if I was scared to go. I answered that I had been asking but nobody would take me. He spoke with my father and told him that instead of my going with the actual fighters into dangerous battles, he would take me with him to a mountainous area that was quiet. Nothing ever happened there; it was more like guard duty. "Let him come," said Raymond. "He will get bored before you know it."

8

MAGNET FOR TROUBLE

PAUL:

I was so excited that day. I got my uniform ready, one passed on to me by my cousin. My mother had to fully re-tailor it to make it fit me. The oversized military belt went almost twice around my waist. There were no military shoes my size, so running shoes had to do. My father lent me his 9 mm Star pistol, which made my pants slip down whenever I walked. I had to slow down and yank my pants back up continuously. I remember thinking at the time, *This thing is so heavy. Why can't I have a 7 mm Beretta or something smaller?*

I waited breathlessly until 7 p.m. Then I was picked up, and we headed for the mountains, not far from the Lebanese presidential palace.

We arrived at a small house just before dark; it was set up as the situation room. Everybody, excluding yours truly, got an AK-47 or M-16 machine gun with a few extra clips of ammunition. I had no weapon save for the pistol, which would be useless in real battle. The leaders did not take me seriously. They assumed I was a guest and would be leaving soon, before night fell, and surely before they headed out to the front lines to relieve the day shift.

That did not sit well with me. All day I had been looking forward to some action, at least to carrying an actual automatic machine gun at the front lines. My uncle had taught me to shoot and clean the models at my aunt's home. He had a large collection, and I took care of it for him.

I was almost in tears, until finally I caught Raymond's eye and he noticed my disappointment. He left and came back with an old World War II rifle. It belonged in a museum, but he told me the rifle was more powerful and accurate than the machine guns. Since this was a mountain region, and the enemy was far-off, a long-range rifle truly was the most important weapon—and he was entrusting me with this jewel. It was a French MAS-36 rifle with a five-bullet magazine. I took some extra bullets and off we went.

We walked slowly down the alleys between the houses until we reached the edge of town, where we waited for our guide. Each man carried some extra food and water because we were supposed to stay until morning. Our guide knew the lay of the land so he walked ahead of us between the olive trees, in total darkness, but not as stealthily as I'd imagined. Some men were chatting, a couple were even smoking. Remember, these guys were normal people, not professional soldiers: plumbers, mechanics, electricians, and so on—and, of course, the most fearsome of all, me.

We got to our location safely and without incident, not because of superior infiltration skills, but because the enemy was not looking our way. This defensive line was nothing more than three locations about a hundred feet apart, a center and a right and left flank, the whole setup consisting of a few hundred sandbags piled about six feet high in a semicircle with a couple of openings in between at a normal adult eye level. The three positions were covered with a dark green tarp overhead. The radio was in the center, hardwired to eliminate eavesdropping; this location was supposed to be the communications control center to the main building. We relieved the day shift, each assuming our assigned positions. I was with Raymond, who was the leader of the center location.

I was watching all three angles at once, excited and ready for some action. I kept asking if I could shoot and the answer was always no. "This is a defensive zone, and we do not fire until we clearly see a threat or an attempt by the enemy to infiltrate!" I had no idea about rules of engagement.

Looking between the three locations, it did not take long to spot some vulnerable areas. If the enemy attacked from the left flank, the right and center locations would be shooting at each other. I was tempted to mention this to Raymond, but I kept my thoughts to myself. They call it friendly fire, though it's not so friendly if you are the one getting shot at.

Nothing happened for a few hours. By midnight, I was getting bored with the whole experience, thanks to my ADHD. My father and his friend's strategy were beginning to pay off. Then, suddenly, I saw a big red flash from the other side and a tracer-like red line that looked like a shooting star. It hovered above us for a few seconds and then exploded, illuminating the whole side of the mountain as if it was daylight. I had never seen such a thing. I was in awe. It was like watching fireworks, or more like being in the middle of fireworks. The more experienced adults knew it was an illuminated mortar bomb; the enemy set one off nightly to ensure there was no infiltration attempt from our side. I thought it served both sides equally, lighting the area so everyone could see who was doing what, but as always I kept my thoughts to myself. After a slow descent, it landed not even a hundred feet from us. A couple of the guys rushed over to see what was left of it and put out any fires. They came back later, carrying a few pieces at the end of a shovel. I was told that if I wanted to touch it and have illuminated hands, I should wait until it cooled. White phosphorus grenades were especially valued in Vietnam for destroying Viet Cong tunnel complexes because they would burn up the oxygen and suffocate the enemy soldiers sheltering inside. We had no tunnels at that early stage of our conflict, so it was purely for illumination. I was fascinated.

Around 4 a.m., I was tired and my vision was blurry. Looking between the sandbags, I started seeing shadows. I mentioned this to the guys playing cards behind me. They told me it was normal. "You're nervous and tired," they said, "and every shrub and shape starts to look just like a human pointing a gun at you." I tried to ignore a couple of shapes about a hundred meters ahead.

Then I saw movement.

"Hey," I said, "there are people moving toward us."

This was met with more laughter—until the imaginary figures opened fire.

Everybody scrambled to their feet and grabbed their weapons. I was left with my antiquated MAS-36, which took an eternity to load and fire. The other guys were shooting a full thirty-bullet clip by the time I managed to fire two shots, and still I had to reload every five shots. The shooting continued for about fifteen minutes from both sides. We were taking fire from three directions, with the center location being in the thick of things and taking the brunt of the assault. We were behind sandbags, but the enemy was behind olive trees and partially exposed. There are no timeouts or commercial breaks when you are in the middle of a firefight. The results are just as unpredictable as any sporting match; however, the duration is a complete mystery. There's no buzzer to end the period.

The attack ended just as quickly as it started, the infiltration was repelled, and the calm that followed was louder than the shooting. My senses were running on overdrive, my ears were ringing, my eyes watering, and the smell of the gunpowder was filling my nostrils. I kept looking in every direction, expecting a second wave. Surely it couldn't end like this.

Without any background in military science, I learned at an early age that it was much easier to defend a fortified position than to attack it without the element of surprise or stealth. Some politicians should take notes here and not divulge their military plans on TV for all to see. I am sure that when they brag about it, it gives the military generals ulcers and increases the casualty count.

We waited an hour in complete silence, just in case there was a second, bigger attack coming and the first one was a test to discover our location and capabilities. Daylight came quickly and a few guys ventured out from behind the sandbags to check things out. I pointed to where I had initially seen the figures move.

One guy harassed me. "You did not warn us early enough," he said. "Your responsibility is to keep watch. This is not child's play! You almost got us all killed."

I was twelve, with a gun in my hand. I knew right then and there that this was the moment to make my mark. I would manage my fear and not let it control me anymore. I stepped right in front of him and looked up, way up.

"I told you about the dark shapes during your card game," I said. "You were the one laughing the hardest and saying that I was tired and scared. Look who's nervous now."

The men around me were taken aback, exchanging

glances; you know, the looks that say "Is this kid for real, are you kidding me?"

I was on a roll. "You guys just come here to play cards," I said. "It's not only you that can be killed. The whole town is counting on us to keep the enemy away from their families."

To defuse the tension, Raymond sent us off in different directions to check out the scene. The bully mumbled under his breath while the rest of the guys were teasing him about his standoff with a midget. We noticed a few drops of blood on the trees and branches, more on the ground, but nothing major. We went back to our positions and waited for the day shift to relieve us.

Sitting quietly in the car on the ride back home, I had a satisfied grin on my face and butterflies in my stomach. Raymond was driving and we were alone in the car when he asked, "Were you scared during the shooting?"

"Who me, scared? I was too busy fussing with the stupid MAS-36 that you gave me to get scared."

"Do you think you shot somebody?"

"Maybe," I said, "but there was so much shooting, I am not sure who did what."

I told him I was sure about one thing: if it had been the PLO or the Syrian army that attacked, we would have been killed. He was surprised and asked why.

Now was the time to prove I was valuable, that I could be an asset. I went into a detailed monologue about angles, heights, numbers, and locations, about what made the present defensive positions so vulnerable.

He smiled back at me, shook his head, and said, "You are one smart dude, Red Devil. I hope you stay alive long enough. We need more like you on our side."

We got back to my aunt's home by mid-morning. Both my parents were waiting on the balcony. They asked about the night and what happened. We exchanged looks and both of us said it had been quite a routine night. Raymond stayed over for breakfast and then left for work. I went inside to find a quiet corner to sleep.

BASSAM:

Bassam knew from an early age that Ghassan was dim-witted and needed to be taken care of. He fucked up the most simple of missions. The idiot was a couple of years older and thought that was a good enough reason for him to be the boss. If it were not for Bassam, he would still be doing guard duty at the PLO gate back in town. He cared only about cars, drugs, and girls.

"Ghassan," Bassam said, "take a couple of guys with you, go up to the highway, and carjack a nice, modern BMW or a Mercedes."

"Why do you need to do this shit all the time?" he asked. "We have plenty of cars."

"I have to go out tonight with an important Syrian officer," the younger brother said. "I want to gift him the car."

"Come on, Bassam," Ghassan whined. "Our parents are so pissed at us. I'm sure they know we shot those three cousins on the street."

"Why should I care? They think we should respect all living things like it says in the holy book. I can't find that verse."

"Why do you need to give the car as a gift?"

"As a goodwill gesture and a sign of respect," Bassam explained.

"This guy is probably a goat herder back in Syria. If we give him a Beemer or a Benz, he will parade it around his town. He will look successful and powerful in his village. He will owe us and will turn a blind eye."

"Should we cover our faces?"

"Of course! The car might belong to a Muslim. Who cares whose car it is? Use your head, man."

"Hey, are you going to a party later?"

"Of course we are. It is a private house. I supply the

madam with hash and pills; she sells them to her girls and the customers for crazy prices. We will be treated like kings."

"Can I come?

"If you get a good car, I will take you with me. Set up a roadblock on the road and wait for the right car. Don't worry who is driving it; our own people are more scared of us than the infidels are."

"A Benz or a Beemer—got it."

That's how long it took to explain things to Ghassan. Bassam knew that it would take him even longer to explain the new recruiting strategy.

9

TRAINING CAMP

PAUL:

Most of the Christian population migrated to predominately Christian territory and soon this became a safe zone. It was small and surrounded on three sides by the PLO and their Muslim recruits, backed up by the Syrian army and their tanks. The fourth side was the sea they planned to drive us into. Our backs were against the wall, or the Mediterranean waters, take your pick. The choices were bad and worse, defend or die. Most of the boys here were students or workers and no match for the trained and better-equipped enemy.

Now that I was a seasoned veteran and no longer a war virgin, I started harassing my aunt's husband to send me with the boys to another location. He was responsible for supplying fighters and soldiers to an area in the center of downtown Beirut. The weapons were taken from the Lebanese army; a few professional soldiers joined the struggle to train the boys. We needed to be able to defend with basic weapons, against the PLO, the Syrian army, African mercenaries, and Muslims.

The decision was made for me as usual: I was to be sent to a training camp for a month before I could see any action. After all, I was by far the youngest and probably the stupidest—that last part they did not say to my face, but I was almost certain they thought it.

The adults in my family thought that after a long, rigorous camp, combined with hard living and training conditions, I would burn playing soldier out of my system. I was the only youngster in the group, small, skinny, and eager to learn. About thirty of us took a bus ride for two hours north and east of Beirut, to a remote location on Mount Lebanon, in the middle of the barren mountains. When we arrived, I was surprised by the size of the camp and the number of people. The camp itself was huge, but everything looked big to me back then. There were other guys from other towns being trained, maybe 300 or so.

A dozen slept in one tent, and we were separated from our original groups, probably to build solidarity and eliminate cliques. In my tent, there was only one guy from my initial group. I had to quickly get used to open communal toilets. I did not take a shower the whole time I was there, unwilling to stand naked with other men. One central tanker supplied the water, and everybody would line up to fill their water canteens. The food would arrive in big pots, and every tent would receive one pot to share; you had to be quick and fill your plate or the food would disappear like in a Houdini act. If you weren't fast and pushy, you went hungry. Hunger and training didn't mix well together.

After a dinner of rice, beans, and one pita bread each, we would line up for an opening speech. The speeches were a nightly ritual designed to boost morale and mentally condition us for the hard days ahead. I fell asleep from exhaustion while listening and sitting on the sand.

The first morning, I woke up to shouting and

swearing. Lebanese can never do anything quietly. Two of the guys in our tent had been stung by scorpions and had to be taken to the infirmary for treatment. This was to become a regular occurrence, just like the speeches. Every morning, half a dozen boys would visit the infirmary. I was on high alert, constantly scanning for these little bastards, hoping to avoid the pleasure of meeting the scorpion kiss.

The days started at 5 a.m. sharp, with a morning stretching exercise, referred to as Swedish for some unknown reason, followed by a five-kilometer run, each day in a different direction. After that, we would split into different groups to train in different skills. The routine was never the same, but we trained in shooting, disassembling, and cleaning the weapons, as well as deployment, strategy and movements, and military tactics. Add to that how to install and defuse land mines. Finally, before dinner break, we had a session of hand-to-hand combat.

We had different trainers for every part, and I excelled in all of it, except—yeah, that's right, hand-to-hand combat. What did you expect? I was at least six inches shorter and a hundred pounds lighter than the smallest person I faced. I got my ass kicked in different ways on a daily basis. This kind of training was called "white weapons," though I never understood why. Our head trainer was a famous martial arts expert who everybody knew, except for yours truly, who was clueless. When he asked on the first day who would volunteer to demonstrate a technique on how to disarm somebody during a knife attack, nobody volunteered. I raised my hand, eager to learn firsthand. The guy beside me kept pulling my hand back down, but I kept raising it until the trainer noticed.

"You are too small," he said.

I almost jumped him. I insisted. I dove into the middle of the human circle, pulled out my bayonet, and told him, "I am ready."

I raised my arm, ready to strike but, the next second I was on the ground with my mouth and eyes full of sand, trying to breathe. The wind was knocked out of me, and I had learned nothing. After regaining some form of balance and dignity, I jumped to my feet, ready for take two.

I was told to rejoin the circle, and he would get another person for the next round.

"I need somebody else," he said. "You can learn more from watching."

My ribs and arm were hurting, but there was no way I would show it. I sat, simmering with anger.

I had watched Bruce Lee movies in our town's small theater, where they only showed Indian and karate movies. The women watched the Indian movies and always left so teary-eyed they drove up the price of Kleenex. But the boys watched the karate movies. After every showing, I tried to jump and kick, and got my ass beat for it by some bigger boy. I had come to the conclusion that this crap did not work in the real world, but now I had a different opinion.

It was an exhausting month, but we did get into shape, physically. We were not trained elite soldiers, but we knew the basics and we would not blow each other's heads off during a firefight. Hopefully.

When I got back home, my lips were the size of cucumbers, chapped and bleeding. As with every other rash or illness, my mother applied rose water to cool the pain, but her homemade remedy just caused more chapping.

I was the only one who decided that now I was ready to help at the front lines. Nobody shared my opinion. The strategy to get the war out of my system had backfired, and I started asking on a daily basis where and when I would be stationed.

BASSAM:

The *Quaidat AlJihad,* had developed a new recruiting strategy; they would send few bullies out to pick on vulnerable and unpopular Muslim guys. The bullies would rough them up before another group showed up and protected them. Before anybody knew it, the two groups became "friends," and the small group looked up to the brave protectors. The indoctrination and radicalization process began soon after. First they went out and had fun, money was flashed around, and then there were regular visits to the mosque, followed by playing ping-pong and cards at the QJ headquarters. The new recruits felt safe and that finally they belonged.

The QJ had grown quickly, and the Syrians gave them freedom in the decision-making. The Syrians also supplied the weapons and training. In return, the QJ hijacked expensive cars and sold them to the Syrian leadership for cheap.

Bassam was always repeating and drilling the same message to his fighters. Everyone, old or new, knew it by heart. "We will not rest until we drive the descendants of the Crusaders back to where they came from. They argue that they were here before the Muslims, but the whole Middle East is ours, and we will purify and cleanse our land of infidels. The rules of are clear. Pay a *jizya,* submit to Islam, or die. They don't want to pay or convert, we will make them leave or die trying."

This is what Bassam said in public, since killing in the name of Allah gave the justification he needed. He did not even tell his own brother that he really only cared about power and money. He did not want to admit out loud that this radical version of Islam gave him the platform he needed to accomplish his own obsessions for power and greed.

As a matter of fact, he did regular business with even the Christians. He kept up a good front when it suited him. He bought hashish from a town in the eastern Bekaa Mountains and shipped it to Europe, a profitable business with incredible margins, something the PLO did not need to know about. He said to Ghassan on many occasions, "I don't know why these European idiots pay so much for this stuff."

The QJ grew so fast that it didn't have enough uniforms and weapons for every man. It was a good problem to have. It was thanks to the drugs and hookers the QJ supplied. The Syrian officers were getting rich and spending their evenings in the bordellos. They never questioned the QJ and were happy to use them on operations that needed to remain secret from the PLO.

10

A CAFÉ WITHOUT COFFEE

PAUL:

At thirteen years old and after two years of waiting and begging to join at the front lines, I was greenlighted. Finally the day arrived, and I was told to get ready. I sprinted home to don my uniform. My mother and Aunt Isabelle were both nervous. I was the only rookie making an official appearance. Joseph, the oldest of my aunt's sons, had returned from med school in France and was joining me on his first deployment. The adults assumed he would keep an eye on me and keep me out of trouble. Well, I have news for you: trouble kept finding me, regardless of who was watching over me.

We assembled at the town's center and displayed our weapons. Rashid, our leader, started with his checklist: roll call, weapons, ammunition, food, water, and first aid kits. This guy was a big, handsome man famous for his skills and daring attitude. I used to follow him around town during my summer vacations; he was the one who taught me how to build kites.

My cousin showed up in full gear, including a helmet

and a bulletproof vest. Nobody else wore a helmet and none of us had even seen a vest before.

We left in late afternoon, in two Toyota trucks the boys had stolen the previous month from a dealership in central Beirut. I sat beside my babysitter cousin on the truck bed, along with the others. Nobody showed any signs of fear or nervousness, of course, though my cousin Joe looked totally out of place in his full gear. He kept calling me Boulous, which bothered me because this nickname was for children, not for a tough frontline fighter like me. He said things like, "When the shooting starts, stay close to me and don't be scared. I will make sure you're OK."

What did he mean? His vest was going to stop bullets for both of us? Or was there some magic in his helmet? I loved him and did not want to embarrass him—saving face was as big for the Lebs as it was for the Japanese. So I listened quietly and bobbed my head up and down, thinking he was the one that needed the sitter.

We waited for a couple of hours at a forward location. Shifts were changed every twenty-four hours in the dark; the area we were supposed to defend was open, located on top of a small hill impossible to get to during the daylight hours. To make matters worse, what separated us from our enemies on the lower side was an apple orchard and a small two-lane country road. The road came toward us on an incline and around a curve, so it was impossible to see vehicles coming until they were right under your nose. But we were satisfied because nobody ever used this road, and we would hear any enemy trucks and tanks approaching.

The building we were in was built to be a restaurant but was called a café. It had a large terrace where people used to sit and enjoy the scenery while having a marathon meal and drinking *arak* (the Lebanese national drink, not unlike the Greeks' *ouzo*). A typical Lebanese lunch took a minimum of three hours to complete.

The café was built of solid poured concrete, not the usual concrete blocks, and was riddled with holes from bullets and mortar shells. Three stacks of sandbags were laid on the large terrace. The fighters took shifts manning these three sites, while the rest were resting, eating, or sleeping in a back room inside. We had to sprint under cover of darkness, or of weapon fire, to get to the forward locations on the terrace as it was totally exposed. Adrenaline rushed through me every time I sprinted across that open space. Every time I crossed, I got a lecture from my cousin.

We were always defending and in no position to attack. We were spread too thin and our resources were limited. The enemy had thousands of trained PLO fighters, the Muslim recruits, and the Syrian army. They were also importing mercenaries from Somalia and Ethiopia; these guys were huge, dark, and scary-looking. We had the advantage of the hills and knowing the lay of the land. Every point of defense had a local to guide us.

Mostly we had light weapons and hand grenades, a couple of RPGs with a dozen rockets, and a .50 Browning machine gun. It was mounted on a pickup truck and parked at the back of the building. This was our prize weapon, and we had to keep it hidden, using it only to repel an attack.

When we were attacked, a driver would pull the truck out from the back, and Rashid would do the shooting while a third fighter held the metallic link chain to keep it from jamming. This machine gun was an old manual model, unlike the new electric models you've probably seen in video games. Basically it was junk, but it was the best junk we had. Once an ammunition box was empty, the truck would be driven back to safety inside the building, where the soldier holding the chain was responsible for changing the box.

All in all, a simple plan, right? Wrong. When under fire and in danger, you had to keep your cool and manage your fear or it would kill you. Like Mike Tyson said, "Everybody has a plan until they get punched in the face." The driver and the two gunners rehearsed their role and agreed they would be ready, just in case an attack occurred.

I was so excited, I made the trip a dozen times between the main building and the barricade sandbags. If somebody needed water, I volunteered. A coffee to stay awake? I went and made some. I got a dirty look from my cousin every time. He was hunkered down behind the sandbag wall, with his helmet and vest on. Being a med student, he was the smartest one of the bunch and knew the danger.

Absolutely nothing was happening. Not a shot was fired, not a person on the other side moved. It felt like they had deserted their location on the opposite side of the hill. I asked Rashid if I could test my weapon, maybe fire a few bullets across the hill. He looked at me and smiled like he knew something I did not.

"You will get plenty of chances," he said. "Just stay calm for now." He was always kind to me.

At two in the morning, we heard loud rumbling sounds. It sounded like tanks rolling down the road from the blind side of the hill. We waited nervously. We only had a few RPG rockets, and we wanted to make sure the tanks were in range before we fired. The men took positions; we were ready to go and everybody was alert. I can never forget the anticipation I felt every time I sensed something dangerous and real was about to happen.

What the enemy did not count on is that we were organized and ready. We ordered an illumination mortar bomb from our infantry. Once the shell was deployed, the whole side of the mountain was illuminated, and what we saw both made us laugh and confused us. We laughed from relief because there were no tanks attacking; we were confused because at first we did not understand what they were doing and why.

They were rolling empty 200-liter barrels down the hill in order to assess our readiness and capabilities. I thought it was a primitive tactic; however, I also thought it was smart. Although we were always calling the Syrians idiots and telling a zillion jokes about them, I knew they were not stupid. I wanted to find out more about their military strategies and ambush manoevres. At this point, however, I did not know where to start.

While we were celebrating our minor victory and patting ourselves on the back for not falling for this trick, another stealthy attack was under way from the other side, from the apple orchard side. They were not so stupid after all. They wanted us to think that this night's attack was a failure, to lure us into a false sense of security, then attack from a different direction. All of us without exception were looking the other way, toward the road.

By a stroke of luck, one of our guys spotted a couple of infiltrators almost ten meters under the terrace. Without warning, he immediately opened fire, and in the blink of an eye, bullets started to fly. We needed more firepower. Rashid, along with his designated driver and the ammunition guy, ran downstairs to the underground garage in the basement and fired up the Toyota. The driver backed the truck up to the top of the hill, and they started shooting at the apple orchard with the BMG. As soon as the first box was empty, the driver was supposed to drive the truck back down for cover so the ammunition guy could load another box.

Except the driver kept stalling the truck: it was a standard-shift truck, and being scared and nervous, he was popping the clutch too fast. The three of them were out in the open and at the mercy of the driver. The gun had a metal shield and Rashid was somewhat protected by it, but not from cannon shots or high-caliber machine guns. Bullets were flying everywhere, and everybody was shooting. The ammunition man and the driver ran for cover, leaving Rashid out there with an empty gun.

I took one look behind me and instantly sprinted to the truck. The driver's door was open and the keys were in the ignition—it wasn't like anybody was going to steal it. I slammed the door and started the engine in one movement, got it into first gear, and drove the truck back underground. Luckily, I had been driving tractors and heavy equipment since I was nine years old. Rashid and I got busy reloading another box of high-caliber bullets.

We got the new full box on, he got back behind the gun, and I reversed the truck up the hill. There I had to turn it off and put it in first gear; I could not leave it idling in neutral on an incline since I did not have the luxury of a hand brake. Once parked, I jumped to the back and assumed the position of ammunition chain feeder. Every time a box was empty I would jump down, go around the truck, and drive it back underground. While the rest of the guys were busy defending the café location, Rashid and I were repeating this maneuver over and over again. We kept doing it until we ran out of ammunition, then I drove the truck back, jumped out, got my gear, and joined the rest of the guys behind the sandbags.

We were successful again. These attacks had only been happening once every few months; I had stumbled into one of the few nights there was action. I told you I am a magnet for trouble.

When I went back to the big room to catch my breath, rest, and get some water, one of the other guys pointed at me and shouted, "Kiss!" This was a curse in Arabic. "You got shot! Look at your ears!"

I remember vividly looking back at him and thinking, *You moron. How can I see my own ears without a mirror in sight?* All of a sudden everybody started talking at once. This was not uncommon—we usually all talked at once—but they were also pointing, which again is not unusual, because we used our hands to make a point. Rashid looked at me and said something that I could not hear, I just saw his lips moving. Then he reached behind my ear and came out with some pink blood on his fingers. Not red, pink. I am a tough guy, right? I checked my body parts and proclaimed myself okay. A little pink blood would not slow me down.

I thought the ringing in my ears was temporary and would disappear soon. I did not know I had just been introduced to tinnitus. Rashid looked at me with amazement. The driver and ammunition guy also looked at me but with embarrassment. I smiled inwardly, knowing I was no longer at the bottom of the ranking. Even though I had acquired a small measure of respect, I knew that anybody could do what I had done. I was too naïve to be afraid, but I was not suicidal.

11

UNCALLED NUMBERS

My actions at the cafe did not go unnoticed. A few months later Rashid selected me to participate in a dangerous mission. We were heading to the outskirts of a Palestinian camp to rescue a diplomat. Seven other guys were also coming; one of them was lucky Emile. He was one of the best-looking guys I have seen, and he was always getting lucky. Tall and slim with broad shoulders, blonde hair, and blue eyes, he was the ultimate chick magnet. But that is not why we called him Lucky.

Nine of us got into three separate cars and headed to Tal el Zaatar (the Hill of Thyme). This was a huge Palestinian camp in the middle of the Christian area. It does not exist anymore. We erased it from existence. The subjects to be rescued were the Turkish ambassador and his driver, both Muslims. They were kidnapped in broad daylight from the main road close to the camp entrance. Thousands of PLO fighters operated out of this camp; they stole, intimidated, and kidnapped for ransom. The Christian Lebanese leadership were planning a full-scale attack soon. However, based on information about the ambassador and his driver, a splinter gang operating outside the main leadership of the PLO were hiding them in an abandoned factory nearby. They robbed the ambassador of his money and car. They made their demand for ransom.

Our orders were simple: infiltrate, extract quickly before the rest of the PLO fighters join the fight. Easier said than done.

Riding in the back of a station wagon, nervous, excited, and scared, I was wondering why Rashid picked me. I kept repeating the same prayer over and over. I was praying in French just in case one of the other guys could read my lips, and I pretended I was silently humming a song.

The whole area was in a blackout. We'd had no power for years. Under a cloudless sky, a bright full moon shone down and illuminated the outline of the factory. We wore dark blue since black is too dark, and the enemy could see our outlines on a night like this. One of the guys commented, "We are lucky, it's so bright we can see what we are doing."

I replied, "Yes, and so can the PLO."

The factory was a one-story, long building. The owner had moved his business to a more customer-friendly location, since you needed the customer to get to you before he or she was kidnapped or killed. We approached slowly from two different directions, windows down, lights and music off. I carried an AK 47, a Berretta handgun, a few more clips of ammo, and four hand grenades that we called pomegranates. Our group was responsible for securing the outer perimeter and repelling an outside counter attack from the main camp. Salim, Lucky Emile, Pierre, and I left the car 300 meters from the factory, rushed to the fence surrounding it, and waited for the second team to take position. The dark blue clothes did not work; we were spotted immediately and started taking fire from inside the building. Emile and I hopped over the fence and rushed to safety behind the structure, below the line of fire. We spotted the shooter hiding inside a room with a steel-barred window; the door was missing. Emile took a hand grenade and threw it inside. We rushed into the room almost as the grenade exploded. We sprayed the room with bullets emptying half of our clips. We pronounced the room safe when we saw the shooter down. I turned and left.

I leaned against the wall outside, waiting for Emile to come out. I saw him stumble and fall down right outside the door. I grabbed him by the shoulder straps of his ammo vest and pulled him away from the door as bullets zipped by my head. We had missed somebody who had been hiding in the room. Pierre arrived from the opposite side, took out a grenade, and launched it upward. He had seen the angle of the gunfire and knew that the shooter was hiding in the attic. I was not going in again, not without making sure no one was still hiding. I took one of my grenades and threw it in for good measure. Pierre and I went back inside and emptied our clips. I shot straight into the room, and he aimed at the attic. This time we swept the whole area and made sure it was secure.

We lifted Emile, who was bleeding from multiple wounds. His back looked like a spaghetti strainer. Pierre drove him to the hospital. I rejoined the fight and went looking for Salim. I saw him lying in a ditch, fully dressed in a flak jacket and helmet.

I nudged him to get up and join me, but he did not move. I shook him harder, but he remained motionless. I turned him over but couldn't find any injury or any trace of blood on him. I panicked. I could not lift him by myself. Even if I could, I would have been totally exposed. I stayed by his side, waiting for help.

Rashid arrived moments later, with his team. They helped me get Salim back to their car. Rashid told me that the hostages and all the terrorists were dead. He looked at me and asked me to sit down. He pointed his flashlight at my legs. I was hearing and feeling a swishing sound in my boots earlier, but I thought that I had stepped in a puddle of water. The color of my pants was darker on the right than the left, covered in blood. The swishing and the sticky feeling were from blood surging in my boot. I didn't know when it happened. But suddenly I knew I was injured and I was no longer able to walk, while minutes ago I was running. I had taken a bullet just over my right hip. I think back sometimes and I believe it was mind over matter.

Happily, my wound was superficial, and I was told I would be fine in few days. But it was not good news for Salim. The doctors discovered that a minuscule bit of shrapnel, smaller than a grain of rice, had gone through his body and into his heart. It snuck its way in just between his underarm and his flak jacket. There is a less than ten million to one chance of this ever happening. Yet it did.

While I was being stitched up, I asked the doctor if we could move Emile's body. He looked at me with a puzzled look. "Emile is alive and being operated on, he is still fighting for his life."

"I saw his back, it was riddled with bullets."

"Yes, twenty-three bullets hit him in the back. We are still working on him. All you can do now is pray for him." I shook my head at the irony. Salim dead from miniscule shrapnel, Emile still alive. And I had gotten shot and did not know it. Rachid and his team had killed the terrorists, which also caused the death of the ambassador and his driver we were meant to rescue. Overall, a total fuck-up.

When your number is not called, you can't cut in line. Emile made it out alive. He got married a couple of years later and was able to have kids, though he walked with a slight limp. Did I say he was lucky?

BASSAM:

The QJ was ordered by the Syrians to participate in the war. "You can't just be a gang. We are planning a major offensive. If we can take control of the high-rise buildings in the capital downtown at the hotel district, we will have control of west and central Beirut. You will have a major role in the attack," Syrian officials told Bassam.

Bassam was waiting for such an opportunity, to succeed in battle, which would give him and his QJ so much more respect and power. He aimed for nothing short of a victory. "I do this and I will be a star. There is no mercy and no room for failure."

The QJ led the attack with the support of African mercenaries the PLO supplied. These paid fighters were poorly trained, not disciplined, and,only in it for the money. They backed off at the first sign of true danger. The homegrown guys were much tougher because they believe in the cause. They were eager to learn and train and they would follow orders to the death.

Bassam looked at his ready troops and whispered to Ghassan, "It feels like I am running a real terrorist university, just like we talked about. They come in green, after fighting somewhere else for a short time, and I help them graduate into seasoned fighters."

Nobody back then used, or even knew about, suicide bombers. But soon they would find out. Bassam had seen a movie about the kamikaze, which jump-started his thoughts. *Why not here*? He had no planes to attack with, but he did have thousands of stolen cars available to him for free. *Imagine a soldier who is not afraid to die—even better, imagine one who is begging to die.* He frowned. *This is scary. I have to think more on this, seriously.* He was lost in his own thoughts until Mohamed nudged him to give the order to attack the hotel.

12

CHECKING INTO THE HOLIDAY INN

PAUL:

From 1975 to 1990, Beirut was split into two major sections, about half and half. The west was under the control of the PLO, the Syrians, Muslim militias, and a few other factions including some mercenaries. The Christians controlled the east; we had our share of factions also.

The fiercest battles were fought in central Beirut. Control the capital and you control the rest of the country: this was the impression, anyway. The two sides were separated by no-man's-land, an imaginary green line. I'm not sure what was so green about it: not a single tree or shrub survived and not one plant grew there. Right in the middle of the line was the hotel district, an area of multiple five-star hotels and resorts, all in high-rise buildings and all of them vacant. Downtown was a ghost town. Control of some of these buildings was important both strategically and for morale. Since none of us had any aerial capabilities, being on top of a high-rise building was a huge advantage for defense and an ideal location for long-range snipers.

Being the veteran that I was now, I was sent with the rest of the boys to the Holiday Inn, right in the middle of downtown Beirut. Not far away and almost across the street from the Holiday Inn was the Phoenicia Hotel. The only way in and out of the district was on foot and through a series of openings from one building to the next. The bravest, most experienced fighters were sent there because the center had to be held. I have no idea why I was there. I was neither.

It was a quiet and hot night. My T-shirt was sticking to my body, and the older guys were making fun of my skinny six-pack. Periodic shooting exchanges between the Phoenicia and the Holiday Inn were heard in the distance; a few bullets were flying high above us from anti-aircraft weapons. Each side had a few of them from the old army's armory. We were twenty inside the building, some behind sandbags on the ground level, some scattered on the floors above.

We received information from our scouts that a big offensive by the mercenaries and the PLO was on the way. We asked for reinforcements and were told it would take a few hours to organize and send help. Basically, the message said, "You are on your own. Hold the building at all costs and do not retreat."

Every single one of us knew what would happen if we were taken prisoner. The Geneva Convention rules and laws didn't apply here. We had seen and heard the stories of prisoners being dragged alive behind the jeeps through the streets of west Beirut. We saw the pictures in the newspapers and read the other side's propaganda campaigns, using naked, dead, young men dragged as a show of force.

You've seen this in western movies, right? How the bad cowboy is dragged behind a horse across the sand until he dies? Well, it was a little different in our Wild West. Crater-sized potholes covered the city streets. The government public works division was nonexistent or had taken an extended vacation. Unless the streets were beside some leader's house or the president's palace, the roads were in a miserable state of disrepair.

The young men would be dragged on hard asphalt behind a jeep. Within minutes their clothes would be shredded, and then their skin and flesh as well. They usually died soon after. If you met these executioners, the Marquis de Sade would look like your kindergarten teacher, all soft, cuddly, and gentle.

Did I make myself clear, that nobody was going to surrender? With no reinforcements on the way, we made a stand.

By accident or sheer luck, I was assigned to a position on the first floor. I was always getting lucky; maybe the elastic band on my arm with a sliver from the cross of Jesus Christ had something to do with keeping me alive that night. Don't laugh; it is what you believe in that can drive you to survive. We believed in the cross, and the men we fought believed that if they died in a holy war, they would go to heaven and find rivers of milk and honey and forty mermaids waiting for them, though I would joke that the bottom half of a mermaid is usually fish. The offensive started with mortar shells flying above us in both directions. They were trying to cut off both our retreat routes and the possibility of reinforcement; our side was trying to give us cover but not doing a very good job of it. Most of our mortar shells were falling short, sometimes hitting the same building we were in.

I think the Eagles got some of the lyrics for "Hotel California" from that hotel. You know the line? The one about "You can check out anytime you like, but you can never leave"? Within the hour, it became clear to the realists among us that we were greatly outnumbered, we were losing, and the enemy was within yards of the hotel lobby. If we had a retreat plan in place, we might live to fight another day. The heroes were not listening: they had decided to make their stand. Rashid told me to jump from the first floor onto the sandbags from the backside with a dozen more fighters and make our way back through the tunnels and buildings to another high-rise building behind the hotel and make a stand there. He and the other guys would provide cover, then follow us as soon as we were in a position to cover their retreat.

By a miracle, we made it to the new hotel and joined the fight. We were covering the street with bullets, but nobody was retreating. I had trusted Rashid many times with my life; it never crossed my mind to question him. We watched in horror from 300 feet away as the battle moved from floor to floor. Some explosions followed flashes on the first floor, and half an hour later it would move to the next floor up. As the night turned to dawn, the battle kept moving up the floors. We tried to help by providing fire support, but there were hundreds of fighters on the other side and only a dozen and a half of us. Our own new location was also under fire: we had to sit tight and watch as our friends were driven farther and farther up, floor-by-floor.

We asked about the reinforcements or if we could rejoin the battle, and we were repeatedly told to concentrate on holding the new positions.

As morning came, it was not the sun shining, the trees swaying in the cool morning breeze, or the birds singing that I saw, not even close. I saw six figures on the roof of the hotel looking down. The roof was to be the last stand. There was no helicopter for a rescue mission. This was it. The remaining six, my friend Rashid included, with the few bullets they had left.

The guys beside me were shouting and shooting at the same time. I knew what would happen next. I would have done the same.

The trapped fighters shut the steel door, the only access to the roof. They were out of ammunition. They stood on the edge of the roof holding hands, and then all six flew like dive-bombing birds to the ground, preferring to die rather than surrender. Watching this happen, I should have been scared or mad, but I am ashamed to say . . . Rashid taught me to make kites and now he was flying just like one, and I was secretly hoping he could fly, that he would land safely and run back to us. I turned my face in the other direction, as I was not able to follow the flight past. In my own way, I imagine them still flying. I know that I am in denial. That is the way I have dealt with the whole period of my teenage years.

Many years later, when I went for parachute training in Israel as a member of the Special Forces and saw the instruction video on how to jump from a plane, I could only think about my six flying friends. My friend, my protector, was dead. I lost confidence in the leadership that day. They lacked the planning and knowledge to assess the battleground. We had been sent to the slaughter.

I did not go to any of the funerals and did not hear the speeches about the heroism and sacrifices the guys made to keep us free. I decided I would no longer be a foot soldier, throwing myself into unorganized battles. I needed to do something bigger. I shut myself off and decided that in order to achieve what I had to do, I needed to be better than Yellow Eyes and his mercenaries. Yellow Eyes represented everyone I was fighting, and what I was fighting against.

That night I did not spot him, but I felt his presence. A strange bond connected us. I took him with me every night, into my nightmares. We became inseparable. I needed those nightmares. They kept me focused on my ultimate goal: to kill Yellow Eyes. They visited me not only at night during sleep; they were my constant companions, even in the daylight hours. My career as a foot soldier was over as quickly as it had begun, though I could think of nothing else other than eliminating the evil that was Yellow Eyes. I was daydreaming and fantasizing about the crazy jihadist, turning Muslims against Christians, neighbor against neighbor, just for money and power. *Where is he now, how many innocent lives has he taken? Did he join in the battle of the hotels?* I had felt this tingling feeling at the back of my neck that night, sure that he had me in his rifle sights when I was running to the back building. *How can I one day defeat him? Will I ever see him again?*

BASSAM:

The battle for the central district was the hardest and bloodiest Lebanon had seen during all the years of the civil war. Both sides took heavy losses.

Bassam did not care about the losses, especially since most of the fallen fighters from his side were African mercenaries. They were a dime a dozen. When they died, he did not have to pay them.

The Christian boys impressed him, he thought begrudgingly. They could shoot and fight. In the end, though, they were no match for his numbers. They preferred to die rather than surrender; they denied him the pleasure of seeing the moment of their death. He looked forward to every conflict, waiting for the moment he could watch the light in their eyes fade, second by second. Many times, he'd come close to an orgasm the moment he saw the last flicker of life leaving their miserable bodies.

But he still dragged their bodies across the city. Everybody in West Beirut knew his name and feared him. The more he terrorized, the more control he had. The innocent and the stupid thought that you had to terrorize your enemy. The reality in population control was to terrorize your own population into submission first; then they have no choice but to help and follow you. Even the PLO leaders wouldn't do anything on a major scale without consulting with him first. He always knew this day would come; he kept the news about the squad of suicidal soldiers he was creating a close secret. The real terror would start soon.

"You know, Ghassan, I swear I spotted a red-headed teenager running away from the hotel. This guy is like ghost with nine lives: every time I try to kill him he gets away. He was too far away for me to shoot him without exposing myself. Anyway, it couldn't have been the same little shit from my town could it? I hate that uppity little shit, and his family. He must be too young and too cowardly to be here".

Ghassan shook his head and grinned. "I remember him in his driveway, peeing himself when we made that final pass. We should have shot him."

"I keep thinking of him, for some strange reason. I feel like we are going to meet again, and when we do, he will take a ride behind my station wagon. I will parade his stupid body in front of our entire town's people. I will make sure he dies an ugly death, a death he deserved long ago, and I will bury his body in the same lot beside his house, where they made us dig for gas. I will make them pay for making me look foolish." Bassam hissed back.

While Bassam was thinking of killing Paul when they ran into each other, Paul was on a mission to make sure that meeting came to fruition.

PART TWO

13

SYRIAN HOSPITALITY

PAUL:

After the hotel battles, I was anxious to surrender my gear and return home. I'd had enough of watching my friends die to last me a hundred lifetimes. On the one-hour drive back, none of us said a word. I jumped from the back of the truck even before it had come to a full stop, dumped my weapons and the rest of my gear by the front door of the control center, and was free to go home. I walked up the hill to my aunt's house, taking my time and enjoying the view of the valley, the rocks, and the trees. I was not a nature lover or a tree hugger, but when you experience something like what I had the night before, life takes on a new meaning. I was thinking, *I might not have returned or ever made this walk ever again.* I had a new appreciation for life. My mother and aunt fussed over me and asked me a thousand questions. They got no reply, I had started living in a shell that I made for myself. It was the easiest way to cope.

The news traveled fast in Lebanon: CNN was no match for gossip. My family wanted to know what happened and who had died. I lied. I said I was not there, that I was at a different location and I did not know. I could not bring myself to say I had left and taken shelter somewhere else. Even though I was following orders, I was still ashamed. I was not a coward, but when Rashid told me to retreat, I jumped at the opportunity. Was it fear, logic, sound military tactics, or self-preservation? I had no answer.

I spent the next few weeks reading and hunting. I walked the valleys and hills with mixed feelings: I felt lucky, and guilty, and happy to be alive. To distract myself, and to pay back the generosity my aunt and her family had shown us, I decided to help in cultivating the fig and grape orchard that my aunt owned on top of the hill above her home. Early one morning I packed some lunch and a bottle of water, grabbed some tools and headed out to a hard day of labor, I was thinking this might distract from the anguish and guilt that plagued me. By midday I made no progress and I was exhausted, so I decided to take a lunch break.

Tony, a teenager a few years older than me, dropped by. He was hunting and was on his way back. Since I knew him very well, I invited him to share my lunch. He took one look at my progress, or lack thereof, grabbed the pitchfork and started showing me the proper way to turn the land. I kept on asking him questions and he kept on working, I was tired and wanted him to keep going. He was doing a much better job than me.

Suddenly, a mortar bomb from a 240 mm cannon landed on the opposite hill from us, between the pine trees. Tony dropped the fork, picked up his hunting rifle and took off at full speed to check it out. By the time I ran after him, he was already few hundred meters ahead of me and gaining, as he was bigger and faster. I slowed down, knowing that I could not catch him.

The Syrians were always using this tactic, drop a

bomb in a certain area and wait for the crowd to gather, then send more. It always worked, as for some strange reason people always gathered, even if there were no casualties to help. Being slow on that day saved my life. The second bomb landed near the first. Tony was there. He was badly injured. By the time I reached him, I knew I could not help him. I took his rifle and started shooting near the homes on the opposite hill, trying to signal for help. By the time a few men made it to us, Tony had bled to death.

I am not sure why I was always getting lucky. Maybe my life had a purpose. The first time on our driveway maybe because I was small, at the café for being quick, in the hotel being on a lower level, and this time because I was slow. The more questions I asked myself, the less answers I got.

My Aunt Cecilia had come for a visit, to check on us. Now she wanted to go back home, to our old hometown, where she still lived. She had been able to stay there, probably because she had bought protection—she had the money.

Cecilia is my father's sister. In Arabic, we have different words to differentiate between the relatives. You don't have to explain the relationship because the words you use will let people know if it is an uncle or aunt from your father's side or your mother's side. Sensing my withdrawal and wanting to pull me back to life, my father asked me to drive her. I was supposed to drive her only to the last Syrian roadblock and then turn back; her oldest son would pick her up there and take her back to town. To show my face back home would have been too dangerous for me and for her.

I took my father's car, a blue Mercedes 220S, and off we went. She asked me about girls and school. She was not aware of my involvement in the war: to her, I was still a baby. She was my father's oldest sister, and to her, my dad was still a baby. Within the hour, we arrived at the last Syrian roadblock on the east side and were stopped for a check. I took both identity cards and handed them over to the young Syrian soldier. He took a very long time checking them over. He looked at the card and picture, then back at me, over and over again. This made my aunt and me very nervous.

Then out of the blue he asked me, "Did you just have a haircut?"

Rule number one when you are at a Syrian checkpoint: Never, ever argue or try to explain. Just smile and say "Yes, sir." *Even if you disagree, don't argue.*

I obeyed the most sacred rule. "Yes, sir," I said.

"You look better now," he said. "Keep it short like that, you hear me, donkey?"

"Thank you, sir. I will keep it short, I promise."

It was only after he handed me back the cards that I noticed he was looking at my aunt's picture. The young soldier could not read and had mistaken me for my aunt. My aunt has thick, coarse, curly red hair. You would never mistake her for a man, or mistake me for her. I told my aunt what had happened and handed her back her own ID card. We had a long, hard laugh once I made sure the guard could no longer hear us. I dropped her off before the next roadblock.

I made a U-turn and started on my way back. This time I was not so lucky. I followed the etiquette rules for checkpoints. Slow down, turn the music off, open the window, put the interior light on, stop, and give them your most stupid grin.

This soldier was able to read. Shit, why do they always have to have one smart guy? I got stopped, then waved to the side. A very bad sign. When you get pulled to the side, you get searched, hassled for money, or forced to give some of them a lift somewhere.

"ID, stupid." They called us all "stupid" or "pig." Sometimes, if they were in a good mood, they called us "animal," and if they were happy, then it would be "donkey." This one was not happy.

"Here it is, sir," I said.

He looked at my ID for a long time. I was starting to get nervous.

"Your name is Bol?"

Pay attention here, very close attention. Most Arabs can't pronounce the letter *P* unless they are fluent in a western language. They pronounce the *P* as a *B*.

"No, sir, it is Paul, with a *P*." Stupid me, I had just violated rule number one and argued. Why did I do this? Because *bol* in Arabic means "urine." I did not want to be called urine, not to my face, anyway.

"Your name is Bol? Your parents must hate you, or they are just as stupid as you are." He started laughing, then called a bunch of his buddies over and explained that my name was urine. They had a good chuckle over that one.

I was supposed to just grin and agree. I knew that. I would have been on my way shortly, but I had to violate rule number two: I showed an attitude, and some pride, a big no-no. The Syrians had come to Lebanon pretending to be peacekeepers, but now they were an occupying army. They wanted to stomp on our pride and humiliate us. If they crushed our spirit and made us afraid to resist, they would control us.

"No, it is not Bol," I said. "It is Paul with a *P*, like Saint Paul. He was from Syria. You should know him."

"You are trying to teach me, you stupid pig-eating donkey? Get out of the car, Bol." Then he smacked me with the famous *sahsouh*. This is an open-handed slap on the back of the neck; it is meant to degrade and insult more than to hurt. When I looked back at him, he saw the flash of anger in my eyes and that set him off. They dragged me out of the car and took turns kicking and punching me. I was tempted to stop them and show them the proper kicking technique.

Then I was invited for a private tour of the Syrian hospitality suite. First, I got to experience the *fallak*, better known to you as *bastinado*, or foot whipping. On the east side of Beirut, we called it a Syrian pedicure. They strapped my bare feet to a piece of wood, not unlike a two-by-four, and placed them in a clamp to hold them still. Using a thin rattan stick, they took turns teaching me how to pronounce my own name. After every ten or twelve strokes, they would ask, "What is your name, pig?"

"It is Paul, sir," I would say. "With a *P.*"

"Are you sure it is not Bol?" For some reason they found this funny.

"No, sir, it is Paul," I insisted. "Read my ID card. The *B* has three dots under it." The Arabic alphabet does not have the sound *P* in it. Many Christians adopted French and Western names, so we invented the three dots under the letter *B* to differentiate *P* from *B.*

The whipping would then go on for ten or twelve more strokes, the same question would be repeated, and I would answer the same way. After a few dozen strokes, you lose feeling in your feet. The pain becomes constant and the reaction to the stick making contact is delayed, which gives the torturer a false impression: they think it isn't hurting anymore. After a couple hundred strokes, they bored of me and transferred me to their spa wing.

Waterboarding is new to the North American market, but we had an older, much used version. I was escorted to the washrooms. The toilets there had not been cleaned in over two years, since the occupying army took over the school that was now serving as their base. It was a small, old building on top of one of the highest mountain ranges in the country, between the Bekaa Valley and Beirut.

The spa treatment did not involve a manicure. It did include a facial and a massage. Maybe the manicure was booked for later or it required an upgrade. Thankfully I did not get the chance to find out.

My face was dunked a dozen times into the filthy toilet, which was full of dirty water, germs, and flies, until I started choking and gagging and needed to breathe again. This was the special hydrating Syrian facial. After every dunk, the same question was asked: "Say that your name is Bol and your last name is shit."

I remember thinking, *oh, this guy speaks English!* Bol. Shit. Get it?

"It is Paul, with three dots under the *B*." I was stubborn then, and I am stubborn now. I wanted to push them and myself to the limit. I did not want them to break me. At the time, I thought this was all I had left. They had humiliated and insulted me, but at least I could salvage some pride. But every person has a breaking point. I was quickly approaching mine. I started praying for death.

Next came their version of the massage. Never try it. I was struggling, so it took a few of them to force me outside and secure me with a rope inside a large rubber tire from a tractor, or maybe a large truck—I was not focused on the actual make and size at that point. Four happy aestheticians and massage therapists rolled the tire to the top of the hill, positioned it, and set it to roll.

"What is your name, pig?"

I said, "Paul." Under my breath, I muttered, "Bol shit." I thought that was pretty funny. I was amazed I still had a sense of humor.

"See you at the bottom of the hill, you stupid pig."

They pushed the tire over the edge of the hill and it began to pick up speed and bounce up and down and sometimes sideways. I got dizzy and puked all over myself; I lost my sense of direction. I closed my eyes and prayed for a quick and painless death. I got bounced around for about a minute, a very long minute; this was not your Disney roller-coaster minute. Finally, the tire made it to the bottom of the hill and fell on its side. My prayers were not answered: I did not die. I had never gone to church unless I was forced to, and I never paid attention in religion classes. Maybe I should have. If I had been a better Christian, maybe God would have answered me. I only lost consciousness.

The next thing I knew, I was lying on a wet concrete floor with about an inch of water on it. The room had a solid steel door and no windows; it was pitch-dark except for a thin ray of light sneaking under the door. I remember looking at the light and thinking, *I am on my way to heaven. Where are the stairs?* I loved that song. I was bruised from head to toe, every bone in my body was hurting, and I stank from the facial treatment and the puking. I was in a semi-conscious state, drifting in and out of reality. I was riding my bike and flying kites in the old neighborhood. I was sitting with my cousins at a family picnic, in the shade under a tree near the natural spring with its icy water, eating my mother's delicious food and waiting for the watermelon to burst. We placed the melon in the cold water, and when it cracked, that meant it was cold and ready to be eaten.

That was how most hostages and prisoners of war cope with the harsh conditions, by retreating and hiding in a comfortable fantasy world, reliving happy moments. I mastered this technique. I could withdraw immediately and ignore the outside world, recreating another world for myself.

A few hours later, the steel door opened and the guard threw something on the wet floor beside me. It was painful to move but I managed to grab it. When I placed it under the door where the light was coming from, I saw it was a stale piece of bread, covered with green mold. I was happy, actually thrilled, and willing to eat it, but my jaw was broken and I was not able to open my mouth. I soaked it in the filthy water for a few minutes until it got softer and then ate it one small piece at a time so I wouldn't have to chew on it. With a bit of salt, it would have been delicious. I should have called room service and asked for some.

I was lucky. Because of my age and the lack of any criminal evidence against me, I did not get the royal treatment. That was reserved for the political or military prisoners. Later, I heard stories from others who had been treated to Syrian hospitality. They were offered services that were not in my spa package. They had their fingernails and toenails removed, and electric therapy applied to their privates. What was that like? Maybe like having a lightning rod in your pants? I preferred not to find out. I did get to be an ashtray for a few of them while standing on one foot for hours. Every time I got tired and put my leg back down, they extinguished their cigarettes on my back and legs—no big deal. All in all, I am glad I wasn't offered the opportunity to sit on bottles or take baths in icy water. Some of the other guests even had to drink their own urine. Why didn't my hosts think of that? Bol drinking his own bol. I told you they were not that smart.

I felt cheated. I should have called their head office to complain. Maybe I could have spoken to Hafez al-Assad himself: he was the CEO at the time. He might have offered me a return visit, on the house.

Finally night came, and with it a break from the pampering. I was not looking forward to my next-day specials.

When I did not show up at home that night, everybody became worried. They formed a search party and started calling. If you had connections, you could find anybody. If you had money, you could buy anybody; if you had both, you could rule. The golden rule applied, especially in Lebanon: The man with the gold, rules. That is what my grandfather always told me.

14

LOST AND FOUND

PAUL:

The search party went nowhere quick. Nobody knew where I was. My mother called her father—he had connections and roots in Syria. Let me take you back a few decades and explain.

My grandfather's father was forcibly recruited into the Turkish army and died in World War I, just like thousands of young Lebanese men. With no military skills, they were pushed to the front lines like sheep to the slaughterhouse, and few of them ever came back. My grandfather's mother, now a young widow, was no longer able to feed the family because food supplies in Mount Lebanon were mostly routed to the military. The civilian population relied on homegrown vegetables, corn, and fruit. To add to their misery, that same year Lebanon experienced the largest attack of locusts in its history. All food supplies vanished. One third of the population died from starvation, not from the war. This happened more than thirty years before Israel was founded, but if you ask a Lebanese about the famine, they will blame it on Israel and tell you that the Jews had farms of locusts they unleashed on the mountain. Almost every disaster is blamed on Israel; Lebanese leaders are not able to take responsibility for their decisions. They give Israel the credit.

My grandfather's mother took her four children and traveled in a caravan-like group toward the Bekaa Valley in search of food and shelter for her young family.

Only six years old, small and weak from hunger, my grandfather got tired during the long, hard march and was not able to keep up. He fell behind and got lost. His mother must have looked for him but was not able to find him; she had to keep up with the group. In order to not risk getting lost herself and endangering the rest of her children, she'd left him to God's mercy. A Muslim family found him crying under a tree and took him home to northern Syria with them.

He grew up with that family, just like one of their own. However, they knew from his name he was Christian, and called him Khalil the Nesrani (slang for Christian). He was sent to a Muslim school with their children and spoke with a trace of a Syrian accent. Eventually, he made his way back home and found his family when he was twenty years old. Every time he told me the story, I felt goose bumps all over my body. His memories were so vivid, especially when he recounted that first meeting with his mother fourteen years later. His mother and siblings had assumed he was dead. By then his mother was almost blind; his two brothers and sister had gone out to a village wedding, and she was left home alone. She instantly recognized his voice without being able to clearly see him. He would tell me that he could still feel her fingers on his face when she tried to make sure it was him. He said, "She could not see me, but she felt me."

One of the boys from his foster family grew up to become an influential and respected sheikh, a true

Muslim scholar, not like the extremists that understand the religion as it suits their purposes. When searching for me, it was to him my grandfather turned to for help; they were like brothers, after all. It took two days to locate my resort hotel and another day to pay off the Syrian commanding officer for my release and get me safely back home. By then I had spent four days on this vacation courtesy of the Syrian army. (Check them out on Trip Advisor; the resort is at the top of its "not recommended" list.)

It took a few months for the concussion, the bruises, the burns, and the wounds to heal, but there was a deeper wound festering under the surface. The hatred was consuming me. I wanted payback and revenge. I was humiliated but I was not broken: that was the only positive I took from this, the knowledge that I was a survivor.

Until this very day, whenever I hear a Syrian accent, I go back to that tire at the bottom of the hill. My cousin is married to a Syrian woman; she is a sweetheart, funny and generous, and she treats me like a king whenever I visit. When she starts speaking, however, I take deep breaths and focus on her beautiful face in order not to jump up and smack her.

BASSAM:

A BMW driven by Bassam pulled into the parking of the Syrian base to exchange drugs for explosives; Ghassan pulled in behind him in a Mercedes. He saw the blue Mercedes 220S that belonged to the Red Devil's father parked just outside the main door. He hoped the sister was there. He would pay any amount to get her.

He asked about the car and who was in it, and got the dirty look from the Mokhabarat guys. These guys thought too highly of themselves. They thought they were feared like the Nazi SS men. Bassam had no time for these degenerates; he was only using them to get what he needed.

He went through the possibilities in his head. If the father and mother were in jail, he would ransom them and sell them back to their relatives. Or, even better, he would have taken them home and given them to his own father as a sign of respect. Then maybe he would talk to him again.

The ultimate prize would have been the Red *Shytan*. Him, he would not exchange. He would kill him and drag his body all over town, even if it caused more problems with his parents.

The Syrians had a better offer for the car and prisoner. They were under orders to release the prisoner and keep the car. They would not tell him who was in jail or anything about the situation.

15

RAMI AND THE MISSING GRAVE

PAUL:

A few weeks later, my family decided to move once more, to a place of our own. My father had secured work as a maintenance mechanic at a college. He would be repairing the buses. We were given a small, two-bedroom apartment in the building next door to the school, where some teachers lived. The apartment was on the ground floor of a three-story building, with one washroom; again, I had to wait to use it per mother's rule. Girls first, boys last.

It was difficult being back home, living like a child under my parent's roof, expected to go to school, when I'd been a soldier and, worse, I'd spent time being tortured in a prison. I'd left childhood behind.

It was a great school, well known and organized. We practically lived in the school, as the walls between it and our home were joined, but my brother, still the iceman, managed to always be late. I have no idea how he accomplished this. All he had to do was jump over the wall and he would land in the playground.

In school, we were taught useless history, Arabic pre- and post-Islamic poetry, geography, and Arabic literature. I sucked and failed at all of it. Not because I was stupid but because I had no interest in any of it. I was resenting all that was Arabic and Islamic.

Math and science were subjects I excelled at. My marks were off the charts even though I didn't study or open a book. I was too busy playing football, which is soccer for some of you. I never bothered to buy the books: I took the money my father gave me for textbooks and saved it for myself.

Every morning before school started, I woke up early to help my father fill the diesel tanks for the buses and do any urgent last-minute repairs. One morning, I was filling up one of the small VW buses that the hippies drove in the sixties; the buses were painted green and white, the colors of the school. I noticed a kid about my age walking around the playground. It was too early to be in school, about 7 a.m., and school did not start until 8:30. Surely my brother was still snoring away at home. The kid came over and asked if he could watch what we were doing, I said sure, and he ended up helping me with my chores every day from then on. His name was Rami.

One day during a soccer match, I was running through center field, when a bigger boy tackled me. We were winning and the other team was frustrated. He fouled me on purpose and tried to injure me to slow us down. He and I started fighting. He was bigger, but I was faster. Suddenly and before I could react, two more boys jumped me and threw me to the ground. Rami dived in the middle of the human pile without concern for his safety and helped me. That same day, he and I decided to slash our wrists with a knife, press them together, and become blood brothers. Rami and I became friends, best friends. Other friends would call us brothers.

We were both sixteen years old and practically inseparable, except during summer holidays, when he used to go with his family to visit his grandmother in the mountains for a few weeks. Rami was always the voice of reason and got me out of trouble too many times to remember. Later on, we would trust each other with our lives, and we protect one another to this very day. He was very tall; even at sixteen and not yet full grown, he was already a giant. He was also very handsome. His black hair was always perfectly combed, and he had big hazel eyes. He also had a birthmark on his right cheek that added to his good looks: it was perfectly proportioned and placed in the middle of his cheek, as if somebody had drawn it on.

A couple of months after we met, he asked if I would go with him to visit his grandfather's grave, something he had never done before. He had always wanted to visit it, but his parents were against it. That made the trip a must for both of us. He knew what city the cemetery was in, but not its exact location. Obviously, we did not tell our parents about the trip—we were not totally stupid, just partially. We wore our bathing suits under our shorts and, to camouflage our destination even further, I took my snorkelling gear and a towel with me and told my mother we were going to the beach. The Mediterranean Sea was a one-minute walk away. Rami and I had been swimming, diving, and fishing daily.

Early on Saturday morning, we retrieved our small savings and took a two-hour bus ride. We were two teenage boys, traveling alone to a city in the north, to a place neither one of us had ever visited. In Lebanon, a two-hour bus ride takes you to the other end of the country. Remember, this was a small country with big problems.

I had heard of this city before: it was famous for its delicious pastries. I also knew a large percentage of the inhabitants were Muslim, which made it risky to visit. However, the civil war was mostly in Beirut at that point and the north was quiet. I did not believe we would be stopped at any roadblocks.

We arrived at the city center. We started our search the old fashioned way, asking questions and talking to people.

When you needed to know something in Lebanon, you headed to a café full of old men. They were the historians of each town and city and neighborhood. They knew the lay of the land. They would direct you, and even misdirect you, but they would never utter the words, "We don't know."

We approached two wizened geezers playing *tawle,* smoking *argile* (a water pipe), and drinking Turkish coffee. We told them the name of my friend's grandfather, his approximate age, and what little information we had, and let them chew on it for a while. Of course, not wanting to say the magic words "We don't know," they sent us on a wild-goose chase, to the wrong burial grounds. We walked around looking for similar last names and found none. Then I spotted an older woman nearby. Women do not have the same phobias as men. They can actually say the words "I don't know." So I asked her. She told me that this name could be at another location, not far from here. She gave us directions.

By a miracle, we found the other cemetery and started our search anew. The first thing I noticed was the difference in the way the graves were arranged and presented. There were no crosses or Virgin Mary statues anywhere.

"Rami, this woman has sent us to a Muslim cemetery."

"Yeah, that is what we want," he said, as if it were the most natural thing in the world. "My grandfather is a Muslim, just like my father and me."

I'm sure the shock on my face was pronounced.

Rami was a name that can be both Muslim and Christian. It had never crossed my mind that he was a Muslim.

There I was, in a city where ninety-five percent of the people were Muslims, walking around cemeteries with my best friend who I had just found out was a Muslim. Oh my God. My best friend and brother was *a Muslim.*

This had to be a dream—no, a nightmare. I had to think on my feet quickly. I acted as if I had known all along. I moved away from him to look for the name in a different row of graves. As I sat under a tree to collect my thoughts and come to grips with this new reality, I heard him shouting for me. He had located the grave with his grandfather's name on it.

"We should go back to the market and get some sweets," Rami suggested.

"I have to be back at home," I said. "I am busy with my father in the garage."

What I really wanted was to be alone and think. On the bus ride back, he asked if we could stop for a swim, but I told him he should go alone because I had to continue on home in order to be back in time to do my chores.

I got home, announced my presence to my mother, and went straight to the roof. I had created my own personal space there by stringing up a tarp around the scaffold that used to serve as a clothesline, and furnishing the area with an old discarded sofa, a couple of chairs, and a small table. This was my headquarters, my hideout. The only two people who visited were Rami, who was not welcome at this particular time, and my younger sister, who came once to deliver food.

So many questions were burning in my mind. *How can a Muslim be living among us? Why is he going to a Christian school? And, most of all, how can I trust and be friends with him?* I could not organize my thoughts and needed an explanation.

On the third floor of our building lived one of the teachers. He taught English as a second language, as well as Arabic literature, a rare combination. He was smart and well read. He once gave me a book about hypnotism. I read the whole book three times and practiced for two weeks. When I tested the techniques on my sister, I failed to make her yawn.

I needed some information now, and he was the only person I knew who might have it.

I knocked on his door. It was Sunday and he was home. I stepped inside and sat on the only couch he owned. He sensed I was wrestling with something. As we started talking about the general subject of religion, he told me he was a Christian from Syria and he had come here after a few years studying in Rome to become a priest. That was a surprise to me. We were fighting the Syrian army. What was going on? Was this a test? I sucked at tests.

I asked him what he knew about the Muslim religion, and he went on about the different faiths, religions, and the many Muslim denominations. He knew my friend and was able to tell me Rami was a Sunni. I asked if he had any books on the subject, and he handed me the Holy Quran. Now there was another small problem. The book was huge and written in difficult Arabic verses, not an easy language even for a native Arabic speaker, much less a teenager. But some research was required.

Why did some Muslims want to kill us? Why did Syria want to occupy us? How could I avenge my family and friends, and terminate people like Yellow Eyes, and at the same time love and trust people like my friend? These people had no beef with us, and my father knew hundreds if not thousands of them. I had so many questions and hardly any answers. However, the more I read, the more I realized that the two religions had many similarities; Jesus and Mary were mentioned many times in the book. I started to understand that the problems and differences were not about religion. They are about culture and politics, power and money.

Knowing that, I did not want to fight and be a drone soldier anymore. I needed knowledge, I needed a different approach, and mostly I needed strength.

Researching and understanding the enemy while developing my fighting skills became an obsession. I had decided the PLO, the Syrians, and their agents were my only enemies. I would not fight against any Lebanese unless it was in self-defense. I gave away my comic books, the ones it had taken me years to collect, thinking at the time I no longer had time for entertainment and hobbies. I read every book I could get my hands on, every military manual, every spy story, every book on military history and tactics. I needed more. I wanted to train in the latest techniques and technologies. My resources were limited. I couldn't find what I wanted.

I remembered the trainer who had kicked my ass in training camp. I asked the boys in school, and each one gave me a different answer about what martial art I should learn. They each thought the one they practiced was the best. I used to feel envy when I saw the boys going or coming from training with their *gis* (uniforms) slung around their shoulders and tied up with the belt. I did not understand the color codes, but most belts I saw were white and yellow. Those were the show-offs. They wanted the world to see they were tough and practiced martial arts. I never saw the black belts flaunting them anywhere.

Not far from the house were a few clubs—karate, kung fu, tae kwon do, judo, boxing. I knew people at every club, and I went to watch them all. I tried to join, but my mother had had enough of violence and would not help me with the money to join or to buy a *gi*.

Rami and I never discussed the differences in our faiths; we resumed our friendship as strong as ever.

During the war, electricity became rare. We only had a couple of hours of power per day. My father made more money installing generators at schools, hospitals, and factories than he made fixing buses. Not everybody had a generator, only institutions and the really rich. Today, electricity is still erratic, and every street has a generator. People pay a monthly fee and share the cost. Back then, propane and candles were the only sources of stable illumination.

I needed money for training, so Rami and I became a candle dealers

I built a small wooden cart, using some discarded wheel bearings from my father's garage. Then I collected the money I had hidden away, that which my father gave me for schoolbooks and which was never spent on books, and bought dozens of boxes of candles.

Rami and I went from house to house, door to door, offering home-delivered candles. Our enterprise was an instant success. My father helped me customize my bike, and I made a trailer I could pull behind my bike while Rami rode his bike alongside. We quickly had many regular customers who waited for us by the door with their money ready. I was told never to skip a day or they would have no candles for the evening. We made a lot of money buying candles at fifty cents and selling them for a lira (one hundred cents).

Everybody called me an entrepreneur, but I had different ideas. The money was a means to an end, not the end itself. I wanted Yellow Eyes and his brother, and to get to them, I needed training and more knowledge. Rami was aware of my obsession and on many occasions told me to drop it. "Those guys are thugs," he'd say. "You don't want to get involved with them."

"You don't understand," I'd respond. "They drove us

out of our home and destroyed my father's business."

"If it was not them, it would have been somebody else."

"I know that," I said, "but it *was* them and I will make them pay. My father will never be the same again. Look where and how we live now."

"You are still pissed off about your blue bike," he would tease me. "Tell me how can I help."

"I don't want you involved in this," I'd say. "It's something I have to do on my own."

We made so much money selling candles, I was able to buy a small motorcycle and decided to join a martial arts club. I went looking for the perfect fit. During my visits to different clubs, I came across the trainer from the military training camp. I figured, why not try this one? I already had proof he knew what he was doing.

I collected my courage, got my nerves under control, and went inside. I used to think of an academy like the ones in the Bruce Lee movies. Boy, was I wrong. The guys were friendly and welcoming, though a few wannabes were showing off their physiques and belts, walking around like roosters in the henhouse. I got my *gi* and registration out of the way, then I tried to put the white belt on properly. I made a mess of it. The *gi* and belt had to be worn just right. One of the guys who was in my class at school helped me. I walked in to the dojo and gave an awkward bow. I didn't know what to do next, so I just stood around, watching some of them do their stretches while others talked amongst themselves.

The trainer walked in and bowed, announcing his presence to the class. The class fell absolutely silent. All I could hear was the ringing in my ears. We lined up in four rows, the white belts (the newbs) at the left, the yellow and green to our right, the blue and brown to their right, and the black belts on the far right. Those guys looked cool.

I took to the art like a duck to water. I was fast and graceful, a good combination. The trainer complimented me on a regular basis. Before long, I was doing moves with more precision than all the yellow belts and some of the green belts. I practiced non-stop. I also saw some guys swinging the nunchucks and immediately went out to buy some. I could not find any, so I made my own from a broom handle and a dog chain. I kept playing with the length of the chain until I got it right.

I was not satisfied. I also joined the boxing club and the judo club. My grades were suffering. My parents lectured me tirelessly. My buddy Johnny forged my father's signature on my report cards, and I returned them to school every quarter. Learning about war and martial arts consumed me. During those years, I did not socialize much with friends. I stayed at home, reading most of the time. My mother was happy. Reading at home meant I was off the streets and out of danger. What she did not realize is *what* I was reading. To keep me happy and satisfied at home, she would make me my favorite snacks and desserts, and that suited me fine.

My older sister walked into the tiny room one day while I was practicing the nunchucks in front of the mirror. By that time, they were almost invisible in my hands. I was in mid-swing when she walked behind me. I hit her on the head and gave her a scar just above her eyebrow. It was an accident—I felt awful. I loved her dearly.

I continued my training without breaks; I went to many tournaments and won them all. My parents had no idea I was competing. My fear of failure kept me from telling them. I did not want to lose in front of my parents. The other kids had their parents cheering for them. I just rode my bike to the tournaments and did my thing.

One day while I was watching a practice session

in one of the other clubs, I saw a little guy choking to sleep big guys twice his size, using a new art that I did not know, and had never heard of. It was similar to judo but had different finishing moves. The next day, I joined the jujitsu class. After four years of long daily training, I earned my first black belt; then I collected one in judo and another in Tae kwon do. I also loved Muay Thai and excelled in boxing.

At nineteen years old, I declared myself fit and ready for the next stage of development. I needed to contribute, but I did not know how or where to start. I was ready physically, but Yellow Eyes continued to haunt me. And he continued to scare me.

I made many other friends from the clubs, and a few of them were also Shia, so now I had friends who were Christians, Sunni Muslims, Shia Muslims, and Druze. Confusing? Not really. Welcome to Lebanon, Habibi.

16

MORNING MIST AT NIGHT

PAUL:

At the college next door, there were always volleyball tournaments going on, but I did not usually attend. Rami, now over six feet, six inches tall, was a good player and the top spiker in the region, and he made sure everybody knew it. He asked me if I would come to watch, and I agreed. He had come to see me in more than a dozen martial art tournaments, and the least I could do was show him some support.

My second sister, two years younger than me, had many friends, and they were always coming over to visit. Most of them were nice to me and I was polite but distant with them, respectful, as was expected of me. One of them was funny, so we joked around a lot, but I wasn't interested in her romantically. None of them caught my attention like that, not until I saw *her.*

I was with friends watching the volleyball match when my sister walked in with her group. Two of them I knew very well, but the third one I had never seen.

I asked my sister if she wanted to sit with us and she

gave me that "are you serious?" look. I had never hung out with her or her friends before. Remember, I told you she was the smart one in the family? She smiled knowingly, winked at me, and came over with her friends.

They sat one row in front of us on the bleachers and watched the warm-up. Many of the girls were really watching Rami and he knew it. I mean, the guy was built like an Adonis—tall, muscular, with thick black hair and almond-shaped hazel eyes. I was shorter but much more powerfully built after years of hard training. My trademark red hair and freckles had faded. Now my hair was dark brown and hardly any freckles remained on my face.

The match started, most of the crowd watched, but not me. I was too busy watching the back of the girl in front of me. She had shiny shoulder-length black hair and flawless white skin. I could see the contours of her neck every time she moved her head back. I made a joke when someone misplayed the ball, and all the girls turned toward me and started laughing. I was a comedian when I wanted to be.

I wish I could say that when she turned to look at me, she turned out to be cross-eyed, was missing a few teeth, or had a big nose. But I can't. She was perfect, flawless. She had perfect pearly white teeth, the kind of tiny Scandinavian nose we call retroussé, the kind that would have cost thousands to have done but in her case was God-given—and her eyes! For me, it has always been mostly about the eyes, the window to the soul. Her eyes were blue, the bluest of blue, like a deep azure Caribbean Sea blue.

She said something in reply to my joke, and I just stared at her. I did not hear a thing she said, partly because of the noise and my tinnitus, and partly because I was frozen. My funny comebacks deserted me, and I was like a deer caught in the headlights. I stammered something stupid, I don't remember what. I don't remember a single play in that match either, or even who won.

After the match was over, Rami came over and as usual got the girls' attention. He started to joke with the stunner, and I gave him that look that only he and I could understand. We even had our own code we had developed over the years. Nobody else could understand it. We'd be speaking our regular Lebanese dialect but we'd substitute certain words for certain other words. If you didn't know the code, it would make no sense. It was only for us.

Rami understood my "off-limits" look right away, even though I had never used it in all the years we had known each other, and he backed right off. I asked my sister if she wanted me to walk her group back to our house because it was late and dark outside. Everybody laughed. They thought I was joking because we lived next door to the stadium. I was not. I wanted to walk home with them and then offer to give Miss Perfect a ride back to her house or, an even better option, offer to walk her home.

We walked home. It took us a whole minute. I asked the rest of the girls if they needed me to walk them home. The funny one just looked at me, smiled, and said, "Oh, in all the years I have been to your house and left late at night, you never offered me your protection."

"You're so funny," I said. "Who would dare give you trouble? You would wrap your tongue around his neck and strangle him."

I offered the stunner a ride or a walk home. and she accepted. I was barely able to ask her for her name.

"My name is Nada," she said. Nada in Arabic means "morning mist." "Thank you. If you can walk me home, I would appreciate it. I am scared to walk by the cemetery at night."

For the first time, I was grateful the cemetery was so

close to our house.

I am usually a fast walker. Whenever I walked my sister back home—she was scared to walk by the cemetery at night, too—she would complain to my mother that she had to jog the whole way to keep up with me. That night I walked slowly and took my time. I did not know where she lived, and if I got her home too quickly, our little date would end before it had even started.

Even walking at a leisurely pace, we reached her home in less than ten minutes. Her parents were outside, as most people are during the summer evenings in Lebanon. Her house was modest but bigger than ours. There were a few steps at the front and a small balcony. I walked with her to the front steps and said hello to her parents; I did not want to give them the impression we were sneaking around. Her mother gave me a questioning look and Nada explained I was the brother of her friend, and I had walked her home after the volleyball match.

When I got back home, a few friends were hanging around the school playground next door. I went to join them.

Rami knew me as well as I knew myself. We had no secrets. I knew about the dozen girls he had dated and had often covered for him. He asked me on many occasions to double date with him because his many admirers would bring a friend along, but I always refused.

He took one look at me and knew I had things to discuss. We said quick goodbyes to the others and headed up to the roof. As soon as we sat down, my blood brother said, "OK, bro, what is happening? You look like you have been stricken by Aphrodite."

"Aphrodite is Greek," I said. "I have been stricken by Abla."

"Oh yeah, Antar," he said, and he started laughing so hard he almost fell off the chair. Antarah was a pre-Islamic Arab hero and poet who lived from 525 to 608 and who was famous both for his poetry and for his adventurous life, which included a long and extravagant romance with Abla. Because of the difference in their social status, he could never marry her. Rami and I were joking then. It never crossed my mind how true these words would be.

"Omigod, did you see how gorgeous she is, bro? She is perfect."

"Relax, you don't even know her," he said. "I hear her family are a bunch of stuck-up show-offs."

I wouldn't listen. I turned my hearing off. All I wanted was for morning to come so I could go by her house.

From that day on, every time I drove by her house in my father's car, she would run to the balcony or window and wave to me. She recognized the sound of the engine. You should always look in front of you when you drive, it is a basic driving skill, but a few times I almost hit the wall beside her house because I was looking up or back at her.

Fadi, a friend of mine from the club, was dating one of her friends, so I asked him if he could arrange a double date with his girlfriend, but he should also make sure that Nada knew in advance that it was me. It took almost a week for him to get back to me. I did not want to appear desperate, but I was. During a break in practice he told me we were going to the movies on Sunday. "Allllll fouuuuur offff usssss," he said very slowly, and he laughed.

I played it cool. "OK," I said. "I will try and make time, no problem." Inwardly, I was counting the seconds. After the sparring session, I showered and left quickly.

On Sunday, we picked up the girls in his car about one kilometer from their homes. They made some excuse, I am sure, and told their parents they were going to visit some friend. A few years back, girls did not have as much freedom as they do now.

Fadi had a red Alfa Romeo sports car that we loved. He was working full-time as a jeweller and made a decent living. I was grateful for the small size of the car. In order to fit in the back we had to squeeze together, so that our bodies touched.

Rocky II with Sylvester Stallone was the hottest movie of the season. I was surprised the girls wanted to see this kind of movie; I had assumed they would choose some romantic picture. When we got to the movie theater, it was mobbed. A few people recognized me from the latest martial arts tournament I had won and came over to congratulate me. Nada was curious about the attention. She asked, "How do all these people know you and why are they shaking your hand? Are you famous or something?"

"No, I am not," I said. "Those are just some guys I know through martial arts."

"So *Rocky* is your kind of movie?"

"I would have preferred *Love Story*. Watching Ali McGraw would have been so much better than Sylvester Stallone." And with that I got punched in the shoulder. I loved it.

During the movie, Fadi and Nada's friend were all over each other. We only held hands. and that felt natural. After the movie we went for ice cream and took a walk by the sea. The time went by so fast, the whole afternoon went by in minutes. Before I knew it, it was time to drive the girls home.

As we approached the house, I spotted her mom on the balcony, watching us. I could tell right away she was not happy.

I did not see Nada for at least another two weeks. These were probably the longest two weeks of my life, besides the weeks I spent at training camp. When I finally was able to speak with her, she told me it would be difficult for us to keep seeing each other. "My parents do not approve of you," she said. "My mom even said, 'From all the boys with good families around here, you have to date this refugee?'"

It was true: I was a refugee in my own country. We were living in the small house given to us by the college, and my father was scraping together a living to raise four kids. I had never thought of us as refugees or second class until now, however. Not long ago, we had been the most comfortable family in our neighborhood, and now the parents of the only girl I had developed feelings for were looking down on me.

We kept on seeing each other behind her parents' back, using friends as couriers for messages because I was not able to call. Fadi's girlfriend was one go-between, and we met most times at her boyfriend's house. We saw each other often for the best part of four years. Then one day, her friend told me that Nada could no longer see me; she was going to be engaged to an engineer who had just come back from Kuwait with money. He had proposed to her, and her family approved.

I was angry and hurt. Deep down, though, I was actually relieved. I had plans of my own, and I did not want to put her in danger. My friends noticed my detachment. Rami said to me, "There are plenty of fish in the sea. Let me take you fishing and cheer you up. I guarantee you will not remember her name after a night on the town with me."

I rarely drank alcohol and did not go out to bars, but that night we went barhopping in the entertainment district, which was full of bars, nightclubs, illegal gambling casinos, and bordellos. The boys were having the time of their lives, drinking, gambling, and whoring. I skipped most of the activities and sat down to watch a high-stakes poker game in the basement of one of the whorehouses.

I found the boys just as a fight was brewing in one of the clubs. As always, I went over and talked them down and got them out of there. Rami left with a girl. He was spending his money on short-time hotels. Nothing worked for me: I was constantly thinking of Nada.

17

FOOD DELIVERY AND THE HUNDRED DAYS WAR

PAUL:

The Syrians were perpetually embarrassed by the small Christian militia. They decided it was time to teach us another lesson. Hafez al-Assad, the Syrian president, was supposed to have an army that could fight Israel and defeat it. That was the message he was selling to his people. He belonged to a small minority, and having big, bad Israel as a ceaseless threat on Syria's doorstep was keeping him in power.

The whole Christian area was surrounded, and the only escape was into the sea. The pounding started one morning without any warning. This was not the pounding of a headache. It was three weeks of continuous, full-scale bombing of the entire area. They didn't care where the bombs landed. Most of them exploded in civilian areas, and hundreds of people died.

We were getting ready for school when it started. My sisters were still fussing with their hair, and as usual my mother was doing her best to get my brother out of bed. When she was lucky, he was only a few minutes late. Rami and I were in the middle of the morning chores, which my father trusted us with. I told him I would go home and make us two *labne* (strained yogurt) sandwiches; these were a favorite of his. I used to add some salt, a little olive oil, and a small sprinkle of dried mint leaves.

Having given up her daily mission-impossible of sending my brother to school on time, my mother was doing the dishes at the small sink. The only running water was cold, so she used to heat water on the gas stove to wash the dirty dishes. I placed the homemade bread on the table and walked by her to the fridge to get the strained yogurt.

"Have you finished helping your father?" she asked.

"Almost done," I said. "Rami is still working. He should be done soon."

"Does he come every day to help?"

"Yes, most days. He likes it; he gets to drive the big buses around the courtyard."

"But you guys are older now and have your own cars," she pointed out. "Why does he still come?"

"He likes to help us," I said. "Driving the buses is just an excuse he makes, since he is not even paid. This way Dad is not embarrassed."

She threw the dishwashing rag at me. I ducked and made her miss. We had a private joke about her aim. When I was younger and got in trouble, which was all the time, my mom used to quickly draw her slippers and throw them at me. I always ducked, so she always missed, but I would tell her that she was a faster draw than Clint Eastwood.

She continued, "You are very lucky to have found a true friend like him."

"I know, Mom. He is like a brother to me."

"Put some cucumber with the *labne*," she told me.

"Rami likes it better that way."

The metal door leading to the kitchen from the backyard was wide open. I opened the fridge door and reached for the cucumbers. Suddenly, the kitchen window shattered, and pressure threw me against the refrigerator. Usually you feel the explosion before you hear it. Don't try it—just take my word for it. It's safer that way.

A large piece of shrapnel from the 240 mm cannon bomb that had just landed behind our house, an early morning gift from the Syrian army, zipped past, a few centimeters from my ear, and ripped through the fridge door. If I had known it was coming, I would have held the cucumbers at an angle and it would have saved me the trouble of cutting them. This is probably a lame joke, but I still can't help it.

I twisted around to look at my mother. Her face was bleeding from the shattered glass, but she did not seem to notice. She was looking at me and screaming. My right leg was drenched in blood, yet I felt nothing. Shrapnel had cut deep, just above the knee. I tried to walk over to help my mother but the floor was too slippery from the blood and I landed on my butt.

I clearly recall her putting pressure on my leg using the wet dishwashing rag in her hand, ignoring her own wounds. I kept insisting it was only a flesh wound, and we should clean her face. But were given no time to argue. The bombs started to land one after the other, too many to count.

Forget going to the hospital: bombs from all calibers were landing at an average of twenty per minute. Driving to a hospital would be suicide; the cemetery was closer. Using alcohol and bandages, she managed to stop the bleeding on my leg and her own face and neck. I assured her no bones were broken, it was a flesh wound, and I was fine. As soon as I spoke these words, she bolted in search of my sisters and my brother.

My brother was finally awake. It only took a few explosions to get him up. The students who had made it to school early were rushed to the basement, where they were soon joined by their parents and the rest of the neighborhood.

Roughly 300 people lived for three weeks in that basement. We placed foam mattresses on the floors and each family had a small area. During the days, men played cards and *tawle*, smoked, drank coffee, cursed the Syrians, and discussed the war. The women, being much superior in a crisis situation, cooked, cleaned, and looked after the children. Rami and I overheard one of the neighbors complaining that she could only use two squares of the toilet paper roll she had, in order to make it last until the end of the siege. She was the prettiest, sexiest woman on the street, an unmarried thirty-year-old, a spoiled, sexy Madonna.

"Use some newspapers," Rami said.

"They have ink on them and they don't clean well."

"But they have pictures of Hafez and Yasser and the rest of the geniuses," Rami pointed out. "You can wipe your butt with their faces."

She took her roll of toilet paper and threw it across the basement. "From now on," she vowed, "I will only use newspapers with the pictures of politicians on them. All the politicians with no exception can kiss my ass."

Rami winked and whispered to me, "They would love to, I am sure. I wish I was a politician."

Everybody was laughing, and then some women started to cry; the tension was high and everyone's emotions were on a roller coaster. Try living with 300 people in a small place, with crying babies and noisy kids, moody women, and eccentric men. Soon you will wish for a direct hit.

"We need food, we need rice, beans, pasta, and mostly bread," my mother said. She was the unofficial director of the hotel. "They are distributing food at the center; we need coupons from every family. Maybe they will give us the food without every person having to be there."

During the siege, the Lebanese Forces—the LF—were distributing coupons for essentials like rice, oil, beans, and baby formula. Most of the families in the basement had some coupons.

"What about the bread?" my mother wondered. "How can we get enough bread? I heard that the bakeries only open for two hours each day and they limit the supply."

"Collect the food coupons from all the families," I suggested. "Rami, Ahmed, and I will go get them every day."

"No, you're not leaving," said Mom. "Every day, people are dying trying to get food."

"If we don't," I argued, "people will die right here. The kids are hungry. They will start getting sick."

Ahmed was a Shia neighbor of ours and a good friend of mine. I knew him and his whole family well. They were the only Shia still living on our street. Ahmed's father owned the convenience store, and my family ran a monthly tab there, just like everybody else. He heard my mother and sent us to get the food from his shop. "Today, go get the perishables and vegetables," he said. "Leave the rest for another day, we will get it when we need it. This way it will not get wasted."

This is how Rami, Ahmed, and I started the food delivery service. We would scavenge food from the store, then we usually waited for a lull in the bombardment before heading to the center and redeeming some coupons for rice and different kinds of beans. I used to drop Ahmed off to wait in line at the bakery, I'd continue to the center with Rami. I picked him up on my way back to deliver the food and bread, driving a VW van owned by the school.

We took care of other shelters, too. We delivered bread to the family of one of Rami's girlfriends. I also made sure that Nada's family got bread every day. When I delivered the bread, I never stayed longer than a few minutes. I would notice her mother looking at me. She knew I was risking my life to make sure she and her family had food. Her looks changed as the days passed, from condescending to respect, and soon enough she started giving me hugs. But I still avoided her.

The sound of a passing bomb is totally different from the sound of one coming at you, or very near you. If you hear a whistle, don't worry: it's passing over your head and will land far from you. If you hear a mechanical sound like a small engine or a grass trimmer, you're in deep trouble. Take cover.

One day while coming back from a delivery, we heard the distinctive sound of an incoming bomb. Rami and Ahmed were in the back of the VW van sorting the food items while I was driving. The van had no doors; we had removed them a long time ago for just such an occasion. I slammed on the brakes, steered the van toward a wall, and the three of us jumped out and dove into the nearest ditch. First comes the pressure. It's like your ribs are flexing and your heart is missing beats inside your body; your bones rattle around, and your skeleton becomes like jelly. Concrete and dust covered us, then we heard the explosion. We stayed down with our hands over our heads until we were sure the dust had settled and the shrapnel had found its final resting place. Then we emerged from the ditch and checked ourselves for any injuries. We had none. I still had my charmed elastic band on my arm. Not sure what those two Muslim buddies of mine had. However, the van was on fire and the smell of burned bread mixed with gasoline and oil overpowered us.

"If we had known in advance," I said, "we could have mixed the rice and water together. It would have been ready and boiling by now."

"Do you always have to be such a smart ass?" asked Ahmed.

"No, only when he is scared," Rami told him. I told you, he knew me better than anybody else. We made our way back to the basement of the school on foot.

My mother still has her scars and so do I. She has three small scars on her face and a larger one on her neck. I have an eight-inch-long scar running down my right thigh, and that is not the only one I have. I have acquired quite a collection since then. I tell people they are from a motorcycle accident.

In all the fighting before and after that day, all the tough martial artists, fighters, and commandos I have met and worked with, I have never seen or met a braver person than my mother. She is cool under pressure and totally selfless. She helped her family survive, and our neighbors.

After that, the whole neighborhood was tighter than ever. When you share a life-and-death experience with somebody, a special bond is created. Later, that bond would save my life.

18

SHOCKWAVES

PAUL:

I did not notice the changes within me, though everybody else did. I was heartbroken over Nada, bitter at our financial situation, and worried about the general state of the war. My friends were telling me that I was being mean and reckless. I had many close encounters with death and stopped caring about my future. I was hoping my number would be called soon. Education was not high on my list of priorities at this point. I was asked gently not to return to the school where my father worked. Apparently I had attitude problems. I joined the rest of my friends at a public high school. There, the girls were separated from the boys; the girls attended from 8 a.m.to 1 p.m. and the boys from 2 to 7 p.m. We used to leave love notes and flirty drawings on the desktops, not even knowing who shared the same desk. We rarely got any replies, and when we did, it was, "Get lost, creep."

The different Christian militias had student committees more powerful than the teacher's committee. Ninety percent of the students carried guns to school;

they stuck them in the back pockets of their jeans like wallets. I preferred to carry mine stuck in the front of my pants under my shirt. Imagine how much authority the teacher is going to have enforcing the rules and demanding attention when he or she was the only one in the room without a weapon. We would close the school any day we felt like it, especially if we had an exam that was too difficult. Rami and I even figured out how to short-circuit the main electrical panel and cause a total blackout. By the time they got an electrician to fix it, we would be at the movies or fishing. On a couple of occasions, we printed notices at my buddy Johnny's uncle's print shop late at night and then papered the front and back gates as well as the walls around the fence, announcing a political strike day. Nobody bothered to check the authenticity of the notices. All the students needed was an excuse to skip. If they were asked why they were absent on that day, the answer was a copy of the notice. High school went by in a blur. Eventually, all exams were cancelled by the government due to the war. Every single student graduated.

The following year, some went to university because they did not know what else to do. A few boys decided to keep on fighting and officially joined one of the various militias. Another group, including me, went to work. A small percentage left to study in another country; those were the lucky ones with good grades and rich parents. Most of them never came back; they built successful, stable lives overseas. Most of the young talent left the country, leaving the poor or the psychopaths to rule. It was and still is a sad situation. The economy was in constant decline due to the shortage in creative skills and thinking; the cultural and artistic fiber that made Lebanon the envy of the whole Middle East for decades was ripped to shreds. We were going backward faster than the speed of light.

Christmas was approaching and I wanted to buy a gift for my mother. I called Sam, a friend of mine and asked him if he could give me a good deal on a pendant.

"Just go to the store near your house, pick up a gift. Don't pay for it, you can pay me later," he said.

I walked down the driveway of our home and saw Rami on the front steps of the old school, chatting with a girl. She gave him her number and left. We decided to go to his home first to drop his stuff and head together to the jewellery store. We were descending the long, wide stair and noticed a man running down the street toward us with a machete in his hand, blood streaming down his white T-shirt, looking back as he ran.

We stayed put and waited for him to pass us, but he never did. A gold color Peugeot 604 came down the street at full speed, the driver put the brakes on and the car slid sideways right behind the running man. The passenger jumped out before the car had made a full stop. He took two steps, aimed his 9 mm Browning gun and shot the running man in the back twice. The running man initially fell to his knees, then a few seconds later he sprawled on the pavement and the machete clinked before him. The shooter calmly approached, stood over him, aimed his weapon and fired three more shots point blank to the back of the head of the running man. He put the safety back on, glanced at the two frozen teens on the stairs, and got back in the car. I did not breathe again until the car disappeared from view. Then I noticed my hand on Rami's shoulder to prevent him from moving.

I was not as brave as my mother. From that point forward, flashes of the drive-by shooting kept sneaking behind my eyelids. For many months after that, every time I walked by that spot, I looked at the three bullet marks in the pavement. It's all that remained of the running man's legacy.

We stepped around the victim and headed instead for

Rami's home, but we never reached our destination that day. Garo, an Armenian neighbor of Rami, lived with his cute, much younger wife and their children in a small rented home next door to Rami's building. Rami lived on the top floor of a four-story building with no elevator. (Even if there had been one, there was never any power.) Garo and his wife sold children's clothes from the front room of their home to make ends meet. My mother always told me to never talk to him, as he was known to practice black magic and spoke to the dead. I never believed her. My belief meter was running on empty; I had taken off my armband and stopped going to the church.

As we approached the entrance of Rami's building, we heard gunshots. For a few moments, I thought my ears were replaying the sounds from a few minutes ago. But no. More shots were fired from an automatic weapon, the unmistakable crack sound of an AK 47. Rami dropped his stuff at the bottom of the stairs, and we went to peek out the side window of his building's entrance, next to Garo's house, trying to figure out who was firing. It sounded like it was coming from inside the house.

Five or six men wearing the Phalangist logo on their green uniforms were approaching from the orange orchard, their own guns at the ready. More than five minutes passed without any shots fired, then we heard a single shot followed by shouts from the men.

We came out to the street as they loaded an injured Garo into the back of their Land Rover jeep. Two more cars took away two more injured people, an older lady and her grandson who lived next door. As they departed, I gathered my courage and went inside Garo's home. I was not ready for what I saw.

Garo's small wife had her hands around her two young children. They were huddled in the corner of the back room. All dead, each from a single shot to the head.

We never found out why. People were saying Satan told Garo to do it. I thought he might have seen her talking to the young man next door.

A week later after recuperating from his wounds, Garo was being transferred to the mental hospital in an ambulance. Two cars cut in front and behind the ambulance, three men opened the back door, and shot him.

After seeing the carnage at his neighbor's home, Rami decided to skip the Christmas shopping and go home. I was left on the street, in shock, with no place to go. I walked with no purpose, in a trance, to the main *Suk* (market) hoping to find Sam.

Good thing he was not there.

The main shopping street was a wide road, lined on both sides with residential buildings. The ground floors were a collection of commercial stores selling shoes, clothes, perfumes, and jewellery. It was always busy and packed this time of year. I walked slowly. Then, just before I turned on the main road, I was thrown against a parked car. Initially I did not understand, I did not hear a sound; I just felt the wind blast. Then I heard the explosion.

Booby-trapped cars were a new weapon, terrorizing the population, as every week, two or three cars exploded in busy areas of the country, indiscriminately killing hundreds of innocent people. Today was our turn. I got up and ran toward Sam's shop.

I got there within seconds and thought I was in hell. I think hell can't be worse. Dozens of cars were burning, hundreds of people were screaming for help and more people were torn to pieces. An older woman about my mother's age ran to me and clutched at my arm. Her hair was plastered on her bloodied face. She was covered with small cuts from the shattered glass of the display windows. I shook her off and ran, knowing there were more seriously injured people who needed help. Sam's display window was shattered, pieces of jewellery scattered over the sidewalk. More guys flooded in to help but I worried there might be another delayed explosion— it is what I would have done if I was planning such an attack.

The next few hours were a blur. I remembered putting out fires. I helped to load people into cars and ambulances. However, I was left with one vivid memory.

The victims close to the epicenter of the explosion were shredded and dismembered. I was obsessing with a small boy's body parts. I wanted him to be buried as a whole, but I could not find his legs. We had his body and head laid out on a stretcher but the legs were missing. One of the guys found a pair of legs and laid them by the body. The pants and boots were similar but they were both right side legs. I gave up and walked around in a daze. Two guys a small ways down the sidewalk were staring at another small corpse. They had it laid out, and had two left legs. The pants and boots were the exact same size and color of the one I just left. I sat down and started crying. I realized the two small bodies were twins dressed the same for a Christmas shopping trip.

The smell of burned rubber and gasoline did not bother me. The smell of charred bodies is another story. There are no words to describe the smell of death. If somebody is ever able to accurately describe it, they have never been in the middle of it.

The next thing I remembered, I was sitting in Sam's car. He was driving out of Beirut toward the northern coast and his chalet. He gave me some of his clothes, and I took a shower, I called my parents to tell them that I was okay, though I would not be home that night. I was sure that my mother was going crazy by then.

Everybody deals with shock and tragedy differently; I wanted to go to sleep. Sam insisted we go out and get wasted. I lost time again, at one point realizing I was sitting in Sam's favorite whorehouse. He was a regular and was treated like a superstar. I was sipping eighteen-year-old Chivas from Sam's private bottle. Chivas Regal is illegally sold in Lebanon. I have no idea how they put that one together, a Jewish–Scottish connection. A couple of hookers came by to say hello to Sam, and he invited them to sit with us. I took a sip and was savoring the taste of the scotch when one of Sam's hooker friend, loudly chewing a wad of gum, put her hand on my leg and asked me, "Are you having a good day?"

Expensive scotch sprayed from my mouth and nose. I can't remember if I laughed or cried.

PART THREE

19

SEEING A SHADOW AT NIGHT

PAUL

By 1980, the many Lebanese Christian right-wing militias consolidated under one banner. They were better organized now and much better trained, and all under the Lebanese Forces command. With my fighting background and martial arts training, I was constantly approached by recruiters to join the different sections of the LF. I never took their offers very seriously. I was eighteen years old with no real job and no prospects. I had read all the books I could find about military tactics, intelligence, and tradecraft, plus I had my years of martial arts training and my collection of trophies. I always knew that one day I would get what I wanted, but on my own terms.

I started working at a scuba-diving club in a prestigious resort. My main duty was helping the master diver with the beginners. I was what we called the sweeper: I would follow the diving group underwater just in case somebody got lost. We also had two speedboats, and I always got the job of taking the children of the rich waterskiing. I was making more money from tips than from salary, looking after the kids and teaching them water-skiing and scuba diving.

I had never thought of myself as good-looking, but I started hearing whispers behind my back and noticing the looks I was getting from the ladies sunbathing around the pool or on the beach. I got a few smacks on the butt and a few propositions; I always faked naïveté and ignored them.

One of the members of the scuba-diving club was the intelligence chief of the Lebanese Forces, Shadow. This guy was ruthless and smart, and everybody knew who he was—a big mistake in his business. He was always throwing his money around—he had loads of it—and he controlled the port, the casinos, the bars, the nightclubs, and the bordellos. Everybody at the resort was at his beck and call. He had a fleet of BMWs, Mercedes, and Range Rovers; even his bodyguards drove Porsches. For security reasons, we only took him on private dives.

Late one evening after a diving trip, he was sitting with a few of his friends under a large awning. He had four or five bodyguards close by. The restaurants and cafés were closed, and it was late. I was in the middle of cleaning up the club and checking the equipment, getting the boat fuelled and ready for the next morning's dives. He called me over and asked me in a friendly way if there was anything to eat. My dinner was untouched in the fridge: a sub and some fruit. I offered my food to him. He thanked me, broke the sandwich in half, and gave me a portion.

I was so naïve. I refused. "No, you can have it all," I said. "I am leaving soon and I will get something on the way home."

One of the bodyguards came from behind me and told me to take a bite. Suddenly it dawned on me: they did not trust me or this food. I took the sub from his hand, thanked him, and started eating. As soon as I swallowed my first bite, he started eating his half. He smiled at me and gave me a $100 bill, which I refused to take. I was happy with my tips, but I would not take charity or be looked down upon by anybody. That was another test, and I passed.

He followed me into the pro shop when I left to lock up.

"Your name is Paul, right?"

"Yes, sir," I said. "I have been out with you a few times."

"I know. I have noticed your skills as a diver and as a boat operator. You move effortlessly underwater."

"The better you are, the less you have to do. Not only underwater, sir."

"Do you live around here?"

"No, not really, I come on my motorcycle; I live about fifteen kilometers from here."

"Where are you from originally?"

I told him the name of my town, and he told me to be ready soon because the Syrian army was planning a major attack on Zahlé. That sent chills through my body because many of my family members and friends lived there. It was the only city in the region that had not fallen under the control of the Syrian army, which was trying hard to change that.

Shadow was a good-looking man and made sure the ladies knew it. He worked constantly on his tan and his six-pack. He had personal trainers before anybody had even heard of them. He gave me a little smirk. "Why don't you come and see me at my office," he said. "I am sure I can arrange something for you."

"I'm sorry, sir," I said, "but I'm not interested in being a soldier or a bodyguard. I have other plans."

The few bodyguards who heard the exchange did not like it. I heard them discussing it outside the door: who is this asshole who fills up scuba-diving tanks and cleans our gear, saying that he is not interested in our job? We drive the best cars; we have the latest weapons, all the girls, and plenty of money in our pockets. He rides a bike and doesn't carry weapons: who does he think he is?

"I will come and see you soon, sir," I said. "Maybe I should go to the city and warn my friends first."

"There is only one way to reach the city now," he said. "It is almost completely surrounded, and the Syrians will be starting their attack soon. As soon as the snow comes, it will be completely surrounded."

"There is only one way to get there? How?"

"By walking through the mountains at night and behind enemy lines for almost ten hours. To deliver food and weapons. Do you want to help?"

"Of course I do," I said. "Dozens of my friends and family still live there."

"I will arrange for you to join the next group heading there."

BASSAM:

The brothers and most of the QJ hated going to Zahlé. This was the only Christian city in the whole Bekaa Valley that had not fallen to them or the Syrians. Every time they went there, they had to keep a low profile. Driving in the car on the main boulevard Ghassan felt like taking a machine gun and mowing down the hundreds of infidels that walked around on the riverside walkway. The arrogant and loud Zahliots were brave and macho. Bassam wanted to unleash his suicide squad among them.

"When the time comes, Ghassan, I am going to poison their water supplies and cut off the food and medicine. The Syrians are not committed one hundred percent. They want to dominate, but they are always worried about international pressure. They should let me use mercenaries. I will show them how I can bring Zahlé to its knees and drive its inhabitants into the sea. I will keep the pretty, stuck-up girls who don't even look our way as a bonus."

The QJ had sent a couple of guys to start a fight at the riverside restaurants to disrupt the businesses; the idiots threw a hand grenade into a children's play area when there were no children in it. The residents and the restaurant owners killed them both before they had a chance to escape.

Ghassan came back with the grim news. " The mission was a total failure, maybe they are really brave, those loudmouth Zahliots. They did not escape, they counter attcked"

"No, they are not." Bassam continued. "We have to start scaring them before the final attack. Terrorism is mostly conditioning. They are not ready to be terrorized.

People have to accept being scared and be ready for it. I have to serve them small doses of fear before the final assault. Let's send a couple of booby-trapped cars, this technique works every time. "

And so the QJ joined the PLO and the Syrians to finally bring Zahle to its knees.

20

THE BATTLE OF SMOKE AND MIRRORS

PAUL:

From the start of the 1975–1990 civil war, Zahlé was a key strategic location. It was on a main artery for the fighting groups, particularly the Syrian army, which occupied the Bekaa Valley in 1976. The city itself lies at the base of Mount Sannine, which is 8,622 feet high. From its peak, you can see not only the entire Bekaa Valley, but the Israeli-occupied Golan Heights and beyond. So by securing at least the base of Mount Sannine, the Syrians could prevent any Israeli or Lebanese forces attempt to scrutinize the occupied Golan Heights and further into Syrian territory.

The Syrians were determined to minimize the strategic importance of the Christian-controlled city. So they blocked the main roads leading in and out of Zahlé. The Syrian forces remained stationed on the outskirts. The Lebanese Forces, however, were inside the city, and were getting military aid from the Israelis. The Syrians were very afraid the LF might hand over the base of the strategically crucial Mount Sannine to the Israelis.

They decided it was time to take the only predominantly Christian city left unoccupied in the Bekaa Valley.

I had gone to school in Zahlé before the war and knew it well. We used to run through the old streets and along the river. I played bumper cars in its famous *wadi* (valley), which was filled with famous, world-class restaurants called casinos—I don't know why, because there was no gambling going on there. The men of Zahlé are probably the most macho of all: they are famous for drinking, fighting, and swearing. They have elevated swearing to an art form. With that said, they are also proud and brave.

The Syrians and their allies laid siege to the city from all directions. For me to reach the city,, Shadow did me a favour, he arranged for me to join the march through the mountains at night. We took foot trails and walked for ten hours up and down the mountain in the snow, cutting down across a river, all behind enemy lines. We went in small groups, about a dozen at a time. Altogether, 120 trained elite members from the LF went from Beirut to Zahlé to aid and mobilize the 1,500 local resistance fighters and the citizens of the city, to prepare for the final battle.

The bridge and main access route to the city witnessed a ruthless fight. The massive Syrian attack lasted from night till dawn, but its army was never able to control that access. During the battle for the bridge, Syrian artillery pounded the city continuously, killing dozens of Zahliots while the Syrian army lost about fifty men. The bridge was also where the "massacre of tanks" took place: the Lebanese Forces were able to destroy more than twenty Syrian tanks that night. Some tanks were destroyed by RPGs or LAW (light anti-tank weapon) rocket launchers, but others were destroyed by brave men who climbed on top of the tanks, with bullets flying everywhere, opened the hatch, and threw hand grenades inside. The tenacity, courage, and effectiveness of the fighters of the Lebanese Forces convinced the Syrians that Israelis were fighting alongside them, which they were not. But we gave the impression that thousands of fighters were defending the city, when in reality only the 120 trained soldiers and the inhabitants were actively fighting.

At one point during the battle, which went on for months, a nun was bringing bread and medicine to the hospitals in Zahlé, along with two nurses. Their car was fired upon heavily by the Syrians, and it slammed into a wall. The Syrians continued shooting at the car even after it crashed. The Lebanese Forces battled the Syrians so the bodies could be pulled out of the car. As it turned out, the two nurses accompanying the nun were Muslim men, which showed the locals that the Christians truly were not alone: the patriotic Muslim population had also had enough of the occupiers. As I've said before, this had nothing to do with religion. Many of the most ruthless senior Syrian officers were Christians. They were even more violent than their colleagues—they had to be, to show their absolute loyalty to their superiors.

One of the Christian residents, Milad, was a good friend of mine from my days in school. Kamil, his older brother, was a few years older than us. He was married to his school sweetheart, and they had two young boys. When the offensive started and the shelling began—an average of sixty mortar shells per minute, twenty-four hours a day for two full weeks—Kamil sent his young wife and two children to stay with relatives in the basement of a high-rise building. They lived in a detached house, and being underground under a large building seemed safer. Most of the city's residents were hiding in churches and schools. But the merciless attackers knew that women and children were hiding in that basement, and they pounded it for eight hours nonstop.

I was with both of the brothers, Milad and Kamil,

at a forward position at the time called "the sandbags of the martyrs." The location was exposed and remote: every day, three to five fighters were losing their lives defending this position and the hill, but more guys kept coming to help because everybody knew what would happen to the town if we failed. We were like a mother bear protecting her cubs. We became braver and tougher, but we didn't become smarter.

When we heard this building was being targeted, Kamil and I rushed back to check on his family. Even now, many years later, I can see the look on his face when we approached and saw the pile of rubble, smoldering cement, and twisted steel that used to be the building where his family was hiding. We ran toward the smoke and the smell. I got there first and stopped dead in my tracks. I actually wished I were dead. The whole building had collapsed, and more than fifty women and children were dead under that mountain of cement and metal. Getting people out alive was impossible.

He looked up at the giant statue of the Virgin Mary that rises high above the town. Most people believed it had been protecting the city for years. Kamil mimicked her pose with outstretched arms and did the unthinkable: he swore at her, tears streaming down his cheeks and snot pouring out of his nose. He swore and prayed to her at the same time. Remember, the Zahliots swear all the time. He was just asking her for help.

The Syrians kept bombarding and shooting at the area, knowing the men had rushed over to help their families. At the end of the two-day rescue operation, we had not pulled out any survivors.

The smell of death is still with me. My nasal passages are permanently infected with this poignant smell. Maybe that's why I like my steak raw; I can't stand the smell of overcooked meat. I am so damaged, it surprises me sometimes that I can manage a normal conversation.

The shelling went on for three months. Food and water supplies were cut off. Attacks and counterattacks were daily occurrences. Hundreds of residents were killed. The city resisted and did not fall. An agreement to end the battle was reached, with the help of some Arab and other countries. All LF fighters would leave the city under the supervision of the Red Cross and international monitors. Ninety-seven of the original 120 fighters left in three buses.

The Syrians were embarrassed that so few fighters, with the aid of the locals, had managed to defend against the might of their army for this long. As usual, they blamed it on the Israelis. Syria produced photographs of some old weapons that didn't work from the battles that had taken place on the Golan Heights years before and showed them to the media as proof of Israeli involvement. Only an idiot would believe the Syrian propaganda. They invented many ridiculous stories, told to the media with straight faces. We had thousands of jokes about them, but some people believed their stories. Whenever they liquidated one of their own people, they would announce that the person had committed suicide. Later, leaked autopsy reports would show that the person had four or five bullet holes in his head. Syrian officers must have been well trained indeed if they could shoot themselves repeatedly in the head.

This was a major victory for the Christians. Pride soared and morale was high again. We had proved to ourselves that we were able to resist superior numbers. As soon as I got back to Beirut on board one of the three buses, I was called down to see Shadow.

21

THE BIRTH OF THE S7

PAUL:

Three months after returning from Zahle on one of the busses, I decided to call Shadow and arrange a meeting. I thought joining the intelligence was the best way to get my foot in the door. I did not want to be a regular soldier, or a sniper, or part of any regular fighting unit, even one of the special units. The intelligence units, which we called Amen, operated in the shadows. They had a lot of influence, and they were feared. They would be the fastest route to getting the training and the know-how that I needed. However, their operations were inside the area under our control. But it would never hurt to listen to what Shadow had in mind.

I got on my motorcycle—with no helmet, of course. We thought helmets were for sissies. I was expecting a regular army barracks or a plain-looking building. As I approached, I was surprised to see huge car-size cement blocks that you had to zigzag through at a crawling speed in order to get to the first security check. After you cleared that one, you had to go through another obstacle course near the gate, at the end of the parking lot. I parked my bike in the visitors' area and approached the kiosk on foot. I gave the guards my name, they checked their book, and I was cleared to pass, but not before I'd had a full body search and left my keys with them.

Once inside the grounds, an escort met me just outside the guard post. I was surprised to see water fountains, flowers, and landscaping, and a whole crew of Sri Lankan detainees at work, manicuring and grooming the gardens. Inside the secured compound, there were only a few cars parked here and there. The compound itself consisted of three small buildings, each about three stories high, painted white with dark anti-glare windows. Upon approaching the main door, I was body-searched again and asked to wait in the lobby. The bodyguards gave me looks—not menacing looks, just curious looks. They recognized me from the diving club and now they wanted to know who this guy was, who had managed to secure an appointment with the boss. After about twenty minutes of waiting in the lobby, I was ushered into the inside office. I had never seen women working with the military before, but sitting side-by-side, behind separate desks, was one blonde and one brunette. Both of them were nine out of ten on the beauty scale; it was like visiting a modeling agency in Paris. I did not mind waiting another fifteen minutes. Then the brunette walked over to me with a smile and announced in a husky voice, "The boss is ready and will see you now."

"I am not ready," I said. "I like it here. Can you please make him wait a few more minutes?"

I got a smile and look from her that said *I like you, too. But this is off-limits. I wish I knew you before, from somewhere else.* How did I get this from one quick look? When there is chemistry and mutual attraction, no words are needed.

I was expected, and he was ready for me, but she

knocked on the door and waited for the command to come in. Then she opened the door, and I walked in behind her. As she stopped to let me by, I got the faint scent of her perfume; it reminded me of the valley in my aunt's town. In one split second, she took me back to happier times and a safe place. I wished I could know her a little longer. But, again, I was in the wrong place at the wrong time.

Shadow had some serious people skills. He jumped up and walked around his desk with a big smile on his face to shake my hand. He told me how happy he was to see me. He was making me feel important, a trick I learned long ago.

My plan was to wait for him to start talking since he was the one who asked me to come in. I had no idea what he wanted, and it was always safer to listen. We chatted a bit about scuba diving, motorcycles, and martial arts. He had a file in front of him with my name on the label in the top corner. He saw me looking and smiled.

"We always do our homework," he said. "That is how we stay alive. I have a complete background check in this file, but I'd like to get to know you as a person first."

"There are no secrets in my life," I told him. "I am sure everything you need to know is in the file." I looked at him. "Maybe if you let me see it, I can fill in the blanks."

He started laughing. "Hey, Paul, that's a very good answer," he said. "I was told you were smart."

"If I am so smart," I countered, "why did I come here? I should've stayed home and minded my own business."

"We are not as bad as people think," he said. "Our business is necessary to protect the Christian area. We are boxed in from three sides, and the sea is our only way out. The money we make from gambling and illegal import-export is necessary. If we have to do business with the devil to survive, we will."

"As I told you before, I am not interested in being a soldier or a bodyguard," I reminded him. "I have done some fighting in the past, and I've discovered most guys can do just as good a job."

"I have all the bodyguards I need, and we don't have a fighting unit," he said. "What I need are people with your skills. Your file tells me you are brave under fire, a master in martial arts, and I know you can dive and are fluent in Arabic, French, and English. That is an impressive package. How did you learn English?"

"I took some private lessons with a teacher who lived in our building," I said. "I washed his car and repaired it for him, and in exchange he taught me English."

"So, you are mechanically inclined also?"

"My father owned a garage, and I was practically born in it. I can fix almost anything."

"Paul, your background checks out and so does the background of your whole family. Let me cut to the chase and tell you what this is about."

"I can't wait—but what does my family have to do with anything?"

"I need you to train a couple of my bodyguards in scuba diving. As you know, I am an avid scuba diver, and I would feel better if I had a couple of them with me at all times."

"Forgive me, sir," I pointed out, "but this kind of service we offer at the club. All they have to do is join a class."

"Of course, I know that," he said, with a pause before he went on. "But we need you to also train them in night diving and booby trapping."

"I have done a lot of night diving," I said, "but not much booby trapping lately. I am not an expert."

"Now we're getting somewhere." He sat back and smiled. "This is exactly the reason why I asked you to come down here. I have spoken with the master diver and the owner of the scuba-diving club. He tells me you are smart, professional, and reliable. We have some plans for you, and a new job."

"Are you going to fill me in on those plans or should I follow blind?"

"Only a fool will follow blind," he said. "I am sure you are not a fool."

He was right about that. "What are these plans, so I can think about them?" I asked.

"We want to start a special unit, a very small, elite unit. I need you to handpick no more than six other guys who have fighting skills, martial arts background, scuba-diving skill, and high IQ. This unit will answer directly to me; your work will be undercover."

I thought for a minute, then I said, "I know a lot of guys with fighting skills, other guys with martial arts skills, and more guys with scuba-diving skills. However, I don't know many that have everything you want."

"Precisely, Paul, and that is why we are asking you to do the selection for us. We need you to pick the top guys in each discipline from our area, no more than six or seven. Once the unit is selected and their backgrounds are checked, you will travel to Israel. Our contacts at the Mossad will take it from there. By the time you come back, you should all be fully trained in every aspect and well prepared for the missions we will be asking you to perform."

This sounded very exciting and right up my alley, but I asked if I had time to think it over.

"This is more your duty than a job," he said. "It should not take you more than a few months to get your team together, and while you are working on it, we have a full gym in the basement. Maybe you can train my first-line bodyguards in jujitsu and boxing. I hear these are very effective defensive arts."

I agreed and said I would do it. "Thank you for your confidence," I said. "I will see you at the gym. This way I can kick your ass without having to worry about it."

Over the next few months I trained in the basement with a few of the bodyguards and the boss himself. They were a fun bunch and open to learning. They parked their egos at the door and were sponging up new techniques and moves that would make them a better group.

22

THE SEVEN MISFITS

PAUL:

I was looking for six special guys who I would trust with my life. I knew sixty such guys, but none of them would qualify for this line of work. I wanted six men who would go to hell with me and maybe come back. The six I settled on did not let me down.

Fadi

Fadi, a black belt in Taekwondo, had excellent boxing skills and had done a lot of fighting in the past. He was small and fast, an excellent combination in tight places. His parents were refugees many years ago from northern Syria, he was from a Sirianni (Assyrian) background, and he had no official papers proving he was born and raised in Lebanon: this guy practically did not exist. I had double-dated with him a few times and sparred with him in the dojo.

One night after training, I hung around and waited for everybody else to leave. I sat on my bike waiting for him until I saw him getting into his Alfa Romeo. "Fadi, you have a minute?"

"Of course, Paul, what's up? Are you still having problems with your Nada?"

"No, that's not the reason I need to talk to you."

"Leave your bike here," he suggested. "Let's take my car and go get something to eat. I am starving."

"Sure," I said. "We can talk in the car. But I don't want to discuss things in a crowded restaurant."

This piqued his curiosity. As soon as we got in the car, he asked me to spell it out.

"Listen," I said. "I know you and your brothers were born here in Lebanon and that none of you have any official papers or registered birth certificates—you can't vote, you can't even get a passport to travel, you guys don't really exist. I think I can help you."

"Are you nuts?" he asked. "This is impossible. My older brother has been trying for years to buy some papers. He is married to a Lebanese and has two girls. They aren't registered either. It's a nightmare to even send them to school."

"I know all that," I said. "That's why I'm here. I've been to your house a thousand times and eaten your mom's delicious food, met your nieces and your whole family—so I want to help. What I'm going to say next is extremely confidential. You can't repeat it if you refuse, and you don't have a lot of time to think about it. I need your answer ASAP, agreed?"

As I started talking, he smiled. He did not hesitate with his answer.

"I have only one condition," he said. "If you can get me official and registered papers for my family, I'm in. I don't need any for myself; I will probably not live long enough to use them, anyway."

"Once we are in this unit," I warned him, "we will have all kinds of documents because we will not be using our real names and identities. If we ever get caught, it will backfire on us and put our families in danger."

"Authentic papers for my whole family, and I am in."

"I will discuss it with the Shadow, and I will make it a condition for your joining. He has many contacts and I am sure we can get everyone registered with predated birth certificates and identity cards. From there, you can get everything else sorted out."

At the gym the next day I asked the boss if we could have a chat. We got into his car, just the two of us, and were followed by a chase car with four bodyguards. He drove while I rode shotgun. We went to check out the new house he was building right above the Casino de Liban—a mansion with reinforced concrete walls on top of a hill with a breathtaking view of the Mediterranean. It was built with security and the possibility of a siege in mind, with underground tunnels and concrete surrounding walls that could withstand direct cannon hits.

In the car, I told him about Fadi. I also told him that most of the guys I'd be picking would have some conditions, since we would need to disappear for long periods of time and we might never come back.

He was sharp. He did not need a long explanation. "Sure," he said. "Tell him to start getting ready. It won't take long to get the documents. I need a list of the names, birthdays, and places of birth."

Once I told Fadi the news, he was ecstatic. He did not care about his own safety. He was all in.

"Listen," I told him. "I have been racking my brains for the last week to find five more guys that can help us. Above all, they have to have the right qualifications and be loyal and smart. You know of anybody?"

He thought a minute. "This friend of mine, Lewis— he has nerves of steel and he is wanted throughout Europe and Africa for diamond smuggling," he said. "He borrows his brother's passport and travels to all these countries anyway. He even wraps the diamonds in a newspaper and carries them under his arm. A few years back, he lost one eye from shrapnel during a battle in the mountains and got it replaced with a glass eye. Now the crazy bastard takes the glass eye out, tapes diamonds behind it, and puts it back in. He is tough and fearless and cool under pressure—but I'm not sure he is trainable."

"I know this guy," I said. "I used to see him at his brother's restaurant? Does he help out over there sometimes?"

"Not really," said Fadi. "He used to hang out there in order to sell the diamonds. That was his meeting place."

Lewis

The next evening Fadi and I drove to Lewis' place; he lived with his mother and brother. We found him on the terrace playing the guitar. His father had passed a few years back from a heart attack. Probably Lewis gave it to him.

Lewis was dark and stocky, about five-foot-eight and almost as wide as he was tall. The boys liked to tell a joke about him. He looked more like an Egyptian than a Lebanese, so the militia was always arresting him and sending him to labor camps to fill up sandbags. But then he'd start speaking in a perfect Lebanese dialect, which only somebody born and raised here can do, and they'd let him go.

I knew I could be mistaken for a European, and he could be mistaken for a North African, a great combination. I did not know the specifics of the missions, but I knew the team would need to blend in with various surroundings.

"Hey, guys, come in." Lewis was the perfect host. "Have a seat and I will make some coffee." Then he shouted over his shoulder, "Mom! Make some coffee!" That is how Lebanese men made coffee or prepared food.

"Who is in the house besides your mom, Lewis?" I had to ask. "Your brother around?"

"Only my mom is here, watching her soap opera. Is there a problem, Paul?"

Lewis had a short fuse. He was always ready for a fight. I had to change that about him, calm him down, maybe teach him to take a step back and count to ten. Later, we would joke about how he counted: it was always, "One, two—ten."

"No, there is no problem," I assured him. "I just want to talk to you."

"Go ahead then, talk." He was on his guard, staring at me with his remaining eye.

"Lewis, what I am about to say should stay between the three of us. If you can't keep it secret, tell me now and we will leave. If you repeat any of it, it's going to cause trouble for you and your brother. Did I make myself clear?"

"Crystal clear—or should I say 'diamond'?"

"This is not a joke," I said. "The next few sentences could cost you your life." Then I explained to him the reason for secrecy and the commitment required. I always explained to each member of the unit the level of danger they were getting themselves into. "I want you to think about it and keep it to yourself," I told him. "Don't take it lightly. You might not be able to see your family for long periods of time. And you might not even come back from some mission. Think of your mother also, as she is dependent on you, and remember, once you are in, you can't get out."

"I need your answer in the next few days," I said at last. "Make up your mind and let me know."

Sam

Sam worked with his father; they owned a chain of jewelry stores. Fadi worked for them. They had loads of money, and Sam was a party animal. He changed cars like underwear, and girls like socks. I don't remember ever seeing him with the same girl twice. I had known him for a very long time. We were in school together and he was a client at the scuba-diving club. I had gotten him out of trouble on more than a few occasions.

Not long ago, one of his friends called me late at night and told me Sam was drunk in a bordello, where he had been challenging a bunch of drunken army soldiers. His friend said the soldiers were waiting for him to go outside so they could teach him a lesson. The friend had abandoned him and called me for help. Who needs enemies when you have friends like that?

I jumped on my bike and got there as fast as I could, which in my case was very fast. Sam was so drunk, he did not even ask me how I got there. When he saw me, he started laughing and ordered more champagne. I carried a few glasses of champagne to the four drunken soldiers on the other side of the bar and started chatting them up. Casually, I told them Sam's last name, which was the same as the name of the son of the highest-ranking Lebanese army general. That gave them something to think about: the last thing they needed was to be roughing up the only son of their big boss. We quickly became drinking buddies. I invited them over to our table, where they drank more and flirted with the hookers—Sam always had three or four at his table. Peace was restored and it was time to leave. Sam was in no condition to drive, yet he insisted he was fine. I asked him to do me a favor and let me drive the Ferrari. He agreed and thought it was his idea. I left my bike and drove his convertible home.

He was so drunk and so happy that I had showed up at his favorite hangout, he took out his gun and shot two bullets into the air to celebrate. The car was a convertible, but the roof was not open. He was too drunk to notice.

We both laughed whenever he was asked about the holes in the roof of his red Ferrari.

I knew Fadi needed the birth certificates, and Lewis needed new identities and passports, but Sam had everything he needed—except excitement. He was an adrenaline junkie, and I could offer him a fix.

I found him late one night at one of the jewelry stores in the main market after he finished with a client, I asked him to take a walk with me. He told one of the salesgirls to keep an eye on the store and said he would be back soon.

Lebanese guys have this annoying habit of putting their arms around your shoulder when you walk with them. It's a sign of close friendship, though it always made me feel uncomfortable. As soon as we started walking down the street, Sam put his arm around my shoulder. I removed it a couple times, and then he noticed. "Why are you always so uncomfortable when I put my hand around you?" he wanted to know.

"Some people might think we are more than just friends."

He laughed. "I can guarantee you none of the girls in the *souk* will think that," he said. "I have dated most of them."

"What about the other few?"

"Their turn is coming. There is only so much Sam to go around."

"Are you SAM six or a SAM seven?" I joked, referring to the Russian antiaircraft missiles.

"I am a Sam sex." He thought that was pretty funny.

I decided it was time to get serious. "Fadi works for your father but he might be quitting soon and joining me in my new business," I told him. "You also know Lewis; he will not be supplying you with any diamonds for a while because he is coming to work with me, too."

"Paul, you are going to be competing with us in the jewelry business? I don't mind—I love competition, it keeps us sharp, but we always win. I never lose, Paul. I love to win."

I chuckled, then I put my arm around his shoulder and gave him a big squeeze. I told him that in my business nobody wins, everybody loses.

"What kind of stupid business are you getting yourself into?" he wanted to know. "It is all about winning, my friend, and I will do anything to win."

"How can you be saying this, Sam? Everyone here is losing ground; our guys are being killed on a daily basis. We have no electricity, no water, and no airport, to name only a few things we don't have. The Syrians treat us like crap and steal our cars."

That hit a nerve. "That pisses me off," he said. "They stole my fucking Ferrari. Imagine, now some dirty little Syrian is driving it in Damascus. I would love to change things, but how can you or I do it?"

"Hypothetically, of course," I said carefully, "if we had a secret elite and highly trained unit that could affect the course of the war and effectively help change things, would you join?"

"Are you joking? This has been my idea for a long time, but no one would listen. We cannot match their numbers but we can outsmart them."

"Hypothetically again—what if I told you that such a unit does exist?"

"I would say you have been smoking too much hashish, and doing a lot of Cadbury." "Cadbury" was what we called cocaine.

"If I was serious, what would you do?"

"I would be the first to join."

"And you would leave your work, all that money, the cars, the girls, and your toys?"

"It sounds like we would be working in a monastery,"

he said. "I don't want to be a monk. I want to be able to make a difference and still have my cars, the girls, and the toys."

"This is not a monastery and you don't have to be a monk," I assured him. "This is real. If you're interested, think about it for a few days and get back to me. Only then will I fill you in on the details. Meanwhile, don't discuss this with anybody, and don't mention Fadi's or Lewis's name."

If Sam committed, I knew he would be a perfect fit. Every operation would need a getaway car or a fast boat driver, and Sam had amazing skills driving both cars and boats. He had participated in many rally races and was a top driver.

Not waiting for Sam's answer, I went after my next recruit.

Michael

Michael was a big show-off, with curly black hair he kept gelled. He worked as a lifeguard at the same resort I did, and usually walked around in his micro Speedo flexing his muscles and enjoying the looks he was getting from the older, rich, and desperate ladies. Being a serious bodybuilder, he had a perfectly jacked and tanned body, which he was constantly checking out in the mirror. I had bought my last motorcycle from him, but I did not like him much. Neither did Sam, because they were always in competition for the party girls in the area.

But he belonged to an elite fighting force we called the Maghaweer, and he was the best sniper that I knew of. In his small Christian hometown of Damour, the PLO had executed his entire family during a massacre in 1976. First, twenty Phalangists militiamen were executed, and then the civilians who hadn't already fled were lined up against a wall and sprayed with machine-gun fire. If this wasn't enough to motivate him to be a warrior, nothing else would.

I put my personal feelings aside because I had to go after the best candidates. I, along with everybody else, knew that Michael had once waited for over forty-eight hours in enemy territory, motionless and hidden from view on top of a hill, until his subject, a Syrian intelligence officer, appeared. On a windy day and from a distance of over 1,600 yards, he had put a bullet right between the man's eyes and made the kill. Only a handful of people on the whole planet could have done it.

When I walked into the bodybuilding gym, I received hostile stares from the heavyweights. Most of those guys were on steroids; you could see it in their eyes, cheekbones, and skin. I approached Michael. He was bench-pressing a few hundred pounds.

"Hey, Mike, do you need a spotter?"

"What's up, man? What are you doing here?" he wanted to know. "Are you changing sides? It took you long enough to realize that martial arts crap does not work in real life."

I played along. "I think you are right, Mike," I said. "I just need one more bit of proof. Why don't you and I go to the back, get into the boxing ring, and test our skills?"

He looked around to make sure no one had heard me: saving face is important to most Lebanese and especially to guys like Mike. He knew how many fights I had won and did not want to get beat in front of his buddies. We joked around for a few minutes, then I told him to go take a shower. I had something to talk to him about, and I would be waiting for him outside.

It didn't take him long. "What's going on, Paul?" he demanded. "You got my curiosity going."

I told him I knew he was working part-time at the resort and fighting with the Maghaweer whenever there was a battle to be fought, and that I knew his parents had been killed in the massacre at Damour.

"I have rent to pay, and expenses," he said. "Even with both jobs, I can barely make it. I'm their top sniper, yet they pay me peanuts." He looked at me. "Maybe I should go into private sniping. I hear it pays well."

"Why don't you?" I pushed him.

"You may think I am a show-off and an arrogant bastard, and you are probably right, but I also fight to prevent massacres like the one that took my whole family from me. The Palestinians and Syrians even cut off the fingers of Christian children to ensure they would never be able to pull a trigger. They killed men and women and children alike. They profaned our churches."

"So," I said carefully, "what you need is a well-paying job, so making money will no longer be an issue, and where you can make a difference in protecting our area. And maybe, just maybe, get some payback for the killing of your town. That sound good?"

He laughed. "I always thought you were a thinker and a quiet, conservative guy," he said. "Now I am thinking you're just crazy. No job like that ever existed, ever."

"What if I told you that I have such a job?"

"Then why are you working at the scuba-diving club?"

"Between the two of us—and keep it this way for now—I am giving notice soon. Why don't you meet me tomorrow in front of the Amen building? I'll meet you in the visitors' parking lot at 11 a.m., and we can talk."

You always have to give Lebanese guys specific times. If you don't, you might be waiting all day. However, I knew Michael would be on time. Snipers are accurate if nothing else.

At exactly 10:59 a.m., he parked his bike while I waited for him by the guardhouse. He surrendered his Beretta 9 mm and his keys, was body-searched—which he didn't like—and walked with me to the basement of building number one, where the gym was located.

Most of the bodyguards working out that morning knew him and came over to say hello. The Maghaweer were well respected, and Michael had a reputation: during a battle in central Beirut, he had jumped on top of an enemy tank, opened the hatch, thrown in a grenade, closed the hatch, and waited for the explosion before he made his way back to safety.

We waited for Shadow to come down and explain the situation directly to him. Michael did not need much convincing. Once he heard it from the boss directly, he was in. He would be transferred from his present unit. The boss made it clear to him that he would be reporting directly to me and only to me: this had to be clear from the get-go. While I walked him back to the parking lot, I told him not to quit his job or say anything until he heard from me, and to be ready to leave at a moment's notice for a long period of time, destination unknown.

Johnny Hypno

The term "assassin" is derived from the Arabic word *hasshashin* or *hassash*, hashish users. Johnny was always high on hashish or something else, he was a psychopath, sociopath, drug dealer, and a smuggler—exactly what we did not need. However, he was also a master forger and absolutely loyal to me. He was serving a five-year sentence in the famous Roumieh jail on fraud charges. The jail is a maximum-security facility, a monstrosity of a building located on top of a hill overlooking East Beirut. I used to visit his mother, pick up his clothes, and take them to a tailor. Johnny needed certain pills in order to control his urges; the tailor would open the waistband, wrap the pills in plastic, and sew them back in. I would also made sure to bring him fruit and cigarettes.

When we were kids, he used to forge our parents' signatures on report cards. Later, he sold forged university diplomas from most international academies, and doctor's prescriptions for his friends to get rohypnol and antidepressant pills—we called him Mr. Hypno. Most of our missions would be outside our territory, and our documents might need some alterations.

Johnny was so fearless I used to think he was suicidal. He was absolutely insane and was always getting in trouble for doing things with no planning whatsoever. I used to knock on his head and ask him to use it once in a while. But I needed him out of jail and out of the country altogether. Once my team was complete, I would ask the boss to bribe an official and get Johnny out.

I was using this opportunity to help my friends and at the same time to build a team I could trust. I did not even need to ask Johnny Hypno.

Freddie

Freddie was a wimp, scrawny and short with a long nose and huge glasses that covered half his face. He was about five-foot-six and weighed no more than 135 pounds soaking wet. Who would believe that such a person was working with an elite, highly trained team of anti-terrorists? He was a loner and did not have many friends. Hardly anybody knew him. He never participated in any fighting, martial arts training, scuba diving, or any other activities—except for one. Electronics were his forte. He could fix anything and reassemble any piece of electronics he could get his hands on. He fixed our radios and TVs; he even custom-made or modified sound suppressors for weapons. He would go on and on, explaining to me about the frequencies of CB channels and cell phones, long before I knew cell phones were available.

He had a small shop on the ground floor of an old building. The only way in or out was through a small alley, and you still needed to look very hard to find the store. But his regulars had no trouble finding him.

He was an Armenian born in Lebanon. We had a huge Armenian community who had escaped to Lebanon from the Turks. He spoke fluent Arabic like a native, unlike most Armenians, who were always confusing masculine and feminine terms. He was also fluent in Armenian and French with a sprinkling of English. He was an only child and still living at home with his parents.

I was going to have some fun explaining him to the rest of the team, but especially to my superiors. They were going to think the pressure had gotten to me, and I had lost it. But first I needed to see if Freddie was able to handle the job and make this kind of commitment.

Fadi and I went to see him together. We parked the Alfa at the end of the street and walked over to Freddie's shop. Fadi gave one of the kids who came over to check out the car 25 liras and told him to guard it with his life. Now the car was secure: the gang's troublemaker got paid, and he did not want to lose face.

We found Freddie hunched over a bench, under the lights, with a big magnifying lens in front of him. He was modifying some gadget using a soldering gun. He became very excited when he saw us and started explaining what he was doing. He might as well have been speaking Chinese because we did not understand anything about circuit boards, chips, or any of the rest of it. We simply nodded our heads in agreement.

Could he close the shop and come with us to help us install a new sound system in the car? He packed up right away and almost skipped to the car. His regulars always paid him for the repairs and his time, but he also loved to help. He was probably the only small shop owner in the area who was not paying protection money. I did favors for the gangs in the area and in return they left Freddie alone.

As soon as we got in the car, he started asking

questions about the sound system, the wattage, how many speakers, and so on. He wanted to see it. I told him there was no sound system and that we needed some privacy to explain a few things to him. Right away he started sweating profusely.

Didn't I say he was a wimp? He thought he had gotten himself in trouble by helping the wrong people.

"Freddie, my buddy," I assured him, "don't sweat it, everything is cool. You know I always take care of you."

"I know what that means sometimes."

"Not for you, baron." We called Armenian men "baron." It's like "mister."

"You had me worried for a minute," said Freddie. "Some guys came over last week asking all kinds of questions about safety switches and triggers. I did not know them. I did not give them any helpful information. They thought I was stupid and they left."

"Do you know who they are? Can you point them out to me?" I was worried about booby-trapped cars. An average of one car exploded every week. Hundreds of people had been killed that way. I needed to know who these men were.

"I don't know where they live, but I think I saw one of them around by the restaurant near your house."

"The restaurant owned by Lewis' brother?"

"Yeah, that is the one," Freddie said. "One of the three guys that came last week used to hang out late at night, outside the restaurant. Two of them looked like they were brothers."

I filed that piece of information in the back of my head so I could check that guy out later with Lewis; he knew most of the guys hanging out at his brother's restaurant.

"The reason we came to see you tonight has nothing to do with those guys," I said. "We might need your help in the near future, and I wanted to see if you are up to it."

Fadi was looking at me like I had lost my marbles.

He leaned over and whispered, "Are you nuts? He's a geek! What are you thinking?"

"Just be patient until I'm done talking, OK?" I whispered back. "Not everybody has to look the same and do the same thing. There are certain things that he can do that we do not understand."

As we drove along the back roads, I noticed Freddie getting nervous again. Then we parked the car at a remote location on a hill overlooking East Beirut. So many people had been assassinated and dumped from that hill that the valley below was called the Valley of Skulls. Freddie thought he was next.

I told Freddie to get out and take a walk with me.

He started shaking. "You know I keep my head down and I don't get involved with anybody."

"Maybe you shouldn't always keep your head down," I said. "It's time you got some balls, got yourself involved in something more productive."

"Yes, right. Because they will give *me* my own Special Forces unit."

"Not your own, but maybe you can be a part of one—a big part."

"Please, man, don't make fun of me. Who is going to give me such a chance?"

"I am here," I said, "to give you exactly such a chance." Then I explained we needed his expertise with electronics and wireless communications. He would be part of the unit, but he would not have to see actual combat or be involved in any field action.

He was ecstatic. "Are you serious?" he demanded. "This is awesome. I am in. When do I start?"

Soon, I told him. The other guys who'd been selected would have a meeting. Until then, secrecy was paramount. Any person leaking information before we got going, during, or after would face serious consequences.

23

THE OFFICIAL STORY

April 1982

PAUL:

It was time to present this bunch of weirdos to the counter-intelligence committee. I arranged for each one of them to arrive separately at a restaurant late one night. The sign on the door said CLOSED. The owner was a trusted member of the Lebanese Forces.

By the time Shadow arrived with his bodyguards in two black Range Rovers, we were all already seated, and each unit member was answering questions about his background, motivation, and commitment. The only one missing was Johnny Hypno, who was approved, out of jail, and waiting for the rest of us in Cyprus, as per Shadow's instructions.

During the recruiting process, whenever I picked a new member, I would send his name down to base, and a full background check would be completed on him. I did not expect many objections to Fadi, Lewis, or Michael. However, Sam, Johnny, and Freddie were a different story. The meeting lasted until the early morning hours.

Sam and Freddie in particular had to answer all kinds of questions about their commitment.

Shadow took me aside and asked me about Freddie. "This guy is a geek, a scrawny wimp—what are you thinking? I can't believe you picked him."

"If you can't believe it," I said, "neither will anyone else, including our enemy. He will not see field action—he will be stationed at headquarters, handling communications, and deactivating car bombs and booby-trapped letters. His role will be mostly logistics, but we need his brains. We might use him to booby-trap things. Nobody will suspect he is a special agent."

"I can see the twisted logic behind it. Not bad," Shadow said finally. "Even when he travels, no one will suspect him. He looks more like a teacher or a doctor than a bomb specialist. I agree, he would make a good choice."

Johnny, a.k.a. Mr. Hypno, already had his cover story; no one was going to miss him, as everyone knew he was in jail serving a five-year sentence.

The rest of us needed cover stories and new identities. Not even our contacts and handlers at the Mossad ("the Institute") would know our real names and backgrounds. The whole unit would never be seen together in public anywhere in Lebanon. We would operate in the shadows from the basement of the headquarters of counter-intelligence.

I was going to France to study mechanical engineering, as per my parents' wishes. At least, this was the story my parents were telling everybody; they believed it to be true.

Fadi, having no official papers or travel documents, needed to be kidnapped. Since he was originally from Syria, from an area they call the Hasake, we staged a kidnapping mission in broad daylight where everybody could see the abduction, and we used a car similar to the ones the Syrian Mokhabarat were driving. The Syrians were kidnapping Lebanese by the thousands each year, and no one ever came back. The guys that performed the abduction spoke with Syrian accents. No one would question the veracity of this kidnapping.

Lewis was a whole different story. Everybody knew that he was wanted throughout Europe, so we spread the rumor that he was caught in Spain with smuggled diamonds and was in jail awaiting trial.

Sam, having a lot of money, had gone to Belgium to open a branch of the family business. Antwerp, Belgium, was the center for diamond cutting and was a logical place for him to be.

Since Michael had no close family, few people would miss him. He was "killed in battle," and a small private funeral was held for him. We watched the gathering from an abandoned apartment's balcony that we used for our meetings.

Freddie's parents were leaving for Canada, anyway. The timing was perfect. The story was that he would be going with them. No one would miss him. He told his parents he would join them in Canada after he sold his shop.

I got the go-ahead to proceed. We had fun and a lot of laughs picking our new identities. Our original names were going to disappear and a full set of documents, including passports, were being acquired from contacts at the Interior Ministry.

We needed names that were neutral and could be either Christian or Muslim. Our area of operations was to include both sides.

My new name for now was Bassam, which means smiling, to always remind me of Yellow Eyes. We would be using many names soon, anyway.

Fadi became Farid (unique).

Lewis chose Latif (gentle).

Sam was now Saber (patient).

Michael was Munir (brilliant).

Johnny was Jamil (beautiful)— "that was a laugh."

Freddie the professor would now be called Faris (horseman or knight). He insisted on a strong, macho name.

These names, along with our new last names, were officially registered with the Ministry of Interior. We would use those names and identities when we were in Lebanon. When we traveled abroad, we would have a totally different set of documents with completely different identities. We were told to go back to base and wait the 24 hours required for the papers to be delivered.

Nobody was allowed to leave base, or have any communications in person or by phone with anybody outside the small circle. Our training had begun. The first lesson was in how to be patient. This was important, because most operations involved long stakeouts.

We had to become experts at waiting.

24

TRAINING WITH KIDON

PAUL:

The order came around midnight: we were told to leave base and head for the port, the private port just behind the main intelligence building. We were heading for the island of Cyprus, which is about 250 kilometers west of Lebanon. To avoid hassle and detection, we split into three groups.

Farid and Saber left from the old port of Jounieh, 15 kilometers north of Beirut. They were heading for Larnaca, the closest port on Cyprus. For many years, we had no access to the Beirut International Airport, so the port at Jounieh was the only way for Christians to get in and out of Lebanon. A few brave captains would dock their rusty old ships at the port, then unload and reload passengers as quick as they could, fearing a surprise shelling.

A few hours later, Latif and Munir left from the same port heading for Limasol, another port city on Cyprus, on a similar ship. There, they would rent a car and make the one-hour drive to the Larnaca airport.

The professor, a.k.a. Faris, and I boarded a private yacht early the next day. A millionaire businessman with ties to the Lebanese Forces owned the yacht. The professor loved learning about the instruments and equipment. He was ecstatic when the owner let him navigate. Checking out the dials and buttons, he was like a kid in a candy store.

Since Lebanese citizens were not allowed to travel to Israel, we were going to Tel Aviv by way of Cyprus. We were using different sets of documents, including Spanish, Portuguese, and Maltese passports. At the airport, we avoided talking to each other, and we boarded separate flights. Munir, Latif, and I were on the same El Al flight, scattered throughout the cabin. When I spotted Jamil waiting for his flight, I couldn't acknowledge his presence. We would not acknowledge each other until we got to the training camp. Even in the Tel Aviv airport, we stayed separate. Jamil and Faris were on a Cyprus Airways flight an hour behind us. I almost had a heart attack when I spotted Saber and Farid flirting with two girls in the departure lounge. I gave them the dirtiest of looks and headed to the washroom. I checked the stalls, making sure all was clear, when Saber came in.

"What the fuck are you doing?" I had to keep myself from yelling. "Those girls will remember you—are they going to Israel?"

"No, they are flying to Athens—they are cute, yes? And you said we should look relaxed and happy, like we were going on vacation, so guys on vacation flirt with girls. You should learn how to relax a little—you want me to introduce you to them? You would blend in much better, Bassam."

I hated that name. Every time somebody called me Bassam, I flashed back to the driveway and those menacing yellow eyes. Why had I picked that name? Because it kept me focused on the ultimate goal.

"No, thanks," I said. "Now get the hell out of here before somebody comes in."

I did not speak to any other member of the unit until we got to the training site in the Negev Desert. We were picked up separately from Ben Gurion Airport in Tel Aviv.

Two casually dressed Mossad agents met me at the airport. You might have expected them to be tough-looking guys in black suits, power ties, and dark shades, like in the movies. Those two guys were absolutely the opposite: one of them wore jeans and a simple blue T-shirt while the other wore khaki pants with a black shirt. They spoke fluent Arabic but with an accent similar to a Palestinian's. However, I could tell they were not native Arabic speakers. They were short and stocky but they looked fit. I put my one small carry-on bag in the trunk, and the three of us squeezed into a blue Renault 12 TS model and headed south toward a town called Beersheba.

At that training camp in the Negev, we would spend the better part of a year totally secluded from the public, even when we went out on simulation missions. We never socialized with the civilian population.

Training was intense and long. Mentally, it was exhausting. Physically, it was a true hell.

A typical training day started at 5 a.m. with a fast five-mile run. At first only Munir (that's Mike, remember?) and I could do it comfortably. For the first couple of months, Faris could not complete it at all.

After breakfast we would have class for two hours with members of the Shin Bet, also known as Shabak (it means "the net," or "the unseen shield"). Their specialty was safeguarding state security and exposing terrorist rings, interrogating terror suspects, and providing intelligence for counter-terrorism operations.

After lunch came my favorite part of the whole day: an intense two-hour training in Krav Maga. This was right up my alley. The instructors even told me I could teach the course. Krav Maga is a self-defense system developed for the Israeli military. It draws on techniques from several martial arts, some of which I already knew very well, like boxing, Muay Thai, Judo, Jiu jitsu, and Wrestling. Krav Maga focuses on real-world situations. It is extremely efficient and brutal.

The highlight of the day came later in the afternoon, when the instructors from the Kidon unit—*kidon* means "the tip of the spear"—paid us regular visits. Most people have never heard of this unit. They are the trained assassins of the Mossad. The details of their operations are carefully guarded secrets, but they handle mostly counter-terrorism, assassinations, and kidnappings. In short, they terrorize the terrorists. And that was what our own unit was formed to do as well.

Some late afternoons and evenings we split up and went to our specialized training courses. Faris, the professor, was being trained in computer programming, data collection, and the making and disarming of bombs. Jamil, or Mr. Hypno, was honing his forgery skills and learning about tactical intelligence. He would work closely with Faris in future operations.

Munir, or Michael, was impressing everyone with his skills. Target for target, he was a match for the elite Israeli Defense Forces snipers. He had more field experience than most of them. "Sniper" comes from the name of a bird, a snipe, whose natural camouflage makes him hard to see and whose erratic flight pattern makes him hard to shoot. A successful snipe hunter had to be an expert shot, and gradually the word "sniper" came to mean a highly skilled military sharpshooter. That was Munir.

You can *train* soldiers all you want, but you will not find out who has the nerves and cool until they are under pressure in a real fight situation. Munir had been doing it for years. The only thing he did not like was when Kidon instructors smeared honey on the back of his calves and told him to stay motionless for hours while the ants feasted on him.

Saber was learning how to drive without being suicidal. He was also being trained on tanks and boats. Latif was quickly becoming a master of disguise. He would handle the different looks, uniforms, and disguises needed for our different operations. He was learning how to build false, double-sided cases and how to break into safes and locked doors.

Farid was specializing in close-quarters combat, tunnel detection, and urban warfare.

I was being trained in all of it, the logic being that since I was the leader, I should be able to step in for any member of the unit who was killed or incapacitated and complete the mission.

Twice a week we would head over to the Mediterranean for scuba diving and other marine-related exercises. We were also trained in using underwater explosives, night diving, and making silent infiltrations.

We spent a year honing our skills and getting ready to put our own stamp on the conflict and start terrorizing the terrorists.

All through our training, we were visited by trainers and agents from European and American agencies. Their role was to teach us how to gather, analyze, and dissect information in order to plan our missions. I got the impression they did not fully understand the situation on the ground: they would pre-plan, plan again, and then re-plan every aspect of a mission. I knew from experience that no plan is perfect and sometimes you have to think on your feet. The problem with those agencies, including the Israelis, is they wanted the plans to be perfect and their own casualties to be minimal. This is not to say that we did not care about our own lives, but we understood the Syrians, the PLO, the Druze, the Sunni, and the Shia better than most of those agencies because we had lived with them all our lives and most of us had many years of experience dealing with them.

Over the next few years, we were able to accomplish more in a single month than all these agencies combined could accomplish in years of careful planning.

Our unit was now nicknamed S7. The S stands for *shayateen* (devils), and you don't need me to explain the seven.

25

MY FATHER WELCOMES ME HOME

PAUL:

We returned the way we had left, in separate groups under cover of darkness. After disembarking at the different ports, each of us made his own way back home.

It was about 2 a.m. when I reached the orange orchard behind our home. No matter where I am in the world, whenever I smell an orange or see an orange blossom, I instantly go back to the small orchard where I played as a teenager. I used the back door and went straight to my bedroom; there was no point waking up my parents in the middle of the night. I knew they would be asking many questions and they would not go back to sleep.

In those years, whenever I had a weapon on me, I worried about my younger brother. What if he was to get hold of it and accidentally discharge a bullet? That was how my cousin Charbel had died a few years earlier, when one of his friends was playing with a handgun and accidentally shot him in the neck.

That night when I got home, I took the magazine and bullet out of the chamber of my Sig Sauer P226; I placed the gun under my pillow and the magazine within reach under the bed. However, I had another weapon that I hid under the bed, also with the magazine out. This was a HK MP5 submachine gun, developed in Germany and rare in Lebanon.

But it was not my little brother I needed to worry about.

My mistake was leaving the magazine nearby. I woke up in the morning with dust over my chest. I could not for the life of me figure out how the dust had landed on top of me. I looked around and noticed a small hole in the curtain beside me. I pulled the curtain. There was another, bigger hole in the cinder block, just about two centimeters above my chest. While I was trying to figure out what had happened, my mother walked into the room, sat beside me, put her hand on my face, and started crying.

"Oh, come on, Mom," I said, "you are acting like you have not seen me in a year."

"I haven't, and you're still a clown, Paul," she said. "It felt like eternity. You should have called, or at least sent some news."

"We were not allowed any outside communication," I explained. "I am sorry, Mom. I missed you."

She looked around the room. "You still don't know what happened last night, do you?" she asked.

"Not exactly," I admitted. "What is this dust? And the bullet hole in the wall? I am so used to the sound of gunfire, I don't hear it anymore."

"Please don't say anything to your father," she said. "He is still in shock. He looks like a trembling white ghost. He heard you come in last night and came by to check on you. You were asleep—but then Rambo saw the machine gun under your bed. Your father says that as soon as he inserted the clip into the gun, it fired automatically."

"This kind of gun is different from the ones Dad used to handle back home."

"Oh my God! You disappear for a year to God knows where, and you were doing dangerous things, I know you were. I always had this feeling and I prayed for you every day. Then, as soon as you get back home safely to me, you almost get killed in your bed by your own father."

"Don't worry, Mother," I said, trying to reassure her. "I have nine lives. I still have six left."

I got up and gave her a hug. She started crying again and would not let go of me.

"Mom, I thought by now you would have breakfast and coffee ready." I was trying to change the subject.

"I did," she said. "It's in the living room. Your father is waiting for you. Please don't give him a hard time. He is already scared, and embarrassed."

As I made my way to the living room wearing only a pair of shorts, I could see my mom looking to see if I was hurt or had any scars. I shook hands with my dad, gave him a kiss on the forehead, and we sat for a few minutes in silence, having breakfast.

To this day my father and I have never discussed what happened that night. There was no point talking about it. Whenever I visited home after that incident, he never touched any of my equipment.

26

DRINKING WITH THE ENEMY

PAUL:

Two days after we got back home, the unit assembled at base in order to start our first briefing on our maiden mission.

It was supposed to be a strictly reconnaissance and intelligence-gathering mission, involving one Abu Mansour, a senior member of the Popular Front for the Liberation of Palestine (PFLP). We were supposed to gather information about his daily routines and movements; this guy was flamboyant and had many mistresses. He housed each one of them in a different apartment in West Beirut. He was also married with four children, so his escapades needed to be done in relative secrecy. When you need your movements to stay secret or inconspicuous, you cannot drive around in a convoy of cars. Instead, when he needed to visit one of his girlfriends, he would give most of his bodyguards the night off and keep two with him in his black BMW 735.

For a full week, we studied him and planned the operation. Freddie, stationed at the base, would handle eavesdropping on the CB radio after he had cracked the frequency. Lewis, being the best to blend into the neighborhood, started selling *kaak* (famous Lebanese street bread) near the PFLP headquarters on a street cart we rented from one of the vendors on the east side. I made my way to West Beirut in a taxi driven by Sam. Posing as a French businessman selling beauty products, I checked into a hotel that had a nightclub in the basement where Abu Mansour liked to hang out. The star belly dancer, Sahar, was one of his girlfriends; she was the newest and hottest one of his collection. He made regular visits.

He did not show up on the first night, however, so I worked on my cover. I was showing products to the front desk clerks and to the restaurant and nightclub waitresses. Women love beauty products, and I was handing out samples with promises of more to come on my next visit. I made sure everybody knew I was making a deal with a major supplier in the area.

At 11 p.m. the next day, Lewis called me in my room, from a pay phone across the street from PFLP headquarters, and told me he was sold out and needed more product. That was code, meaning Abu Mansour had left and might be on his way to see his hot dancer.

I headed to the nightclub and found a table near the back wall where I could see the entire room and the front door. I ordered a drink and an ashtray, and I started to smoke. I hated smoking, but most Frenchmen smoked and I needed to stay in character. One small mistake could cost me my life.

Around midnight, Abu Mansour showed up with one bodyguard; the second was left outside with the car. The bodyguard sat at the bar while my subject got a VIP table at the front between the dance floor and the main stage. He was treated like royalty as he was throwing his money around, but he was no match for the Saudis and Kuwaitis flaunting stacks of money, who were opening dozens of champagne bottles for the mediocre singers and sexy dancers. But he was feared and so he was given the best table.

Abu Mansour was drinking and smoking heavily. I knew that before long he was going to be drunk. Once Sahar showed up and started her number, he got loud and excited and ordered a couple of champagne bottles to be opened at the stage by her feet. I was noticing everything at once, including the nightclub manager sitting with the Saudis and Kuwaitis, telling them that this girl was off-limits, and not to offend the boyfriend at the front table. I knew I had to leave the club before Abu Mansour did and get to the lobby so I could see in which direction he was heading. If he went upstairs to one of the rooms, I needed to know what floor.

I paid my bill and was heading out, minding my own business, when Sahar saw me. She waved to me with a big smile while wiggling her sexy hips to the rhythm of the music. I had given her some cream and perfume samples the night before. This did not sit well with my friend at the front table, as he felt she belonged to him, and how dare another man hit on her. The bodyguard intercepted me at the door. He put the palm of his hand on my chest and pushed me back toward the table. I lifted my hands in a nonthreatening gesture and sat down beside Prince Charming.

I asked in French, "Is there is a problem, sir?"

He did not understand what I was saying, but the manager noticed what was happening and rushed over to our table.

"*Ya rayes*," he began—slang for 'leader'—"Mr. Ollard is a client at the hotel. He sells beauty products and perfume and he gives lots of samples to all the ladies—that is how Miss Sahar knows him."

Abu Mansour kept staring at me with those dark, empty eyes, trying to understand my motives. I sat quietly at his table, waiting for permission to leave. This suited me fine since it gave me the opportunity to be close to him.

Suddenly he burst out laughing, reached for an empty glass, put some ice in it, and poured me a large amount of Johnnie Walker Black. He tapped my glass with his and said, "*Kessak!*" (cheers). I said, "*Sante!*" (cheers in French), and we drank to Sahar.

One of the waiters delivered a message to me from the front desk operator that said, in French, "We have to deliver new inventory." That meant that, if it was safe and possible, we should proceed with the extraction of the subject tonight.

I knew that by now Lewis (Latif) would be near the entrance of the hotel with his *kaak* cart and Sam (Saber) would be waiting nearby posing as a taxi driver in a dark green Mercedes. At that time, most taxis in Beirut were Mercedes.

I needed to get Abu Mansour as drunk as possible and then find a way to get into his car with him. I started drinking faster and politely ordered him a Courvoisier XO cognac—he had offered me a drink, after all, and the least I could do was reciprocate. He smoked Cohiba cigars and enjoyed the cognac so much that he drank three or four more glasses in less than an hour. Sahar did not need to wiggle as much; I was sure the whole room was spinning by now. Then I hit the jackpot.

Fatso suggested giving one of the bodyguards the night off, so then there'd be enough room in his car for me to accompany him to another club, to pick up another dancer. We could continue the party at the home of one of his friends. We would find more girls and play poker with some of his friends. I told him that I loved poker, and would be more than happy to go with them if I could just go up to my room to get some more cash, along with my diabetes medication. All this was translated through the club's manager.

He told me that was no problem; more cash was always welcome and U.S. dollars were preferred. He sent the bodyguard with me, just to keep me company.

Waiting for the elevators, I spotted through my peripheral vision three men coming toward us. I felt them before I saw them.

Bassam, Ghassan, and their cousin Mohamed were crossing the lobby toward the elevators.

I had dyed my hair black, even my body hair, and I had blue contact lenses and glasses. I was confident they would not recognize me, but I started shaking. I put my hands in my pockets hoping they didn't notice my trembling hands. I remember thinking, *what kind of spy are you Paul? You're scared and shaking, and you are going to be killed before your first operation has even started.*

The elevator arrived and I started breathing again, thinking we were going to make it up to the room before they spotted me. The bodyguard knew them, however, and held the elevator door open for them saying, "Hello, comrades, are you going up also?"

Ghassan answered, "Yes, thank you, we have business upstairs." I have not heard the brothers' voices in years, but I felt my whole body tense. I averted my eyes from the magnetic yellow eyes and tried to look relaxed. I shifted my gaze down and to one side. Being stuck in an elevator with four armed men was not good odds. I was quickly calculating and rehearsing my moves if one of them tried to take out his gun. I was going to disarm him and shoot Bassam first, than go on autopilot from there.

Bassam glared at me and asked, "You don't say much do you?"

I kept my blank look painted on my face and smiled.

The bodyguard answered for me. "He is French, he can't understand us. We are taking him with us to a poker game tonight; if he wins, he won't be back." They all laughed and I sweated.

The elevator stopped. Bassam informed the bodyguard that he might join the game later and to leave him the address at the hotel's reception desk. He gave me one last glance and they exited.

I was not sure I was breathing or not. I was dizzy, and the elevator cabin felt like I was in a blender. I took a couple of deep breath and stumbled out. I heard the guard asking me if I was okay.

"Yes, yes, I am fine, I think I need my medication."

In the room I made a show of putting some drops in my eyes, then I switched bottles and put one in my pocket. I also showed the bodyguard a hypodermic needle and told him it was for my diabetic condition; just in case I went into shock, I showed him how to use it. I took cash out of the safe and declared myself ready for a night of drinking, whoring, and poker playing.

With one less guard, security was very relaxed. This guy felt safe because he was connected to the CIA, who needed him alive; he guaranteed the safety of the American citizens teaching at the American University of Beirut and the staff of the U.S. Embassy. This made him an off-limits target to the Israelis. However, they wanted him taken care of, so they commissioned us to do the dirty work.

I climbed into the front passenger seat of the Bimmer beside the driver. Fatso was in the back seat, fondling the gorgeous dancer, who had thick blonde hair and a small, tight, sexy body with curves in the right places. She could have not been older than twenty-three.

Just before we took off, I noticed Lewis getting into another car with Sam. They followed at a safe distance. I am not sure there is such a thing as a cold-blooded killer—I was hot and anxious. I was always like that before an operation, though once the action started, my training took over and I had no time to think or second-guess. The shaking and the knots in my stomach usually intensified after my adrenaline stopped pumping.

I waited until the driver started to slow down in order to make a slow, 90-degree turn, then I reached over and grabbed him by the collar of his suit jacket, jerking him violently toward me while landing two solid elbows on the side of his head and the bridge of his nose. He went to "sleep." The car smashed into another vehicle parked on the corner of the narrow street, but no one was injured since we were traveling at a very low speed. Fatso had his pants down and was pushing Sahar's head down between his legs, forcing her to go down on him. He was laughing as she was gagging, but then the situation dawned on him. He tried to pull his pants up while reaching for his handgun, but he was very slow and ungraceful. Within seconds, I disarmed him, stuck the needle in his neck, and sent him into a deep, snoring sleep. Sahar started to panic, screaming. The last thing I needed was a screaming woman after midnight in West Beirut. I grabbed her by the hair and knocked her out with one punch, partly to shut her up but mostly to give her a chance during the ensuing investigation. The big facial bruise might save her life, make them believe she had nothing to do with Abu Mansour's abduction.

Sam drew his car up beside us, and Lewis helped me drag Fatso out of the back seat of the BMW and dump him in the trunk of the Mercedes. This was only half the mission, as we still needed to get him out of the area and back to the eastern side of the city before they shut the passages down.

The Lebanese Army was acting as a buffer force between east and west. They had roadblocks on every road crossing between the two sides. We knew we had to pass through at least one of the checkpoints. Three guys in a taxi late at night would definitely be searched and questioned, but we had an ace in the hole. A Christian Lebanese Army captain was responsible for one of the crossings. We knew he would be present at the checkpoint and that he would have a trusted crew manning the point throughout the night.

We got to the checkpoint without incident and were stopped, as expected. As was customary at checkpoints in Lebanon, we turned off the music, turned on the interior lights, and rolled down the windows. Regular army soldiers, who asked us for our papers, approached us from both sides. Our papers were in order, so they handed them back to us and asked us to open the glove compartment. It was empty. Then one of the soldiers asked me to step outside and open the trunk. I got out as calmly as I could manage while trying to decide what to do next, wondering if this was one of the captain's guys or not. I opened the trunk for him, he shined his flashlight and looked inside, then he looked at me, smiled, and said, "Have a good trip." I am sure he could see the shocked look on my face, but he kept on smiling. I got back in the car and saw the same look I had repeated on Lewis' and Sam's faces.

"Sam, go, just go," I said.

"What the hell, he just let us go with a 250-pound man in the trunk?"

"He even wished us a good trip."

We drove the last five kilometers in silence and made our delivery to the jail located in the building next to ours.

Instead of celebrating the completion of our first mission, Lewis looked at me and asked, "What are we going to tell the cart owner? I left the fucking thing at the Roucheh." The Roucheh is an upscale district in Beirut, famous for restaurants, clubs, and the Roucheh Rock formation.

Sam laughed, hard, and told Lewis we would give

the cart owner the Mercedes instead.

I started laughing also, mostly from relief, and told Lewis not to worry: I would make sure the man was fully compensated for his cart.

Back at base, we were met in the parking lot by the rest of the S7, along with Shadow and his entourage. Shadow was beaming because we had accomplished in one week what the Mossad had been trying to do for over a year. High fives, cheers, and hugs were going all around me, while I came crashing down from my adrenaline rush. Again, I stuffed my hands in my pockets as they were shaking. This made me look cool, like it was no big deal. But I knew better.

"The Israelis are going to be shocked that you guys pulled this off," said Shadow.

"If they are shocked, that means they did not train us very well," I answered.

"You know," Shadow pointed out, "their problem is extraction. If they had done this operation, they would have had to come in from the sea and go back the same way. It is very risky and it is logistically impossible."

"That is why they need us, boss," I said. "But remember, they only help us because they can use us. The first lesson during training was, 'In this business do not trust anybody, maybe not the members of your own unit. Even your own fingers.'"

"Don't worry, Bassam." Shadow knew how much that name bothered me, so he took every opportunity to call me Bassam. "I know this game, and I know how to use them, also, for weapons, training, and equipment. We need them."

I stayed behind to file my report while it was fresh in my mind, then I drove the 25 kilometers to the town of Tabarjah, where the members of the unit lived in a high-rise building in one of the country's top resorts. I shared a two-bedroom apartment with Lewis. All the S7 guys were already there, playing cards and drinking beer. There was a mood of celebration with relief written on their faces.

Lewis said, "I should have at least brought that *kaak* with me. I'm hungry."

Freddie replied jokingly, "Are you sure you did not eat it all before you left the cart?"

"Maybe I did," said Lewis. "I don't remember. I was munching all day. Being nervous gives me the munchies. This is not good for my health."

I did not join in the celebration or the card playing. I sat on the balcony, put my feet up with a beer in my hand, and gazed at the city far off on the horizon. The view was breathtaking and we were doing a good job destroying this beautiful piece of heaven. I was thinking, *God is angry.*

The sun was rising out of the east, and the city was starting to wake up. I was pleased with the completion of our first mission, but I did not like the quick change of plans, and the immediate decision to perform the extraction at high risk on the spur of the moment. Would we be this lucky next time?

I knew in my heart that we would not be.

PART FOUR

BASSAM:

The QJ were feeling threatened on many fronts, for the first time since its inception. Christians could come in and actually kidnap a friendly officer right from under their noses. The worst part was that they saw the operation unfold and did not notice. Bassam had felt something strange about the man in the elevator, and he had hated him instantly. For some reason he hated him as much as the Red Devil.

"The day will come when we meet. I have to think of some new torture technique for him; dragging him behind a car will not satisfy me."

The QJ were told to help the Druze to attack in the mountains. The QJ had other plans for the Druze, though. After they finished with the Christians, they would finish off the Druze.

The biggest threat to the QJ were the Shia. The Iranians were helping the Shia train and get organized. The Syrians were on their side—no surprise, because they were almost the same sect. They would have to fight them eventually. For hundreds of years, the Shia were treated like second-class citizens. They were the poor, they did the manual labor, and they had babies. Now they had the most fighters. The Iranians were paying them salaries to join, and providing free educations for their kids and free medical for the whole family if they did. The Shia had no jobs and no prospects, so they were joining in the thousands—this was a dangerous situation.

It is one thing to fight the infidels and another thing altogether to fight another Muslim. But it had to be done at some point, so the QJ found a new, innovative idea to get them to fight with the Christians and Druze. It was a win-win situation: let them kill each other while the QJ watched and played both sides.

27

BACK TO SCHOOL

PAUL:

In 1982, months after invading Lebanon all the way to Beirut and the surrounding mountains, the Israeli Defense Forces (IDF) decided to quickly withdraw their troops from their positions in the southern suburbs of Beirut and from a section of the Beirut–Damascus Highway. They didn't bother to warn us: the Israelis were loyal only to Israel. Immediately, heavy fighting started between the Druze militias and the Lebanese Forces.

By this stage of the war, the Druze were 17,000 strong. Joining them were another 10,000 fighters from the Syrian Social Nationalist Party, which backed the idea of a Greater Syria, and the Nasserite Murabitoun (Sunni). The Amal militia (Shia) had mobilized another 10,000 fighters. Both the Amal and the Druze-led coalition received the discreet but crucial backing of the PLO and the Syrian army, which provided logistical and artillery support.

On the opposite side, the Lebanese Forces militia had about 2,500 lightly equipped Christian militiamen in the Chouf Mountains. They were mostly tied down with garrison duties.

Can you see what was coming? On one side: 37,000 well-equipped fighters backed by the PLO and the Syrian army. On the other: 2,500 well-trained but lightly equipped soldiers scattered across a large area.

As soon as the last Israeli units left the Chouf in early 1983, the Druze launched a full-scale offensive against the Lebanese Forces. Warned at the last minute by our contacts within the PLO of the imminent Druze attack, the LF command began evacuating Christian civilians from the villages around Deir el-Qamar, but there was no time to evacuate all of them, which left the surrounding countryside virtually undefended. This is the same town where I went to boarding school as a boy. I knew both it and the surrounding hills very well.

The ferocity of the assault caught the LF garrison forces completely by surprise. Hopelessly outnumbered, supported by obsolescent field guns and some jeeps, heavy machine guns, and recoilless rifles on gun trucks, and anti-aircraft mounted on wheeled armored personnel carriers (APCs), they tried desperately to hold their ground against a determined enemy that was now equipped with Soviet-made tanks, tracked and wheeled APCs, and long-range artillery, supplied on loan by Syria.

It took only two days to force the Lebanese Forces troops to fall back to Deir el-Qamar, which held 40,000 Christian residents and refugees and was defended by 1,000 LF militiamen. The Druze slaughtered 1,500 people and drove another 50,000 out of their homes. We were not used to such quick and decisive defeats. The leadership had to respond and to open a supply route in order to deliver food and medicine to the besieged town.

The S7 did not get involved in the regular day-to-day fighting. Our mission was to find and liquidate the top military leader of the offensive.

Piece of cake, right? Penetrate behind enemy lines, assassinate the leader, retreat, and try to make it back to safety. Not great odds, but we never stopped to calculate. Our focus was always on the mission. After growing up and living for years in the middle of the battlefield, most had lost the sense of fear. Was I the only scared one? I asked myself the same question over and over, but never aloud.

Fadi, Mike, and I had to move into position quickly, before the different troops solidified their positions and secured the areas with roadblocks and checkpoints. There were so many different groups and factions, they had a hard time working out who was supposed to cover what and where the borders were. We took advantage of the confusion and the disorganized situation.

In the middle of the night, Sam drove us to a mountaintop facing the Chouf Mountains. We descended the mountain into the valley and found a hiding place before daybreak. The whole first day we stayed motionless under the cover of some shrubs and a small camouflage net, waiting for darkness so we could make our way up the opposite mountain and start our search. I promised myself never to complain about a hard pillow, as I laid my head on a stone slab. It took most of the next night to get to our observation point behind enemy lines.

Well-hidden and camouflaged, Mike assembled his Heckler & Koch PSG1 sniper rifle and scope and took up a position between two rocks overlooking the main base of the Druze fighters. Fadi was spotting for him, and I was covering their backs from another location 200 above them.

Late in the afternoon we started hearing a rumbling noise from the opposite hill, about 400 yards west of our location. Through his spotter scope, Fadi located a yellow Caterpillar bulldozer moving back and forth. He signalled to me that there were three people in the vicinity of the dozer. I told him and Mike to stay put and I would go and scout.

Moving silently through the woods during daylight is a very slow and tedious process: it took me almost two hours to cover 300 yards. Knowing that Fadi had me in his sights and that Michael was covering me, I could feel the crosshairs of Mike's scope on my back.

What I saw next sent chills through my body.

The Druze forces were digging a grave, a mass grave. Not far from where the dozer was working, I could see a pile of bodies, about 50 of them. I couldn't tell if they were old or young, but from the sizes of the bodies and the colors of their clothes, it wasn't hard to guess that they were mostly women and children. I was sure they were slaughtered Christians.

I watched the driver pick up a dozen bodies at a time in the bucket of the tractor and drop them into the big hole, like rubble. Next they threw lime powder over the victims. The two men on the ground motioned to the driver to start refilling the mass grave with dirt, as they walked back to their parked truck to have a cigarette break.

I gave Mike the signal to shoot them; in seconds, they were both dead, each with a bullet in the head. The driver did not hear a thing, since the dozer was very loud and he was looking the other way. I approached him from behind and climbed on top of the machine, right behind him. When he stopped to reverse direction and get another bucketful of dirt, I bayonetted him in the neck and pushed him to the ground quickly. I did not want his blood on my clothes or to have his smell on me in case I needed to approach someone else, but mostly I did not want to be reminded of my acts. Never take souvenirs when you want to forget.

My experience driving bulldozers as a kid came in handy. I took the seat, collected the three gravediggers, and threw them on top of the rest of the bodies. Next, I crushed the small pickup truck and dumped it into the hole. Finally, I finished their job for them and covered the whole grave with lime and dirt.

It was starting to get dark and surely it wouldn't be long before somebody missed those three. Having given up our positions, we had to quickly change location and get closer to our target.

I waited for Mike and Fadi to join me; we spent the whole night moving quietly through the woods to another location. We were sure our target would be inspecting the siege and military positions around Deir el-Qamar.

As the sun rose, I started to recognize the different landmarks of the town. Everything looked smaller than it had before; even the big cross that dominated the hill opposite my old school looked smaller to me. From a distance, I was able to locate the school.

We were less than 500 yards behind the enemy's forward lines—and a total of 800 yards away from our LF defensive lines. We had to keep radio silence. It was going to be difficult to complete the mission and head toward the town. Both sides would be shooting at us.

The enemy's main position consisted of sand-filled barrels topped with a few hundred sandbags in three locations on top of the hill. Mike was in his sniper mode, totally motionless. Fadi was doing his reconnaissance with the spotter scope when he suddenly signalled that two vehicles were approaching. As if on cue, our target got out of one of the vehicles. The Druze fighters were overconfident. They were on the offense, and not a shot had been fired in the last two days from either side. I was 100 percent sure the Lebanese Forces scouts were watching the same thing we were. I was hoping that once the mayhem started and the time came for our sprint to safety, they would recognize which side we were on.

One of the leaders came out from behind the sandbags and approached our target. He did not salute him—this was not an organized army with official ranks—but they shook hands and spoke for a few minutes. The leader handed our target a pair of binoculars. Our target then made a 360-degree sweep of the area, starting with the town and the surrounding hills.

I knew that Mike had the guy dead in his scope. What I did not know was when he was going to pull the trigger. Mike waited until the binoculars were pointed in his direction. I can only imagine the shock on the face of our target when his binoculars located the sniper. Just as our target started to say something, his binoculars exploded in his hands. Mike had put a shot through the right lens and disintegrated his head.

Everything was happening at once. Some Druze soldiers were running around in a panic, others were shooting at the Lebanese Forces' positions, and some were trying to attend to their leader. This was our opportunity to make a run for it. I broke radio silence and started to communicate with Freddie at our base in East Beirut; he was quickly relaying the information to the operations room in the besieged town. The LF opened fire at the disorganized Druze soldiers and fired a few 60 mm mortar shells to get them behind the sandbags.

We had started moving seconds after Mike delivered his shot, since we were still about 400 meters from safety behind our sandbags. I know that the Olympic runners can cover this distance in less than forty-five seconds, but we were not sprinters and we also had our equipment. The three of us were running down the hill as fast as we could, totally exposed, finding cover behind some rocks here and there, but we were taking fire. This run felt more like forty-five minutes. Fadi, the fastest one of us, was the farthest down the hill and the closest to safety. I was still hiding with Mike behind a rock when I saw Fadi fall. I was not sure if he had tripped or been shot. Bullets were flying everywhere while Mike and I held our position between the two sides. Since we were below the enemy lines, they started to throw hand grenades our way. We were pinned, but we seemed to be protected from metal and rock shrapnel, as the grenades kept landing on the rocks around us. I knew if we lost our nerve and moved, we would be dead. We kept our heads down and waited for the LF guys to cover us with mortar fire. Every time a 60mm shot was fired, we heard it and anticipated its landing; I knew from experience and from the sound of the whistle how long we had before it landed. I also knew that because we were under the landing site we would not get shrapnel directed our way: shrapnel traveled in a direction like a reverse umbrella. We would count thirty seconds after we heard the shots fired, then we would both run down the hill and take cover behind other rocks. We did this four times before we made it behind the sandbags of the LF side.

As soon as we made it back to relative safety, I went to check on Fadi. The LF had pulled him over to their side and had set up a makeshift field hospital and two medics were frantically working on him. I did not need to be a doctor to understand the gravity of the situation: he was covered in blood from the middle of his back to his feet and was losing blood quickly. The lack of a proper operating room and a surgeon made it hard to save his life. The medics were pumping what little blood was available into him. I donated some myself since I knew we both had B positive blood.

While I was holding his hand, watching him fade away, he only said one thing, "Make sure that the papers we got for my family are all in order."

"Don't worry, buddy," I said. "As soon as we get back, you can make sure of that yourself."

He smiled weakly at me, but I was very familiar with this look.

"You are such a bad liar," he said. I opened my mouth, my lips parted but the words escaped me, I watched him close his eyes and fade.

Hot tears burned my cheeks, my grief fresh and raw, but I had no time to mourn. Most people will not be able to understand the feeling that survivors have when somebody close to them dies. Initially, you feel guilt and a sense of failure for surviving while not being able to help your friend. After a while, though, you become so hardened to the culture of death, you expect it and even accept it. Every day I used to wake up and ask myself, "Is it going to be me today?" On most missions and during deployments, I would look at my unit members and others and wonder, who will die and never come back? On this day, it was one of my closest buddies.

The following morning, with one priest from the town and a few soldiers, Mike and I buried our friend in an unmarked grave in a strange town that Fadi had never been to. No flowers will ever be laid on his grave, and not even his parents will know where he is buried. We were not in this for the glory or the recognition. We did it because we needed to.

That afternoon I went up the hill and visited my old school. It did look much smaller. I recognized one of the priests sitting on a bench under a large tree that we used to play under during breaks. He was reading a book. I went to sit beside him.

"So, you are one of the fighters that took refuge in this town?" he asked me.

"No," I said. "I missed a few semesters of school and came back to complete them."

He took a closer look at me and started to laugh. "You haven't changed and can't fool me. Your hair is darker, the freckles are disappearing, but I can tell from your eyes that you are still the same troublemaker."

I knew the priest came from a small town about halfway between Deir el-Qamar and the Mediterranean coast. If we could reach the sea, the LF had the stronghold base by the beach to transport soldiers from East Beirut to the Chouf Mountains. Mike and I could make it from Deir el-Qamar to the sea by travelling at night, but we needed a safe place to hide during the day. Most of the small towns on the way were a mixture of Christians and Druze. I asked the priest, "Do you think your relatives will take us in during the day, on the way to the sea?"

"Absolutely, without questions," he said. "Go to the house behind the church in Kfar Matta. Give them my name and ask for sanctuary."

That night, Mike and I met with the Lebanese Forces military commander and told him we were going to attempt to get through the enemy lines and get to the sea in order to make it by boat back to East Beirut. We also needed to contact our base and tell them to have a boat ready for pickup.

"You guys are crazy," said the commander. "You're lucky you made it here alive. Your friend was not as lucky. Don't do this. It's nuts. Wait until the Red Cross and the international community get us some help."

"We are going tonight," I said. "If you don't hear any shots, it means we made it behind the lines."

With the complete shortage of fuel for cars, some guys stripped a VW Beetle of its steel, leaving only the frame and seats, then harnessed an unlucky donkey to pull them around town. Whenever they came to a small incline in the road, they jumped out and helped push the frame. They had even offered us a ride earlier in the day. We felt sorry for the poor donkey and declined.

Two a.m. is usually when the sentries and guards become tired and careless. We could have killed a couple of them stationed at the southernmost end of the town and closest to the Druze headquarters. They never expected an infiltration to come from this direction since it would have been suicidal. We passed right under their noses, not even 100 feet below their post. We heard them talking and saw them smoking. We needed to stay totally undetected. We did not want a search party on our tail, since we were going to be spending the whole day in a town under their control.

By 5 a.m., just as the sun was coming up, I knocked on the back door of the house behind the church; a man in his mid-fifties opened the door for us. I could see shock on his face: he opened his mouth and started to say something then changed his mind. He looked outside in both directions and motioned for us to hurry in. We did not need an introduction. Our unit logo was hidden under a Velcro cover, but he knew who we were from our distinctive black and dark gray camouflaged outfits. He was astonished that we had made it into his town.

"Do you know where you are?" he asked.

"The priest at the boarding school in Deir el-Qamar sends you his regards."

"The priest is my brother," he said. "However, you don't need an introduction for me to hide you at my house. In the open, you're sitting ducks."

"We just need to stay until dark," I told him. "We will be on our way tonight."

"This is crazy!" he said. "It is impossible for you to make it through another dozen towns undetected. The whole area is crawling with so many different factions, it's hard to tell who is who."

"Then this is a perfect opportunity for us," I said. "If we get spotted by one group, they might think that we belong to another."

He went into another room and told his wife about us. She came over, still in her pajamas, and got busy making breakfast.

Our host was understandably nervous; our presence put them in danger. He said something I already knew: "You know if they find you here, they will kill us all."

I promised him we would be leaving that night as soon as it got dark. "Until then," I said, "don't receive any visitors, and we will stay under the windows' line of sight."

That day, Mike and I took turns sleeping on a foam mattress on the floor. When darkness came and we were getting ready to leave, the woman of the house provided us with a few snacks and sandwiches for the road. We thanked them both and told them that if we got spotted leaving the house, the story would be that we just came in and stole their food, and that they had never met us before.

Nobody in the area had electricity, and it was pitch-black when we made our way out of the back door and into the fields. Again we walked the whole night and made it all the way to the top of the hill overlooking the beach base of the LF.

Another challenge lay ahead: we needed to get around the last of the Amal (Shia) checkpoints to approach the LF defense lines. With no communications available and no warning of our approach, they might take us for the enemy.

Circling wide around the checkpoint was easier than approaching our own base on foot, dressed in army fatigues and carrying weapons. It would only take one nervous soldier with a happy trigger finger and that'd be the end. We had to wait for one of the patrols to come out and make ourselves known to them before they could hose us down. This base was basically an island. It was located on land but surrounded by enemies on three sides. Even the sea side had to be constantly monitored, as the Amal party had acquired boats. The LF soldiers had to monitor four directions at once. They were on the alert and nervous.

We made our way as close as possible and started singing LF military songs. We were sure we would be asked to come out and show ourselves, and this is exactly what happened next.

We let them surround us; they sent a whole squad to smoke us out. Our military units always came in multiples of three. We operated in a triangle format for both attack and retreat modes. A fifteen-man squad, almost a full platoon, took their positions.

There is nothing friendly about friendly fire. It would have sucked big time to be killed by our own, after we had eliminated one of the enemy leaders, lost one of our friends in the process, and spent two days escaping from behind enemy lines. We did not even have a white flag to wave.

I had a bright idea. "Mike, what color underwear are you wearing?"

"Why don't you wave yours?" he asked.

"Mine are black."

"So is mine, but you're whiter than me, so maybe I could try and wave you around, Bozo."

We threw our weapons out from behind the rocks where we were hiding, but these guys were too experienced to fall for such a simple trick. We were dealing with suicide bombers long before the west had heard of them. Like the sail, the alphabet, and the ink in Phoenician times, Lebanon invented suicide bombers. The soldiers ordered us to come out slowly with our arms over our heads. This was all easy stuff, but the Amal snipers were on the top of the hill and that would leave us exposed to both sides.

"How about we crawl halfway and naked?" I shouted.

"How many are you?"

"Two, we are from the LF."

"How did you get here?"

"We walked for days, from Deir el-Qamar."

"What were you doing there? There is no Amen there. Don't answer that. We got an encrypted message about this possibility two days ago. We never thought you would make it. Come on out. You can keep your clothes on."

Mike and I walked around the rocks slowly, making sure we were not exposed to sniper fire, and approached the platoon.

I looked at one of them and did a double take. "Oh my God, you're going to shoot your first cousin?"

"What the fuck are you doing here? I thought you were in France." The platoon leader was my cousin Rony.

"I am," I said in French. "Is this not the Cote d'Azure?"

"You are trying to be a comedian? Let's get the hell out of here, quick."

We hugged and kissed; Lebanese kiss each other three times, unless it's a hot woman, then there is no maximum.

The main barracks was a converted electricity generation station no longer in operation. There was no fuel delivery to keep it going. The whole area used candles and some kerosene lamps. I wished I had my candle cart close by, I would have made a killing—no pun intended.

We waited for the extraction boat to arrive, and under cover of darkness they fed us boiled rice and beans. To this day, many years later, it is still my favorite meal. That same night we took the boat back to East Beirut without incident.

This time, back at the base, there was no celebration of any kind, no backslapping or congratulations. We were mourning the death of our close friend Fadi. I had the unpleasant task of delivering the news to his family. Sam and Lewis came with me to deliver the sad news, while I sat there silently crying.

Our unit name did not change. We would always be the S7, because our fallen comrades remained a part of us.

28

GOING ON HOLIDAY

PAUL:

We were going back to Cyprus, again by boat because Christians still couldn't get anywhere near the airport. However, this time we needed to enter and exit Cyprus with different identities. Our mission was to eliminate a member of the Libyan intelligence services. I know what you're thinking: how could there be any intelligence in Libya during the Gaddafi regime?

This guy's name was Mubtasem, which means "smiling." He actually did smile a lot, because he was living the good life, spending money like water and facilitating the delivery of funds and weapons into Lebanon. The Shiite Amal movement wanted to get their hands on him as well. They hated the Libyans more than us. The Libyans had been responsible for the kidnapping and disappearance of their well-read, moderate, and respected leader Imam Musa al-Sadr in 1978. Gaddafi invited him and two companions to visit Libya. They went and never returned. The Libyans claimed they had left for Italy. Italy had no record of them entering the country.

Mr. Smiley kept an apartment in a small, two-story building on a quiet street in Nicosia, the capital of Cyprus. The landlord and his family lived on the ground floor, and our target lived in the two-bedroom apartment upstairs. He was a frequent visitor to the island and had many contacts and friends there; he usually met with his contacts in a Syrian restaurant on the outskirts of the city. Flamboyant and generous, he made sure that when he threw his money around, people noticed. He was a regular at most of the clubs and bars and knew almost every Eastern European hooker by name.

All visitors to the island have to register with the police. When you check into a hotel, the police will photocopy your passport and send it to Immigration. Cyprus was small, so it was easy to keep tabs on most visitors.

Johnny left alone, two days ahead of Freddie and me. He registered as a Portuguese tourist in a hotel in Larnaca, left his luggage at that hotel, rented a delivery van under a different name with another fake passport and credit card, and drove it to Nicosia. We were staying in an apartment practically across the street from our target that had been rented a couple of months earlier.

Freddie and I arrived two days later, via Rome, and headed straight to Nicosia. Our contacts on the island had already secured the material we needed. Freddie was both nervous and excited, as this would be his first field operation.

Johnny knew our target split most of his time between the Syrian restaurant and the different cabarets, so he was looking forward to following Mubtasem around and studying his movements. Johnny was changing looks and disguises three or four times a day. He would take his morning walk dressed like an old man walking with a cane. Some afternoons, he would go out on a bicycle and ride around the neighborhood a couple of times before returning to the apartment and going out again as a businessman. Every time he came out, he looked like a totally different person. Anybody monitoring the apartment would have thought there were several different people living there.

Johnny's favorite part came late at night, after our target finished his meetings and dinner and went out for his nightly escapades. On an unlimited budget and with carte blanche for spending, Johnny was partying harder than Mubtasem. I had warned him not to attract attention to himself. "You don't want anybody to remember you after we are done with this job," I said.

It didn't help. "Why are you so worried?" he asked. "Everyone's going to remember somebody that looks totally different from me and with another name. Perfect cover. They will be looking for a ghost."

"Whatever happens, don't go with the target into the apartment."

"Don't worry," Johnny assured me. "I have it under control."

I had to give him one more piece of advice, even if he wasn't paying any attention. "If you get to meet him, and sit down with him at one of the clubs on zero night, get him as drunk as possible. If he is sick and too drunk, he might skip taking a girl back with him. Maybe we can spare the girl's life. And remember, don't approach him until we let you know that we are ready."

Mubtasem operated as a publisher of books and other printed materials. This was the cover the Libyans used to invoice money into and out of the island banks.

Waiting is usually the hardest part. We spent the entire first day monitoring the apartment and waiting for the go-ahead. On zero night, Freddie and I parked the delivery van a couple of blocks from the apartment.

Johnny arrived by taxi around midnight, went inside wearing a suit and a tie, and came back out wearing casual clothes. He did not order a taxi; he just kept on walking. Once he got close to the parked van, he knocked twice on the front passenger window to let us know that Mubtasem was on his way to a cabaret. At that time, we still used classic tradecraft drop boxes and signals. There were no cell phones, texting, or emails.

We waited another hour to make sure the target did not come back too soon because he had forgotten something. I helped Freddie get onto the back balcony of the apartment building, then went straight back to the van to resume waiting. Freddie and I had handheld radios, but I kept communication to a minimum; we would only use the radio in case of an emergency. Freddie picked the lock in ten seconds and was in before I got back to the van. Another twenty minutes and Freddie was knocking twice on the side of the van to let me know that he was done. He got in and we drove away at a leisurely pace, to avoid attracting attention. We dumped the van in an empty parking lot a few blocks away and made our way back to the apartment on foot.

"How did it go, genius?" I asked Freddie.

"Perfect."

It was hard to get Freddie to talk. He was a thinker and he always spoke in short sentences and to the point. Trying to have a conversation with him was more like an interrogation.

"Are you sure it's going to work?" I prodded him.

"On the first flush, or this operation would literally be flushed down the toilet."

It was the longest sentence I have heard him speak in a long time. Freddie was making a joke. He had planted four kilograms of C-4 in the toilet tank of the washroom in the master bedroom. The bomb would detonate as soon as somebody pushed the lever to flush the toilet.

With binoculars we could see into the living room of the apartment if the lights were on, and just like clockwork Mubtasem arrived by taxi around 3:30 a.m. However, he was not alone. He had picked up a hooker from the club, and she was struggling to hold him up. He got out of the taxi and stumbled up the four steps before trying to unlock the single door that led to the upstairs apartment. He dropped his keys a couple of times before he was successful.

A few minutes later, the lights came on in the living room, and we were treated to a show. Freddie and I were taking turns with the only binoculars we had, until we got tired of fighting for turns and put our heads close together, each one of us looking through a single lens.

Valentino (Mubtasem) was sitting on the couch sipping straight from a bottle of vodka while a gorgeous, tall Eastern European blonde was giving him a striptease show. The guy had just left the strip club, and now he was home and wanted his private show—he could not get enough. No wonder his boss had a private harem and his personal bodyguards were all women. The show went on for about twenty minutes, then she started giving him a lap dance while he was fondling her. Freddie and I almost forgot about the mission. Then her head disappeared below the window line, and we lost visual contact for five minutes.

Freddie and I were both relieved when we saw her emerge again. She got dressed and helped him stand up and put his pants back on. He reached into his pocket and gave her some money. It was ironic: he was thinking that he just got lucky, while we were thinking that this girl was the luckiest hooker in Cyprus.

While the girl was waiting for the taxi downstairs, the back windows of the apartment disintegrated into a million pieces—she was lucky again because she was standing on the opposite side of the building. Our target must have gone to relieve himself before going to bed and still had the presence of mind to flush the toilet. I guess old habits die hard. And even good habits can kill you.

Johnny never came back to the apartment. He went straight to the hotel in Larnaca, where he waited for a next-day flight to Athens. Freddie and I left the apartment within two minutes of the explosion, before the police arrived or a crowd gathered; most people were asleep at that hour. We got into another car we had rented at the Larnaca airport when we arrived, made the thirty-minute drive to the airport, and waited for our early flight to Rome.

To this day, every time I flush the toilet—an average of six times a day—I flinch in anticipation, as I think back to that day.

BASSAM:

Not only was there a secret unit kidnapping PLO guys in West Beirut, right under the QJ's nose, they now had killed their best contact in Libya, the man who supplied them with money and weapons—and they had done it in another country.

The QJ had reasons to believe that it was the Israelis and their allies. Time for a payback, and payback was a bitch.

"Hey, Ghassan! Come over here and close the door. We have a disaster on our hands."

"What's up? I was winning the ping-pong match."

"Pay attention or all your heads will bounce like ping-pong balls."

"Why are you so upset? Some shipment got busted?"

"Why am I pissed? You want to know? While you and your idiot buddies are playing games, our contacts are being killed, and now the Shia have boats, and control shipping routes into West Beirut. Maybe they liquidated Mubtasem—remember the issues they have with Libya? All while we watch and play ping-pong."

"It's the Iranians, brother," said Ghassan. "They give them equipment and money. We should get the Saudis and Qataris to give us funding."

"You're not so dumb sometimes, Ghassan. Maybe now the Saudis will listen to us. Shia domination and control of Beirut is not good for their influence or prestige."

"Yes, exactly—they don't want the Iranians to have more influence."

"The only problem is that we tried this route and the answer was no. The Saudis will not do it. They say we are terrorists, and they don't support our kind of movements.

I am working on getting Iraq to help us. Saddam hates the fucking Iranians, and we have just started to develop contacts with him. Anyway, the reason I called you here is not to discuss politics and strategy, I want to you to do something for me."

"If you want me to go alone, it means you're preparing something big and secret."

"Just go down to the pier, count how many boats there are now, and report back to me. Do not tell a soul or start to show off."

"OK, I'll get some ice cream and walk around a little. Can I chat with a girl if I see one alone?"

"What part of secret don't you understand?" Bassam sighed. "Just go walk alone and come back. It's that simple."

Ghassan came back and reported the number of boats, all equipped with heavy machine guns. This was the opportunity the QJ had been waiting for.

They set up a double-cross operation with their contacts in the east.

"If I feed them some intelligence, the mission will partially succeed or partially fail depending on your point of view and what side you are on. For me, it is a double win." Bassam had a nagging feeling in the back of his head that the man from the elevator had something to do with it. *It had to be the Red Devil*, he thought. *Why else would I think of him again, so many years later?*

Bassam knew enough to trust his gut. It had kept him alive this long.

29

LIVING A CHARMED LIFE

PAUL:

As the months went by, we were being asked to perform some minor duties in our own area. I hated these jobs, like keeping the gambling casinos in check and collecting money from the bordellos. It bothered me, I imagined myself becoming more like Bassam than myself. I was afraid I was becoming the man I hate. The whole unit was aching to get back to work, do what it was supposed to do, and not get involved in politics or power struggles between the different Christian factions.

The six of us were restless to the point of quitting. Johnny Hypno got back to his drug habit; he denied using cocaine, but the signs were there. I told him one day that he had to stop or he would be kicked out and probably land back in jail. He got very defensive and swore up and down he was not using anything.

All of Lebanon had seen the movie *Deer Hunter*; it was a big hit and probably the number one box office draw, along with *Mad Max*. As I was bringing lunch in one day, carrying two big trays of food and some packs of pita bread, I saw a few of the bodyguards and Johnny playing Russian roulette. They had a few hundred liras on the table, and the betting was hot.

One of them was spinning the cylinder with the lone bullet in one chamber. When I passed behind him, I knocked his elbow with mine, and just as I was starting to say, "Stop this shit," the gun fired and the bullet ricocheted back from the ceiling and onto the table. They were staring at me with their mouths wide open. The shooter, who was supposed to be dead now with his brain splattered over the room, dropped the gun and gave me a hug that made the trays fall to the floor.

"Look what you just made me do!" I yelled. "I dropped the lunch. Which one of you suicidal idiots is going to clean it up?"

I wanted to deflect attention from what had just happened, but the guy was screaming, "You just saved my life! I owe you big-time."

There was too much of this sort of thing going on in our down time. And, unfortunately, Russian roulette was a tame game compared to a contest we called "last man standing." The fighters, having nothing better to do, invented this game. It was both simple and stupid. Two guys faced each other as in a Mexican standoff, on either side of a three-foot-tall, cinder-block wall. It was an extreme game of chicken: the men removed the safety pin from a hand grenade, placed it between them on top of the wall, and started counting. The first man to duck for cover beside the wall was the loser; the last man standing won the pot.

Early one morning I got the call for a briefing on a new mission. The members of the S7 never drove together as a unit in the same car unless we were working. We knew every intelligence building would have some informants, and we did our best never to be there at the same time.

On the rare occasions when we went there for a meeting, we arrived separately at different intervals, went straight into the conference room, and kept contact to a minimum.

Once we were assembled, Shadow walked in with his assistant, Roger, an ex-banker. Roger always gave the impression he was the smartest person in the room, but he was not. He was not liked by anybody but his boss. Nobody trusted him. He had this condescending attitude that gave me the urge to stand up and smack him. Of course, urges are different from actions, so I kept it under control and did my best to listen.

"OK, listen up," he said. "I am going to explain the mission quickly the first time. Don't interrupt until I am done. I will answer any questions at the end of the presentation."

To my surprise the guy was prepared and had a full set of diagrams and maps with exact locations printed out.

"As you all know, we travel to the Chouf area and to Israel by boat. We have enjoyed this luxury for two years now. Now, however, the honeymoon is over as our friends at Hezbollah, the well-funded Iranian Shia faction, have obtained four speedboats equipped with heavy machine guns that can chase us away from the shore. This presents a serious danger to our logistics and supply routes."

We had questions that we wanted to ask, but we kept quiet and allowed him to finish.

"The mission is complicated," Roger went on. "It is a dangerous mission, as all your missions are. As you can see on the diagrams, this is the location where they dock the boats at night. The only way to get to them is to come in from the sea. The boats are well-guarded 24 hours a day, and you have to destroy them all in order to be able to get back to your waiting extraction boat. If you don't get them all, the remaining boats will chase you and kill you at sea. Any questions?"

Any questions? We had about a million questions each, about timing, the extraction team, and on and on. However, this was not the guy to ask or rely on to plan our mission. As always we would plan the operation ourselves. Desk jockeys had no idea about field operations and contingency plans. In his mind, a few charts and pictures were enough to execute the search-and-destroy mission in the heart of enemy territory.

We had developed many informants on the other side, and we needed to crosscheck the information we got from them. They could be moving the boats from time to time to a different area, or they could be out at night, guarding their shore.

We never divulged the details of our missions to anybody, including members of the Amen. This was by design, to eliminate any leaks that could jeopardize the mission.

We decided all six of us were required for this operation. Freddie got the explosives ready. Sam was responsible for driving the boat and navigating in pitch-black conditions; he got busy with his charts and compass. Mike, Lewis, Johnny, and I were the diving team.

We were receiving constant updates from our contacts in West Beirut and cross-checking the information we received. We were checking the weather and the moon cycle. We needed darkness and a calm sea. Freddie started leaking a few tidbits of disinformation about a separate mission being planned for a date much later than the date chosen for this mission.

Thanks to the numerous trips we had made by sea to the Chouf area, or to Israel, we knew precisely the distance from the shoreline and the time required to clear the tip of West Beirut. Our best and fastest boat was a cigarette with twin, 500-horsepower Mercury engines.

We were confident that with 1,000-horsepower, we could outrun any pursuing boat. Our top speed was over 150 kilometers an hour.

Zero night was calm and moonless. The six of us got into the cigarette just after midnight. It did not take us long to reach our destination. Sam operated with no lights; he even placed his jacket over the small, dashboard-mounted compass in order to eliminate any reflection. Three kilometers from shore, he turned the engines off and let the boat drift for a while in the water of the calm Mediterranean. We anchored the boat and checked our bearings; the four members of the diving team had our underwater compasses recalibrated, in case we got separated. Each of us needed to know his location and be able to get back quickly to our boat.

Each member of the diving team carried ten kilograms of high-explosive C-4 equipped with a strong magnet. According to the information provided, the shaft of the motor was the only metal section of these boats; the hulls were fibreglass. So each of us was supposed to place a charge on one boat and swim back to our waiting vessel. We had no other weapons except our titanium diving knives and our scuba-diving spear guns. Simple, right?

In order to conserve air and keep our tanks full, we used our snorkel tubes and swam just under the surface for the first two kilometers. We were operating in total darkness, total silence. About 500 meters from shore, I gave the signal to dive below the surface and reach a depth of ten meters; we also needed to keep our breathing in check to minimize the air bubbles rising to the surface. The four of us made it under the dock without being spotted.

I went to school—I could count: there were six boats docked there, not four. I knew right away we had been double-crossed. We had been given only partial information. The guys were asking me in sign language if we should abort. Leaving two boats undamaged would cause a huge problem for us. The enemy would discover our waiting boat before we even got there.

While we were having the sign language meeting under the dock, a guard approached, walked onto the dock just above us, and started shining his flashlight into the water. The decision was made for me when I saw the look on his face: he spotted one of us. Johnny shot him with his spear gun, the guard fell into the water, and we dragged him under the dock. Then we went to work. Within minutes, all the charges were placed, and we were on our way back to our waiting boat as fast as we could swim.

We reached it quickly and without incident. I was starting to think we might get away with it, but as soon as Sam got the engines started and pushed the throttle to full power, we heard a loud noise from inside the engine compartment. Freddie went down to check it out and came back up in no time to tell me that the four engine brackets were cracked and out of alignment.

It did not take a genius to figure out our mission was compromised from the beginning. Our boat had been tampered with. Every time Sam put on any power, the boat would only crawl along as the engines revved with no power delivery. Then, all of a sudden, we heard four explosions within seconds of each other.

I knew it would take Hezbollah a few hours to figure out what had happened—unless they also had been given some partial information. With limited tools and resources, Freddie was trying to improvise a quick repair job; he was able to partially realign the engines with the help of some wires and screws. We couldn't go faster than five kilometers an hour, but we were sure we could make it back to East Beirut while it was still dark.

It was as if somebody was reading my mind. No sooner had I thought this than a half-dozen heavy machine guns from West Beirut started firing toward the sea. They did not know our exact location and were just spraying the waters; the tracer bullets were landing far away from us as we continued crawling out to sea, away from the coastline. This did not present an immediate danger, but then I spotted a much larger, fast-moving object shooting in our direction.

There should have been two boats chasing us but I saw only the one. The fifth boat must have been damaged by the explosions. Then another thought snuck into my brain. How could a single boat locate us this fast in the dark when we were more than five kilometers away from the shore?

I promised the guys and myself that if we made it back, a lot of people were going to answer for this. Starting with the marina staff, all the way up to Roger, the boss's assistant, and maybe even Shadow himself, not to mention my own informants.

That single boat was approaching so fast we could not outrun it. They knew our position and their .50-calibre bullets were now landing a few feet from our crippled boat. We had our Sig Sauer automatic rifles and a few hand grenades on board, but to use them effectively the chasing boat had to come within a few feet of us, and we could not allow this to happen. Mike had brought with him a M72 LAW rocket launcher. These can destroy tanks, and this one could destroy the approaching boat. However, hitting a moving target when your own boat is tilting and swaying is another matter altogether, even for a trained elite sniper.

We took the first hit on the starboard side while Mike was getting ready.

"Mike," I said, "you have one shot only. Make it count or all of us are dead. No pressure."

"I have to stand up and aim," he answered. "I need you and Johnny to hold me still."

Freddie was sitting low and keeping his head down, Sam was driving, and Lewis was holding the wires that Freddie had installed to hold the makeshift engine brackets together.

A spray of .50-calibre bullets hit the boat from bow to stern on the port side. Fiberglass shards were flying around like a thousand arrows.

Freddie and Johnny were hit and killed instantly. I was soaked with Johnny's blood, invisible against my black wet suit in the dark; the heavy odor of iron clung to my nostrils.

"Come on, Mike—fire the damn thing and kill those motherfuckers."

"I need them to get a little closer before I show myself and the rocket."

"Do it now—they are not getting any closer, and they have the firepower to pick us apart from a long distance."

"It will be a wasted shot."

More bullets hit the boat. Lewis swore. "Fuckers, they just hit the engines. There's oil all over the place."

I was hoping they wouldn't get lucky and hit the gas tanks when suddenly our engines went quiet and Sam announced that we had lost all power.

Mike stood up. I tried to hold him still. He took aim and fired. He never missed with his sniper rifle, but on this night, under pressure and with two of his friends dead, with their blood all over him, he missed the enemy boat by a few meters. Our only shot was wasted.

The remaining four of us took out our Sigs and started firing in the direction of the incoming boat, knowing full well it was a waste of both effort and ammo. But we were not going to surrender or go down without a fight. They sprayed our boat with bullets and not one of them hit me. I was feeling immortal. This is when most fighters get killed: it is like standing in the middle of a thunderstorm and not getting wet. I guess you had to be there.

They had us immobilized and vulnerable, our boat was sinking, and they loved it. They were enjoying the moment. They stopped firing, not even 200 meters from us. We looked at each other and decided to stop firing, as well, until they got closer or fired back. Not one of us ever considered surrendering; we knew what would happen to us and our families if they discovered our identities. Lewis was keeping low, arranging the scuba-diving gear—the plan was to jump ship with the equipment and go underwater, and if we could throw a few air tanks and regulators overboard quickly, we might be able to survive this.

We never had the chance to do it.

Like an angry ghost, a large dark shape appeared out of nowhere, bearing down on us. It was approaching fast, high above us in the water. Before we even knew what type of vessel this was, they fired a missile at our tormentors and blew their boat and the five crew members to smithereens. This happened so fast, none of us reacted. We just stood in our sinking boat, frozen and shocked.

Once the enemy boat sank, the Israelis sprayed the water with hundreds of bullets from their own .50-calibre guns until they were certain no one on that boat survived. They approached us slowly; using a loudspeaker, they spoke to us in Hebrew and asked us to identify ourselves and to put our hands up and not move.

Lewis was shouting, "We are from the Amen, we are Amen!"

As they came closer, we could make out the shape of the boat. This was an Israeli Dvora patrol boat—we called them Dabur, for "wasp." A voice called out in broken and heavily accented Arabic, "Don't move or we will blow you to pieces."

As they came within a few feet of our sinking cigarette, I noticed the difference in size between the boats. They had two .50-calibre machine guns and four M-16s aimed at us. If we had made any sudden moves, we would have been shredded in under a second. As this thought was going through my mind, I noticed Mike slowly reaching for his Sig. I moved my foot just as slowly, like it was due to the swaying of the boat, and stepped on his hand. If they noticed him, we were toast.

"You don't look like Amen. Do you have any papers or badges?"

"No, we don't," I said in Hebrew. "We are on a mission and ran into trouble. Our boat is sinking and we need your help."

They threw two lines to us, which we tied to our boat. They pulled us closer so we were now rafting with them. They also threw a rope ladder into our boat.

"Everybody stay still," said the voice. "Only one of you climb the ladder and come aboard."

I told Mike, Sam, and Lewis, the only surviving members of my unit, to stay absolutely motionless and not to get any dumb ideas. I moved my foot away from Michael's hand and nonchalantly kicked the Sig away from him. Once I made it onboard the Dabur, they cuffed my hands behind my back and walked me up to the officer in charge.

"What are you doing here, and what was your mission?" he wanted to know.

"We just finished blowing up four boats and damaging a fifth in West Beirut," I said. "They had more boats than we had been led to believe, and they were chasing us. You just sank the last one."

"How do we know that you are from the Amen?"

"Call your headquarters and get in touch with the Mossad or the Kidon. Tell them members of the S7 are asking for assistance, and they will confirm our identities."

I was led outside while he was making his radio calls.

A few minutes later, the captain came back out and told the soldiers to help get everybody on board. They threw two body bags over, into our boat. Once I was uncuffed, I helped with the transfer. It was closer to 5 a.m. now and the light was coming fast; if we stayed any longer, we would be easy targets for the machine guns on the shore. We loaded our two friends' bodies on board, the rest of the guys made their way up and cut the lines securing the cigarette to the Dabur. Then the captain backed his vessel about fifty meters from the cigarette and gave the order to sink it quickly. The Israeli soldiers opened fire with two .50-calibre machine guns. Fibreglass and equipment were flying all over the place and within a minute the boat was gone.

I could not wait to make it back to East Beirut, as I had many urgent things to do and a few unpleasant visits to make. I asked the captain if that's where we were headed. He told me they never dock in any port in the open, even in friendly territory. We were heading to the port of Haifa.

Our Mossad contacts were waiting for us before we even got to port. I went to meet with them and told my guys to take care of our fallen comrades' bodies. I needed to start leaking a disinformation campaign immediately. I did not want the informants, the marina staff, or Roger to be alerted and start covering their tracks. Everybody was a suspect now, and I was pissed.

The official story was released through the next day's morning papers in Beirut and over the shortwave radio. The headlines read: "BATTLE FOR SEA SUPREMACY, SEVEN BOATS SUNK, DOZENS KILLED."

30

CATCHING ROGER RABBIT

PAUL:

I look back now and wonder if this was the time when I lost my capacity to feel love. My heart went still and cold and was replaced by a pump. A big hollow cavity was in my chest. I was terrified to love anybody. I started conditioning myself to forget Nada once and for all, and I forced myself to stop thinking about my family.

It took three days to secure a ride back to East Beirut—the longest three days of my life. I was worried about my family. The harder I tried to ignore my feelings, the more I thought about them. What news did my parents get and how was my mother holding up? She must have been thinking I vanished at sea.

It was during this time that I met my first CIA contact. I was training with Izek, one of my oldest Mossad contacts and a Krav Maga expert himself, when I noticed two figures watching us. I recognized the short, stocky, dark man who was talking to the tall blond man, who seemed to be in his mid-forties. Both of them were watching my every move.

The blond guy opened with, "So, you are the guy terrorizing the terrorists?"

I had never heard this expression before, especially spoken in English. "Yes," I joked. "I am the Terrorist University headmaster's worst nightmare."

"Yaakov here has told us all about you, and we would like to get to know you a little better. Maybe you can visit us one day."

"I would love to," I said. "Let Yaakov arrange it with your superiors."

He left, and I did not think about it again.

We buried our two dead friends in unmarked graves, and after three long days of waiting, we left them behind in Israel. The heat and the nature of the mission made it necessary. The boat supplied by our Mossad contacts was barely large enough to carry us, our personal weapons, and a couple of extra jerry cans of gas for the 120 kilometers from Haifa to East Beirut. We wanted to get home. We were adamant about getting to the bottom of this.

With the danger now eliminated from West Beirut and with absolute radio silence, we docked the small boat in a private marina ten kilometers north of our own marine base. Everyone thought we were a pleasure craft docking for breakfast after a night fishing trip. Dressed in civilian clothes and with our weapons hidden in our knapsacks, we quickly blended in with the regular clients and staff of the marina.

We had no way to get to base, so we walked as naturally as possible out of the marina and into the parking lot off the strip plaza. It took Lewis less than two minutes to break into a blue Fiat Supermirafiori.

We could not go to our base or make contact with anybody at the Amen headquarters—we were officially dead at sea, and we wanted to keep it that way. The four of us were angry and betrayed; we did not know by whom, and right now everybody was a suspect.

"Where do we start?" Sam asked me.

"We can talk to the mechanics later," I said. "Let's go pay Roger a visit at home, before he gets to headquarters and before we get spotted."

Roger lived with his wife, two kids, and a maid in a very large two-story penthouse apartment fifteen minutes northeast of the Amen headquarters. His only escort was a driver who called himself Marco. Marco acted tough because of his boss's position and because he carried a gun, but he was just that, a driver. I used to see him watching our jujitsu training sessions.

We left Sam in the car, approached the building from the underground garage entrance, and waited for Marco to show up. You would think that as an intelligence officer, Roger would have been varying his timing, routes, and routines. But he was a banker, and bankers are used to routine. Roger wasn't worried about security, as he was operating in the shadows.

Mike was behind a big pillar, Lewis by the entrance, and I was waiting by the door that connected the main building entrance to the garage. We saw Marco park the car, a BMW 545i. He kept it idling and was listening to music. An amateur mistake. He should not have been listening to music. Instead, he should have been out of the car looking around for dangers. We did not complain because he was making our job easier.

Roger showed up like clockwork. He was reaching to open the front passenger door when I stepped in behind him, grabbed him by the collar, and pushed him toward the back door that Mike had just opened. As I was stuffing Roger into the back seat and tying his hands with lock ties, Mike was inside the car, holding a gun to Marco's head. Lewis joined us seconds later and opened the Beemer's trunk.

Mike said, "Marco, give me your gun slowly. Don't be brave and don't get any bright ideas or you will die today. And shut that fucking music off."

As soon as Marco gave Mike his gun, Lewis reached for him, yanked him out of the car, and walked him to the open trunk. We needed to separate them, in case they had any valuable info. We did not want them communicating.

Lewis said, "Marco, you know what to do."

Without any complaint, Marco climbed into the trunk. Lewis joined me in the back seat, and now we had Roger between us. Mike was already behind the wheel. We left the garage slowly and naturally, and Sam followed us with the blue Fiat.

Roger said, "I thought you guys were dead. Thank God. Where are you taking me?"

I knew right then he was guilty. A superior officer being cuffed—and not very gently, I might add—and his driver stuffed in the trunk would not say, "Oh, thank God you're alive." He would be saying "What the fuck are you doing, I am going to kill you all," or "You idiots are going to jail for this," etcetera, etcetera.

We drove them to a safe house in the country that we kept in case we needed to hide one day. It was secure. Nobody beside the S7 members knew about it, not even the Amen bosses. We never met with informants there and never spent the night; one of us would come twice a week and check for bugs or any surveillance. It had a small private road, with access via a hidden driveway by the side of a cliff. We had the entrance secured with a locked chain. It was located in a valley between two small hills and far away from nosy neighbors.

We chained Marco in the washroom and brought Roger into the living room to question him on how he got his intelligence and about the four boats. The first thing out of his mouth was "I did not know they had six boats, I swear."

"How did you get all the charts and diagrams?"

"My informant gave them to me."

"What is his name? Describe him to us."

We knew that the name would not help. Informants are usually double agents. They sell information to many sides and for the highest price, and they use different aliases.

"All I know is that he is a Sunni Muslim from West Beirut," said Roger. "They did not like it that Hezbollah had established a marine squad and were dominating what used to be their territory."

"So you just believed him, right?"

"He had a good reason, why not?"

"Where did you meet?"

"I arranged to meet with him at a safe house near the green line."

"Is it one of the Amen safe houses?"

I asked that question because the Amen had people with cameras taking pictures and keeping an eye on the safe houses they used. They also voice-recorded the conversations.

"Yes," he said. "I don't have my own houses, so I asked Marco to arrange it with Steve."

Steve was the head of the Tanassut unit, a tech spy unit who specialized in bugging, taking pictures, and following the movements of suspected spies both with and against us.

We moved Roger to one of the bedrooms and Lewis brought Marco in.

Marco was hysterical—not hysterical as in humorous. Hysterical as in scared shitless.

"Marco, I heard you are now involved in operations?"

"No, Bassam. Please believe me, man. Roger asked me to go to the green line and pick up some guy. He also told me to ask Steve if we could use a safe house nearby for a meeting. That's all I know. I just drove the car."

"You know what will happen if you lie? Roger is saying you knew the guy and you arranged the meeting with him."

"No way. I picked up that guy as soon as he got dropped off in a back street near the green line and I drove him to the house. I did not attend the meeting. I was told by Roger to wait in the car."

"What kind of car dropped him off? Did you get the plate? Don't answer that—the plate will be a fake anyway."

"He was in a black Mercedes; two other people were with him."

"What did they look like? Tell me every detail, as if your life depended on it—which, in this case, it does."

"I did not see the driver very well; he had a thick black beard and a hat on and was on the other side of the car."

"What about the passenger?"

"That guy I remember," said Marco. "He scared me just by looking at me. He had these strange-looking eyes and a smirk on his face."

"How strange? Describe them." I needed to keep this going and the guys knew better than to interrupt.

"I am not sure I can explain—this guy's eyes were like yellow. He was dark-skinned but his eyes were like a bird's or an eagle's. They were freaky."

A cold chill went through my body. I only knew one guy with eyes like that who was smart enough to send an informant with partial information to set up these two idiots. If it worked, it was win-win for him. Eliminate the Shia domination and the boats from West Beirut, and at the same time take care of whomever the Christians sent to execute the operation. The Shia and the Christians fighting while he sat, watched, and waited. It was a dream scenario.

We brought Roger back into the room.

"Who knew about the operation, and the boat we were going to use? If you lie to me, I am going to get your wife and kids and kill them right here in front of your fucking eyes."

I would never have done that, but the S7's reputation for violence and no mercy had been exaggerated a thousand-fold—leave it to the Lebanese—and I was going to make use of it.

"I am not lying," said Roger. "I saw the mechanics getting the boat ready the day before. I was with a friend at the same marina. I might have said something about the boat belonging to the Amen and that it was the fastest thing on water. No specifics."

"Who is the friend? Was it your mistress and secretary?"

First he looked shocked, then he admitted that it was. "Please, Bassam," he pleaded, "She doesn't know anything."

I told him to contact the informant and set up another meeting. "Let him know you are happy with his work, and that you want to work with him on another operation."

That night Lewis and Sam picked up the mistress. After a few hours of interrogation, she admitted she had been sent by a military leader in West Beirut to meet high-profile officials and get them to say things during pillow talk. The best part was when she described this "military leader." He had freaky strange yellow eyes.

We could not drive the BMW or the Fiat to town. The BMW belonged to Roger and all of the Amen would be looking for it. By now probably half the city knew the Fiat was stolen. It would be spotted, too. However, we had our own silver Range Rover parked behind the house under a tarp.

Roger was able to set up a meeting with his informant, with the promise of money as an advance on the information he needed without giving specifics. The informant insisted on meeting in West Beirut as he could not arrange a safe crossing on such short notice, but he was eager to meet and collect his money.

We left Marco chained in the washroom with a bottle of water, and I left with Mike and Roger for the meeting.

"Roger," I warned him, "remember this if you betray us. The other guys know where you live. Right now you are just an idiot who got fooled. Don't become a traitor and let your family pay the price."

Mike had a camera equipped with a huge zoom and got himself into position to take some photos of the driver and, if we were lucky, the mastermind. The Mercedes arrived on time, with three people in it.

I was acting as Roger's driver, and as they slowed down to drop off the informant, I got a good look at both the driver and the passenger. They did not recognize me. I had on a full beard and glasses, and besides, those two had not seen me since I was ten or eleven years old and again disguised in the elevator of the hotel. The driver was Ghassan. The passenger was Bassam, Yellow Eyes himself—the two brothers who shot the three cousins on my street and killed the family next door. Behind them was another escort car with four guys in it. I was sure they were armed.

Mike and I were good, but we were not suicidal. We were not about to start a fight in West Beirut with seven armed guys and without advance planning. The only reason they wanted to keep Roger alive was so they could use him again. I watched in silence, my nerves tingling and images of my murdered neighbors rushing through my head, as if I were seeing it for the first time.

But I had the information I needed. Bassam was alive and active. I would get him and his brother sooner or later. Revenge was a dish best served COLD.

In the middle of the night, Lewis and Sam had gone

to pick up the mechanic from his home and deliver him to the Amen jail for interrogation. We met with them there and dropped Roger off. He and, later, Marco became the newest residents of the Amen prison. The guys at the door did not know how to react to Roger and Marco. Keep them separate and alone, we told them, until Shadow comes by.

Before going to see Shadow, I needed to see my parents, and the other guys wanted to see their families, too. We had to do it without any of our neighbors knowing. Sam dropped Lewis and me close to our homes and took Mike with him to his house. Mike had nobody to see. They were going to pick us back up in two hours.

I sneaked in through the back door and woke my mother. I tried to do it as gently and quietly as I could, but as soon as she opened her eyes she screamed, "Oh my God, oh my God! I can't believe my eyes. Paul, is that you? I can't believe my eyes."

"Mom, be quiet," I half whispered. "So much for sneaking in. You just woke the whole neighborhood."

"We heard so many rumors," she said, "and nobody was able to give us any real news about you and your friends. I did not know if I should keep wearing black and mourn you—I have just started thinking of going to dark gray. So I just prayed and died a thousand deaths."

Can you tell I got my sense of humor from her?

I told her about the guys who were lost. We talked quietly for a couple of hours until the rest of my family woke up. I knew this was probably the last time that we would all sit together and share a meal. I was savoring every moment, while I was silently saying goodbye to my family.

I told them I was going away for a very long time. "You are going to hear many different stories," I said. "Some of them will say that I am dead, others that I am a traitor, but don't worry. Don't discuss this with anybody outside this family. My boss, Shadow is starting to sleep with the enemy. He is starting to make deals with the Syriansm and I need to put some distance between him and I. There is no way I am going to help the Syrians against our own people, regardless of his political ambitions."

I packed a duffel bag with my personal items—nothing that would give away my identity—we said our hushed goodbyes, and I left that house and my home for the last time.

Sam picked me up, and the four of us went back to headquarters together, breaking procedure. Shadow was there, waiting with his bodyguards. As soon as we pulled in, Shadow and his bodyguards rushed over and started speaking at the same time.

"Did I hear Steve right?" Shadow asked. "You have Roger and his driver in custody?"

"Yes, boss—the guy was operating on his own; he was running his own operations. He probably had different ambitions, or he is a double agent. I am going to leave it up to you to decide his fate, after you finish questioning him. Your bigger problem is his assistant: she must have leaked very valuable information to your enemies."

"Leave Roger to me. I will get to the bottom of it," Shadow promised. "I set him up with her, without him *or* her knowing it. It was a test and he failed. We have time for all that; he can stay with Steve for a while, in a small dark room, so he can think. That will soften him up. Walk with me a little way. I have something to tell you."

Whenever Shadow told me to walk with him, it meant he had something important to tell me that he wouldn't trust to anyone else.

BASSAM:

While watching an American movie, Bassam saw the stupid teenagers drinking alcohol through a hose connected to a funnel. This gave him an idea. The QJ began their newest experiment—they forced a prisoner to drink gasoline through a funnel and hose.

Bassam liked to give speeches. His followers cheered—they could not get enough. He encouraged and motivated them, and they were ready to kill and die for the cause.

"My brothers and fearless Mujahedeen," I told them, "the Americans, French, and Italians, all descendants of the Crusaders, are now occupying our city under the pretense of being a peacekeeping force. They think by showing up here they can shut us down. But they are not smart—they play 'fair' and worry about 'human rights.' We have something to show them. We will strike them in such a way that the Americans will wish they were still in Vietnam, and the French will miss Algeria."

Ghassan brought out Mr. Flames.

This was the guy who had been drinking gasoline. They placed him in the middle of the yard and shot him with tracer bullets. He started burning from the inside out, and then he exploded. The QJ fighters were cheering and chanting. This was more exciting than dragging prisoners through the streets, which was getting old.

"I wish it was the Red Devil. His father made me dig all night for gas once. He made me look like a fool. When I catch the Red Devil, this is how he is going to die. I will make him drink less gas so he will burn slower."

Then the QJ blew up the American embassy.

Bassam and his men used the first kamikaze they trained and graduated, and the world blamed the bombing on Iran and the Shia. The *Quaidat AlJihad* could not believe that the world's biggest superpower could be deceived so easily. They were giving the QJ carte blanche to do whatever they want without ever having to answer for it. Because of their differences and failures with the Iranians, they blamed everything on the Shia.

The QJ began preparing an operation that would make bombing the embassy look like a rehearsal.

Bassam did most of his creative thinking while he was smoking his opium Argile. Both brothers were addicted. "It's so easy to motivate people to do the suicide missions. We should start advertising a Terrorist University for *all* the revolutionaries and outlaws in the world. They can send their people here, and I will send them back as fearless, suicidal psychopaths."

Ghassan liked that idea. "Another revenue stream," he says. "The only university on the planet with only one form of homework. Your first test is your last."

"Ghassan, you're a comedian. Did you find the truck?"

"You mean the water truck?"

"What am I going to do with you, man? Yes, of course—the yellow water truck."

"I found a similar truck. All it needs is a paint job and it will be identical."

"When will it be ready? I only have a small window here. The subjects might change their minds; it's hard to keep them in a trance."

"I have the trucks. One will be painted yellow, the other white. You will have them in the morning."

"Make sure you don't fuck up and send the wrong colored truck to the wrong location."

"I have it all planned out," Ghassan replies. "Once the concrete slabs are in place, we will send the big yellow one as a gift to the American *Shaitan*."

"Make sure the slabs are thick," Bassam explained

slowly. "Place the explosives on top of them. I want the explosion to go skyward."

"I got it, it is all under control, but you have to keep the drivers focused."

"Don't tell me what to do. I have been planning this for months. They are ready and itching to die in the name of Allah. They keep praying and meditating while listening to propaganda."

"How do you find these guys?" Ghassan wanted to know.

"There are some criteria you look for. They have to have at least three of them." Bassam counted them off on his fingers. "A loner with nothing to lose. Somebody that lost a close family member in the fighting against Israel. An extremist at the mosque without much education. These are the three main signs for a prospect. You convince them it is a holy jihad in the name of Allah, and if they scream Allah Akbar before they blow themselves up, they will go straight to heaven, and enjoy timeless life with seventy-two virgins. I say this with a straight face. But there are other variables."

"What about the woman driving the truck tomorrow?"

"Never worry about women—they are braver than men. When they make the decision for martyrdom, they will go through with it. This one lost almost her whole family to the Christians and Israelis during the camp's massacre last year."

"Bassam, are you really going through with this?"

"Don't worry, we are not taking credit. We will leak information pointing to the Shia groups and the Iranians. Let the sons of Crusaders take their revenge on them. Tomorrow morning, the whole world will hear about a new jihad group. They will not even know where to start looking for it. They will be pointing fingers in all directions."

"I will have the trucks ready—you get the drivers

and their cover stories."

"Don't worry. We have been dropping hints that those guys are Iranians. It pisses me off that the Americans think they are smarter than us because they have a bigger army."

"Maybe bigger, but they are not braver, bro."

"We are about to show them a new fighting technique. My graduates are ready and eager."

31

ROCKING THE WORLD

PAUL:

I walked with Shadow through the parking area between the buildings. He was more nervous than I had ever seen him. He was in the middle of a power struggle with the military leaders. The Syrians were killing and kidnapping more Muslims than Christians by now. The Christians were fighting among themselves.

Rumors were circulating that Shadow was changing camps, getting help from the Syrians and distancing himself from the Israelis. At first it did not make any sense. I could not believe it. After I did some more digging, the reasoning became clear. Another charismatic Christian leader had taken full control of the LF and installed his own cadre. Shadow had been pushed out of the inner circle. To get back in, and take control, Shadow had made his deal with the devil.

It was a mess, and I wanted out of it, but I did not know how to make that happen. I was not getting any closer to my ultimate target.

"We are getting intelligence reports from different

sources," Shadow told me. "There is a second major attack in the works against the peacekeeping force in West Beirut."

"Have we been able to cross-check these reports with our own spies?"

"Not accurately," he admitted. "There seems to be a new, very secretive, but growing group out there."

"Do we know where and when?" I asked. "Can we eliminate them before they strike?"

"Our spies are only getting hearsay info. We have warned the Americans, the Italians, and the French. They won't listen. They think they are secure in their bases."

"What about the Mossad? Do they know something?"

"They are not saying anything," Shadow said flatly. "This is a new outfit that has not been infiltrated. If the Mossad know anything, they are keeping it close to their chest."

"Can it wait a few days? I just got back, we lost two members, and I need to inform their families. If I find out anything I will contact you."

The very next morning, the windows in our apartment shook and rattled with two explosions that turned out to be twenty-five kilometers away. Minutes apart, two truck bombs had struck the barracks housing the American and French members of the multinational peacekeeping force, killing 241 American and 58 French servicemen.

A group calling itself Islamic Jihad claimed responsibility for the bombings, a group no one had heard of. The Terrorist University students had graduated, and the world was introduced to a new kamikaze group.

The Americans were expecting a yellow tanker truck carrying water. The truck that arrived was carrying tons of explosives instead. The suicide bomber drove his truck through the chain-link fence, all the way into the lobby. The American guards were operating under a passive rule of engagement: no magazines in their weapons or live rounds in the chamber.

When I went to HQ that morning, Shadow pulled me aside. "Paul, did you read this? The guards had no bullets to fire on the driver."

"We can't start second-guessing now. Nobody was expecting a suicide attack."

"Reports are pointing to the Iranians."

"It is too early to know for sure," I cautioned him. "If you ask me, this new jihad group is a terrorist extremist movement that doesn't answer to anybody." Then I got to my real point: "Have we been asked for help? We can go in easier and faster to check things out."

"No," said Shadow. "The Americans are pissed, and they want revenge. However, our contacts in Israel are saying that the Americans can't make up their mind on how to respond—their leadership is split."

"I am afraid that by the time they get it together, this group will have packed up and moved on."

"Just be ready," Shadow said. "I know you are short on manpower. We might need to identify the leader of this group and take him out."

He paused, then he went on. "We gave the Israelis everything we had about the threat, but the Americans were completely unprepared. We think the Israelis are keeping some secrets from their allies to serve their own interest."

Was Shadow saying the Mossad knew when and where the attack was going to come, but only gave general information to the Americans? "This is serious," I said. "Are you sure the Mossad knew the details and did not tell the CIA?"

"We are going to stay out of this one," Shadow said. "We need them both. This conversation never happened. Just activate and pay all the informants. We need to know who these guys are."

BASSAM:

With only two trucks, the QJ had rocked the world. The Shia would be blamed and the QJ needed to get out of the Beirut. Both the Americans and the French were promising revenge. *Thanks!* thought the Jihadist.

Ghassan is nervous. "Did you see the French president and the U.S. VP promising to hit the criminals?" he asked me. "Should we be worried?"

Bassam exhaled a long stream of heroin smoke and answered slowly. "What do you expect, brother? They came all the way here—they need to make a brave statement. The fools don't know who to hit, so they will pick a few soft targets and make a gesture. They want to look good for the elections and for TV. Turn it on."

The TV anchor reported France had launched an air strike against a group called the Islamic Revolutionary Guard Corps.

Who the hell were they?

The anchor said everyone was praising the Shiite Hezbollah for carrying out the bombings, even though Hezbollah officially denied any involvement. He said that many people see Hezbollah as "the spearhead of the sacred Muslim struggle against foreign occupation."

"Turn that fucking TV off," Bassam yelled. "We do the planning, training, and work, and now the Shia and Iranians get the credit?!"

"You were hoping they would get the blame, remember?" Ghassan answered.

"Yes, the *blame,* genius," He had no patience with his brother's less than brilliant comments. "So a few token bombs get dropped on them for 'retaliation,' but they are also getting all the *credit.*"

"For a movement like ours, it's better not to draw

too much attention," said Ghassan slowly. "The Syrians supplied the explosives. They know who the real heroes are."

"Ghassan, the first part of what you say is true and smart, especially coming from you, bro. But as for the Syrians? I am afraid if the Syrians know, the Israelis will know next. The Syrian Mokhabarat leak worse than the old fishermen's nets."

"What do we do next? We can't stay here. Hezbollah and the Syrians will be after us now. They want to keep their involvement in this operation secret."

"I have planned for this and made contacts with a rich Saudi. Using his private jet, we will fly our men and equipment to Pakistan and later on to Afghanistan. We will help our brothers the Mujahiddeen kick the Soviets out."

"This is funny, bro. Now the Americans will help us and give us weapons to help fight the Soviets?! This is one crazy world. When do we leave?"

"Saddam is giving the Christians weapons to fight the Syrians and, indirectly, the Iranians and their agents. It's a crazy mess—but I love crazy."

"Everything will be ready to go in two days. I don't want the Syrians to know. Tell all the guys we are going on a training mission. Don't tell anybody our destination."

Ghassan asked to go home to say goodbye to their parents. Bassam frowned. A list of reasons why this was a bad idea filed through his brain, but finally he agreed. "Just leave tomorrow morning, be back the same day, and don't let anybody know."

Ghassan paused and then asked, "Can I take Mohamed with me?" Though Mohamed was a cousin, Bassam was sure this was increasing the danger to Ghassan, and to their plan. But again he agreed, knowing he had to trust Ghassan at some point. He warned him, however, not to tell Mohamed where they were going until they were on the way.

32

HADAKA JIME

PAUL:

Lewis and I lived together in an exclusive resort full-time. The main reason was privacy: only owners of the overpriced chalets were able to enter the secured grounds. The unit had been confiscated from a gang of amateur forgers who made poorly copied U.S. dollars and sold them for ten cents on the dollar. The bills were of such poor quality that none of the banks would touch them, not even the most corrupt, and all the merchants rejected them. After we moved in, we found a large stash of hundred-dollar bills behind a hidden opening in one of the closets. Sam and Michael spent them in one of the cabarets, paying the bill with real money and throwing the fakes at the feet of the belly dancers.

The evening the call came, we were at home, in no mood to party. We'd hardly said a word to each other. Lewis was making spaghetti, and I was on the balcony overlooking the bay, reading a book. I had a premonition as soon as the phone rang. The actual call lasted less than five seconds.

"Hello."

"You are to come to base immediately."

It was the knockout brunette from Shadow's office. I wanted to flirt with her, but she hung up. Lewis turned off the gas stove while I was getting my keys. I was driving a red Fiat Ritmo 135 at the time, a chick magnet. We were changing cars so often, we often did not know who was driving what.

At least we didn't have to worry about speeding tickets—who did? There weren't any street cops or traffic lights anywhere. The highways did not have any marked lanes. Only the brave or reckless drove fast. I guess I was both.

We were speed-checked through security at the gate. I was one of the few allowed to drive a car into the actual complex, and the red Ritmo was expected.

I was hoping to stop and chat with the brunette, but she pointed her manicured finger toward the inner door. "They are waiting for you."

My instincts have kept me alive this long. I sensed the anticipation and the energy as soon as I entered the room. Shadow was there with Sam and another person I did not know.

"This is Walid. He has been working with us for a long time and has done a great job in the past. We hope it is going to continue. Tell the guys what you have just told me."

Walid was from the Bekaa Valley, like me. He was a professional informer and probably a double agent. We paid them very well.

"I know for a fact," he said, "who designed and planned the attack on the UN forces' barracks."

"You mean the Americans and French?" I asked. Without exception, always clarify and double-check with informants. I could hear the Kidon trainer telling us this.

"Yes, that's it," Walid confirmed. "The American

and the French barracks. I was visiting my sister in the village next to ours, and I saw two guys driving a BMW. They were received like heroes. I asked my brother-in-law about them, very casually, and he told me they were the brother and cousin of the mastermind of the attack on the U.S. embassy a few months ago, and probably the UN barracks."

"How does he know that?"

"Right after the embassy bombing, the two brothers came to visit their parents. The father and the boys had an argument. They were shouting, and the father told the younger one never to come back, that he was ashamed of being his father."

"How do you know what happened a few months ago? How often do you visit your sister? You must really miss her."

"I wasn't there, my sister told me," said Walid. "After my first conversation with her husband, he left to go and shake hands with the two, as a sign of respect. They were welcomed like heroes. My sister and I kept talking, and she told me about the argument. She thought the parents were ashamed of what the two brothers were doing, especially the younger one. Dealing drugs, weapons, and stolen cars—and now sending suicide bombers to kill indiscriminately. She also added that the younger brother would have been a good husband for her daughter if he was a nice man, since he was very handsome and had the most amazing eyes."

I was busy trying to piece the information into a clear picture when Mike asked, "What is so amazing about his eyes?"

"She said they were like a hawk's eyes, almost yellow in color."

This couldn't be happening. I didn't believe in coincidences.

Yellow eyes.

From the Bekaa.

Two brothers.

Stolen cars.

Drugs and weapons.

It smelled like a setup. It was too good to be true. Shadow and I went into his office, leaving Walid in the room with Sam and Mike.

"What do you think? These guys are from your hometown. Do you know them?"

"If the info is accurate, I know exactly who they are."

"Do you think we can set up a snatch operation this quick? We have to do it. We have other assets in the area that can watch them."

"Does it have to be a clean snatch op?"

"Try for a clean op. If we can't do it on such short notice, kill them. We can cash in huge favors with the Americans and the French for a very long time, even if they're dead."

"Keep this Walid here, and make sure he understands that if this is a setup, he will never leave here alive. Make sure he gets it."

"We think he is also working for the Syrians," said Shadow. "They wanted him to give us this info. They probably supplied the bombs to the brothers and now want to eliminate the link back to them."

"Why don't they just kidnap the suspects? They are now in territory under the Syrians' control."

"Because nobody would work with them if they did that. They need the link eliminated but without them being involved. Since when do you care about politics?"

"I don't," I said. "I just don't want a repeat of the last fuck-up."

"Get going," said Shadow. "If you need help, let me know. Viper and his guys will help you."

Right. Viper was the head of his security detail. We were shorthanded, but the four of us could manage this snatch op. The last thing I needed was a bunch of hot-headed "helpers" who shot first and asked questions later.

We took a large truck that Steve and his small army of landscapers used. Lewis drove, and Sam followed in a stolen Mercedes, one of dozens we used. We drove near the last Syrian-controlled checkpoint and parked the truck on a side street. Lewis stayed behind, waiting for my call. The three of us continued in the Mercedes as close as we could get to the checkpoint without risking being spotted or stopped. This was where I had spent some time at the "spa," experiencing Syrian hospitality, and I did not want to pay them another visit. I was still waiting for my refund from the last one.

We were watching for a gray Toyota; the driver was one of our operators. His job was to drive a few minutes ahead of the black Beemer Ghassan and Mohamed were riding in.

Mike was on the side of the main road, trying to look busy fixing a phone line while keeping an eye out for our guy's Toyota.

When he spotted it, Mike sprinted back and got into the car. We took off immediately and made sure to stay ahead of the Toyota. We passed Lewis, then turned onto a side road that would take us through an industrial area to East Beirut without going through any more checkpoints. If traffic was heavy, and that was almost ninety percent of the time, many people took this detour to get to the east side of the city. It was a gamble. The road was right in the middle of the green line. The area was hotly contested; and the road was blocked. If you made one wrong turn, you could easily get killed by snipers or be kidnapped on the west side.

When we reached our designated point, I radioed Lewis to get ready; he was still waiting on the main road. He took off slowly, keeping an eye on the traffic passing him from behind. The gray Toyota was right behind him. When the Toyota driver spotted the black BMW coming up fast in the far left lane, he changed lanes to block it and accelerated to pass the truck. Lewis then swerved the truck into the next lane, hitting the Toyota and causing an accident—and an instant traffic jam. The detour exit was a hundred meters behind them. We counted on Ghassan turning around and using the detour, in order to save a couple of hours of waiting for the car wreck to clear the road. In Lebanon, you had to wait for a licensed expert to arrive, take pictures, write a report, and determine who was more at fault. It took hours to clear even small fender benders.

Minutes later, Lewis made contact on the radio. "They detoured; they're coming your way."

Sam stayed in the car. Michael and I split up and took positions on opposite sides of the road. Sam saw the Beemer coming, shot away from the curb and T-boned it, right at the front wheel axle. The Beemer's front end collapsed like a fat, gut-shot hippo. It wasn't going anywhere. Sam jumped free from the car and took off running in the opposite direction, heading straight to a warehouse where we had a Range Rover parked for our getaway car.

The cousins came out of their car, drawing guns they had jammed into the back pockets of their jeans like wallets, which was how most guys carried their weapons. They both took aim at Sam, who hadn't reached the warehouse yet. Mike and I arrived behind them, from opposite sides of the road. Mike immediately placed two bullets at point-blank range in the back of Mohamed's head.

I kept walking until I reached Ghassan, who by now was confused but trying to take aim at Mike. I disarmed him and took him down to the ground in one quick move. He struggled but he was fat and slow. I sat behind him on the ground, put my legs around him, and applied a Hadaka Jime, or naked strangle—better known these days as a rear naked choke. I did not squeeze to complete the choke and put him to sleep. I should have, but I had waited almost a decade for this and I wanted to savour the moment. Even if it was not the ultimate prize, Yellow Eyes' brother and cousin were a close second. I had seen this bastard shoot the three young cousins in my quiet neighborhood long ago; he and his brother had lived in my vivid memories for a long time. A fast kill would not do.

Mike was shouting at me, "Kill the fucker! Break his neck! Let's go!"

Sam had brought around the Range Rover and was idling nearby. Regular traffic was building behind us. Some drivers were honking their horns while others were turning back and leaving the scene. The Mercedes and the Beemer were blocking traffic.

"Hello, Ghassan," I said. "How is Bassam doing?"

"Who are you? I am going to kill you and your whole family, and your pets."

"I am the one killing you now. Do you want me to send your best to your brother? Do you want a funeral in our town?"

As soon as I pronounced the name of the town, recognition dawned on him.

"The fucking Red Devil! I should have shot you many years ago."

"I agree. You should have. It would have extended your useless life."

I started squeezing my legs and arms together. This is called a "blood choke" because it restricts blood flow to the brain via the carotid arteries. When it is done correctly, it causes unconsciousness in a few seconds. I had practiced it thousands of times and used it at tournaments a hundred more times. The chances of

Ghassan escaping were zero. Within seconds, he started to fade and went to sleep.

Sam could not wait any longer. He stopped two feet from me and popped the trunk. Mike and I carried the fat Ghassan, threw him inside the Range Rover, and took off.

"What were you doing there?" Mike asked me. "Asking him out on a date?"

"Yes," I said. "He turned me down. I had to choke him out. Do you think he will change his mind later?"

"Where do we take him?"

"He will not be sleeping for long. We're going to handcuff him and tape his mouth, then head straight to the U.S. embassy."

After the bombing of the American embassy in West Beirut, the U.S. had moved its embassy to the eastern section. Being on friendly grounds, it was much easier to defend. They had built a fortress impossible to penetrate. It would take a commando unit many hours to penetrate the security perimeter.

On the way, I contacted Shadow, briefed him, and asked if he could facilitate our entry into the embassy. "We don't want to get shot by the marine guards," I said.

"Just keep driving in that direction until I get you an approval. What are you driving?"

"A black Range Rover with three, plus one sleeping in the back seat."

"I thought there were two men in the BMW?"

"The other one did not make it. We need a clean-up team to take care of the cars and the body. It's on the side of the road."

"Hang up. I'll call you soon."

Within ten minutes I got the go-ahead to slowly approach the compound from the rear. Civilians lined up at the front gate for normal embassy business. Even with advance notice and approval, we still had to wait for the car to be scanned for explosives and for us to surrender our arms. The Americans were not taking any chances, not after two embassy bombings and the bombing of the barracks. Nobody was going to get near them without going through a colonoscopy.

Once we drove into the underground garage, the huge automatic door closed behind us. We found ourselves surrounded by six Marines in full combat gear, weapons drawn and at the ready. The CIA station chief was there along with two more suits who were probably registered with the Lebanese government as commercial attachés.

We started our delivery procedure.

"What do you have here?" asked a marine sergeant.

"A big fish. Not the whale himself but the big shark. This is the brother of the mastermind and leader of the group that bombed your embassy and barracks in Beirut."

The station chief and the suits exchanged looks. Even the other Marines were interested now.

"Is he dead?"

"No sir, just sleeping. We would not bring him here if he was dead."

The station chief turned to his aides. "We have to get him out of the country immediately."

"You have a few hours to extract him. Only a few people on the street saw the capture in progress. Nobody has identified him yet. We also killed his cousin, who was an active member of their outfit, during the operation."

"Excellent, we will take it from here. Give my best to your boss and tell him we will speak soon."

The American fleet was just off our shores. They probably transferred Ghassan by a private vessel to one of their ships and took him to one of their high-value prisoner camps. Having delivered the prize, we took off and returned the Range Rover to the body shop. By the next day it would have a different color and new plates.

BASSAM:

Bassam was worried about the whereabouts of the two idiots. It had been hours since they left town. They were probably high, lounging around in some whorehouse. The road back from town was full of them.

Ghassan probably told Mohamed that they were leaving for Pakistan. He couldn't keep his mouth shut. Bassam was sure they wanted to say goodbye to the party for a while, though there were a ton of drugs over there. Maybe they were worried about the lack of available women.

He sent a car to drive back along the road they took and check every whorehouse on the way. The arrangements were done, and the QJ were leaving that night. If they were not here on time, they would leave without them. The Saudi millionaire's jet was waiting. If they weren't there, they could walk, barefoot, and meet the QJ in Pakistan.

33

HIDDEN SHADOW

PAUL:

We returned quickly to the Amen building for a tense debriefing with Shadow and his aides. The senior aide we called Priest was directing the show.

"You were supposed to perform a clean snatch and kidnap op. What happened, Bassam?" He was using my code name to aggravate me.

"The cousin was taking aim at Saber while he was running for cover to get the Range. Munir had no choice but to shoot him. I preferred him being dead over Saber, wouldn't you?"

"I ask the questions, just answer them."

"I just did."

"Where is the Range now?"

"It is at the shop being changed over."

"What about the Beemer and the Benz?"

"We asked for a clean-up team."

"You should have had a clean-up team at the ready. Why didn't you?"

"I had them on standby. I was not sure where the

location zero would be. We only had a small window of opportunity, and we had to take it or lose them."

"This is not acceptable. We expect more from you as professionals."

"We planned and executed this operation within hours of identifying the targets. This kind of op usually takes weeks of planning. I am sure the Americans are tickled pink with the results. Maybe the Mossad are embarrassed—give them some of the credit and they will be happy."

At this point, Shadow stopped the interview. We were being blamed for our success. He called an end to the session and took me to his office.

I was hoping the knockout brunette would be there, and she was. I lingered one step behind Shadow and asked for some water. He spoke over his shoulder. "When you're done getting your thirst quenched, follow me in here and close the door."

This guy noticed everything, even the quickest look or gesture. He was acting strange. When May came out from behind her desk, she made it a point to wiggle her hips all the way to the fridge to get me a bottle of water.

"Thanks, I could have gotten it myself."

"This way it will taste better, don't you think?"

"I definitely agree. I am going to savor it. Maybe I should come back and ask for another."

"I am giving you an open invitation, anytime you want. The fridge is stocked."

"The fridge is always cold. I wish I drank coffee. Sometimes I like hot stuff."

"Stop squeezing the bottle so hard, it's going to explode."

"Better the bottle than me."

I heard my name called from inside the office and I had to break it off. She gave me a smile and went back to work.

"Sit. How is the water—hot?"

"No, it's fine, it's cold."

"I meant May. She is hot, but off-limits."

"May" translated into Arabic means water. He was jealous. He had a reputation as a playboy and probably had something going on with her. I did not answer; I knew there was no point discussing it.

"Remember when you were training with Kidon and the Mossad? You met an American CIA officer."

"Yes. He even asked me if I would like to go visit Langley one day."

"He was at the embassy today, watching the exchange on screen."

"I had no doubt we were being taped."

"They still can't believe we were able to identify the organization and get their number two guy this quick."

"We are local. We blend in and have resources. We know the culture and the area better than anybody."

"They have requested that we send you on loan to them. Being a native, speaking Arabic with a European look and background, they have some plans for you. Do you want to go to the U.S.?"

I had a double motive to agree. First, my boss was becoming a double agent. Soon all of us who were working for him would be labeled traitors. Second, I felt like I lived in vain: I was not helping the Christians anymore, and I was not any closer to finding Yellow Eyes. "We started this unit for a reason. If my going to the U.S. will help achieve our goals, I will go. But if it is only to serve their interests and the interests of the Israelis, we shouldn't even consider it."

"They need to use us, and at the same time we can use their help. They have the manpower, the technology, and resources that we cannot dream of."

By using the resources available through the Mossad and the CIA, I can track down Yellow Eyes and make sure that he gets what he deserves.

I was starting to feel regret for not killing the fat Ghassan.

PART FIVE

34

PROTECTED BY THE ENEMY

PAUL:

This could only happen in Lebanon, Beirut international airport that was crawling with Syrian intelligence and their many allies. Shadow arranged for me to leave Beirut through the same airport. He was able to organize it through our contacts with the UN monitors stationed on the green line between the two sides.

Early that morning in 1984, my father, my brother-in-law, and my best friend, Rami—remember my blood brother and Muslim friend, the tall handsome guy with the birthmark on his cheek?—drove to a Lebanese army barracks close to the green line. We had coffee with the officer in charge while they were making the arrangements. Rami and my father wanted to come with me to the airport. However, the officer made it clear that I would be the only one leaving with the two soldiers. While they were getting ready, Rami and I took a walk outside.

"Boulous, my bro," he asked, "why are you leaving for the unknown?"

"I am going to use every trick, and everybody, to get to Yellow Eyes," I told him.

"You know, the Americans and Israelis will only protect you as long as you have value to them. They might even sell you out to Bassam."

"I know the game, bro," I said. "We are all users. I am using them, and they are using me."

"So what can I do to help? I want to put an end to this obsession you have with the yellow-eyed monster."

"I wish you could. I would not trust anybody more than you to have on my side, but I think Yellow Eyes is in Afghanistan now, at least the last I heard."

Then my father called us back, gesturing that it was time to go. We embraced and said good-bye.

I threw my duffel bag into the back seat of the Land Rover with the soldiers and got into the front. We hadn't gone more than one kilometer before we stopped again, at the Hezbollah barracks. I was sure that once again I had been double-crossed. My mind was racing as I assessed my options, all the while trying to stay as cool as possible and continue to act like an awkward, bespectacled student going abroad to continue his studies.

The Land Rover stopped beside a Toyota truck with the yellow and green Hezbollah flag on top of it. Three bearded fighters of that party were waiting in the truck. One of them stepped out and came around to help me with my luggage. He was surprised I had only one small bag.

"That is all you have? You must be leaving for only a short period."

"This is my second year at school," I told him, hoping he believed me. "Most of my stuff is still in Brussels."

"I can see you are nervous," he said. "Don't worry; we are going to take good care of you."

Taking good care of me could only mean one of two things: getting me safely to the airport and onto the Sabena flight, or taking really good care of me and shipping me to the famous Mazza prison in Syria. Thousands of Lebanese, both Christians and Muslims, have gone on a one-way trip there. Nobody had ever come back alive.

I got into the truck. Not much was said between us on the way to the airport. Once we got there, two of them came with me inside the terminal. They did not even let the Lebanese customs official search my bag, and one of them stayed close behind me when I went to the washroom. They made sure I got safely on the plane before waving a friendly goodbye to me, wishing me good luck.

The strangest thoughts were going through my mind as I sat in the plane waiting for take-off. A few weeks ago I was blowing up their boats, and today they were escorting me so I could board the plane safely and go finish my studies. This war was making no sense to me. My best friend was a Muslim. Some of my other friends were Druze and Shia. We had relations with the Syrians, the Israelis, the UN observers, and the Americans. The whole thing was becoming very confusing.

I was en route to Canada via Belgium. I was supposed to layover in Brussels only for one night and then continue to Montréal.

Upon arrival at the Brussels airport, with my impeccably faked set of documents and an authentic Canadian stamped visa, I was thoroughly searched. They were not very welcoming to anybody with a passport that showed you were from Lebanon. During the search, the metal detector beeped every time I passed through it, because of the few pieces of shrapnel left under my skin long ago. I had never bothered to remove them; they were a reminder of when my cousin was killed not even ten inches away from me. After I was asked to take off my shirt, they noticed a few scars on my body. Immediately, I was surrounded by four cops in full gear and ushered to a private room.

The Belgian security officers noticed the bullet scar I had on my hip; they added it to the *born in Beirut* on my passport. They took me through a different set of doors to a holding cell.

"Why are you coming to Belgium?" they asked me in French.

"I am not," I told him. "I am on my way to Canada. That is what my visa says."

"We don't welcome people like you in Belgium. You can't stay tonight in the hotel that was booked for you through the airline. You are going to be our guest here at the airport until your flight leaves tomorrow. This way we can guarantee that you left."

"Do you have room service?"

"You think you're funny? We will see about that."

This did not bother me. Staying in a holding cell crowded with Moroccans, Algerians, and Tunisians at the airport in Brussels was like staying in a five-star hotel. I had been the guest of the Syrians, where I experienced their many creative ways of interrogation. However, as soon as I stepped into the holding cell, all eyes turned to me. As I've said before, I do not look like an Arab. While the rest of them had olive skin and dark features, I was totally the opposite. They assumed I was a European troublemaker and that I would be deported the next day just like the rest of them. I was fit and young. They left me alone and started talking about me in Arabic, not realizing I understood every word.

35

BLACK INK, BLUE INK, AND
THE REVOLVING DOOR

PAUL:

Early the next morning, I left my roommates behind and was escorted by two security officers to board the flight to Montréal. I was tired; I had not slept the whole night. Right after take-off, I went straight to sleep. I was going into the unknown. I had no idea who would be meeting me on the other side, or what my next move would be.

I was woken up by the friendly middle-aged man sitting beside me. The food was being served, and he wanted to make sure I was awake to eat. I readjusted my seat, opened my tray, smiled at him, and thanked him. That was a mistake. He wanted to know everything about me and why I was coming to Canada. I just shook my head as if I didn't understand a word of English and smiled back at him.

They had an in-flight movie showing, though I didn't pay attention. I spent my time leafing through the airline magazine. However, there was no information about Canada; it was all about Belgium and Europe. I did not know much about Canada. I had heard of Montréal because some of my friends carried Hurstal Browning handguns that said *Made in Montréal.* In all the years of training, we never even mentioned Canada. I knew it was a cold place north of the USA.

After eight or nine hours in the air, as we were approaching Mirabel airport and my final destination, the flight crew started handing us Canadian landing forms. I took my black ink pen from my bag and filled out my form on the French side. I noticed that the man sitting next to me was simply holding his blank form. He gestured to me that he did not have a pen. I was more than happy to offer him mine.

He thanked me and started to write his name on the top line of the form. Suddenly he stopped and handed me back my pen. Why did he refuse to use my pen? I had been nice to him—I'd got up twice so he could go to the restroom, and helped him get to his luggage in the overhead bin. So I said, in intentionally broken English, "Excuse me, sir. My pen. Is it wrong for you?"

"No, there is absolutely nothing wrong with it. It is a perfect pen."

"I could not help it but to notice, that you did not use it before returning it to me."

"I don't like writing with black ink," he said. "I prefer blue ink. It looks better on white paper." Then he asked a passing flight attendant if she could give him a blue ink pen.

Once he finished filling out the form and handed the pen back to the flight attendant, he proudly showed it to me and said, "You see how much nicer is the blue ink on white paper?"

At that moment, my jaw dropped, though I tried to hide it from him. I smiled back and nodded agreement. I was almost tempted to give him a hug, but not because he had such perfect cursive writing, or because he had been a good travel companion and left me alone most of the flight.

Because at that moment he reminded me of something I had lost as a child.

I had spent the better part of my life dodging bullets and trying to survive and help my people. My dilemma was how to stay alive until the end of the day, because I might get my head blown off at any moment. The Canadian man next to me also had a dilemma: black ink or blue ink? A very hard choice to make. I had this big grin on my face. I closed my eyes, put my head back, and started thinking. *This Canada place must be so easy to live in. How lucky these people are.* In life, you can get lucky just by being born in the right place.

But I was not Canadian, so I had another problem: I had to figure out my next move and what I would do if nobody met me on the other side.

I knew that Freddie's parents lived in Edmonton, a city I had never heard of. And a relative of mine lived in Ottawa. I had both addresses written down and tucked in my pocket.

As the plane started its descent, I was trying to look over the landscape. The first thing I noticed was the large expanse of land and thousands of trees. However, the strangest thing I noticed was the emptiness, and the lack of homes, cars, and humans. Lebanon is one of the smallest countries in the Middle East. Four million people lived, died, and fought over the 10,452 square kilometers of land.

My paperwork was in order. Getting off the plane and going through customs was as easy as 1-2-3. It took a very long time for the luggage to arrive. Were those Canadians trying to decide if they should organize the bags by color or by size? Once I collected my bag and passed through the last checkpoint, I found myself in the public area of the terminal. The big sign said in both English and French: WELCOME TO CANADA. BIENVENUE AU CANADA.

That was easy, I thought. I started looking around without being too conspicuous, to see if there was someone picking me up. Seeing no one who looked like they were waiting, I decided to stretch my legs after the long flight. I looked outside. The sun was shining, the sky was cloudless, big, bright, and blue.

Back home whenever the sun was shining, it was hot, or at least warm. I had on a thin black leather jacket made for the fall in Beirut. I saw the revolving door that led to the parking lot, and I decided to go for a walk before I made my next move. It was an afternoon in late November. I remember it as if it were today. I pushed through the revolving door—and the extreme cold weather hit me like a punch in the gut. I had never experienced such cold, even in the winter, high in the mountains of Lebanon. A temperature of −24 (Celsius) was alien to me. I pushed the door around full circle and walked back inside. I decided that if no one was meeting me, I would go back to an airline counter and buy a return ticket. All I needed was a ticket to any country other than Canada. Once there, having no visa I would be deported back home at the expense of the host country. The only problem was, I did not have enough money on me to buy another ticket anywhere. I was legally in Canada, and they would not return me at their expense.

I waited for an hour inside the terminal and did not spot anybody waiting. I decided to take a taxi to one of the addresses I had tucked in my pocket. I pulled out one at random and handed it to the French-Canadian taxi driver. He took one look at it and threw the paper back at me with a barrage of French-Canadian dialect that I did not understand a word of, although I had been speaking French since childhood. However, I understood his body language: he was telling me to get the hell out of his car.

That did not need translation.

I found out later that I had handed him the address in Edmonton, which is almost 3,000 kilometers from Montréal. I am sure he did not want to drive four days to get there, and I am more sure that I did not have the money to pay him.

I went back inside the terminal. I had changed my mind about Canada. It was not as easy as I had thought it was going to be. It was freezing, I didn't understand the language, and they were not friendly. I walked to the counter that advertised bus routes to the major Canadian cities. In my impeccable French, I asked the attractive girl behind the counter about ticket prices to Edmonton and to Ottawa.

"Monsieur, oh, non, c'est st st jjdyd."

Again I did not understand anything except *"monsieur."* And I figured that French was not going to help me, so I switched to English and repeated the question.

"Sure," she said. "We don't have a direct bus to Edmonton, but there is a bus leaving for Ottawa in half an hour, and the cost is $13 each way."

"Great, please give me a one-way ticket to Ottawa."

"Of course, it's my pleasure. Here's your ticket, and a complimentary map for the city of Ottawa."

The Canadians were friendly after all, but first they had to understand you. I found a pay phone and dialed my relative's number in Ottawa; he answered on the first ring and was surprised but happy to hear from me.

"I am arriving in Ottawa in a couple of hours; I was hoping I could visit with you. Maybe you can recommend a reasonable hotel nearby for me to stay in?"

I did not want to impose by asking if I could stay with him.

"You don't need a hotel," he said. "You can stay with me. I have a spare bedroom, and you can use it. I have not seen you since the war started. I will meet you at the bus terminal. I hope I can recognize you."

I told him the bus number and the time of arrival and hung up. The two-hour bus ride went by quickly. I was busy checking out the landscape and the strange collection of people riding with me on the bus. From beautiful young students who were practically making out in public to older couples holding hands. Showing affection in the open was strange to me. Almost everybody wore hats, gloves, scarves, and something else on their ears that made them look like aliens. Later I learned they were called earmuffs. I was intrigued by the flatness of the land, but mostly by the emptiness. We passed some houses but they were few and far between. I remember thinking that you could fit all of Lebanon in the area between Montreal and Ottawa—why not bring the Lebs here for a year during the winter, let them freeze their asses off, then send them back. Maybe they would appreciate what they have and take better care of it.

Upon arrival at the terminal, I immediately recognized the man waiting for me. Khalil had not changed much, he was just an older version of himself. He had gained some weight and lost some hair. He also looked a little whiter—from not spending too much time outside, I guessed. Who would, in this giant freezer? I approached him with a big smile and spoke to him in the Lebanese dialect used back home. I could see the surprise in his eyes.

"Wow, you have grown so much," he said. "I remember you as a ten-year-old, zipping around the neighborhood on your blue bicycle. If I had not known you were coming and simply ran into you on the street, I would not have recognized you

"As much as I have changed," I said, "you have not changed at all. I would have recognized you anywhere, Khalil."

"Let's go. My car is just outside, in the parking lot. After you called, I prepared dinner—you must be tired and hungry."

"Thank you, I am. How can people work outside in this cold?"

"You will get used to it one day," he assured me. "Canadians are very proud and clean people. The first thing you're going to notice is the lack of garbage on the streets."

We left in his white Ford—another first for me, as Fords are illegal in Lebanon. For some crazy reason, the Lebanese government decided that Ford is a Jewish company and so Fords cannot be sold in Lebanon. Don't ask me why. I know it's absurd, as are one million other things that go on over there. Within ten minutes, we had arrived at his apartment. He lived alone in a nice, well-furnished two-bedroom apartment.

"Make yourself at home, don't be shy, you can use that bedroom. While I'm preparing dinner and setting up the table, go ahead and take a shower. You must be exhausted."

"Thank you very much. I will," I said. "In the next couple of days, I hope you can help me to look for a place."

"Don't rush it," he advised. "Get a feel for the place and learn the city. Once you know the system, you will get to appreciate how organized it is."

After a dinner of lasagne, which I loved, I helped him with the dishes and the cleanup—another first for me. He asked me if I wanted to watch TV, and I said sure: let's find out what the Canadians watch. He started flicking his remote control up and down. Almost every other channel showed a strange game played on ice with players who tried to put a small black rubber disc into a net. I had no idea what was going on, or that this sport was going to be my favorite. I just liked the speed and the contact.

He kept flipping up and down between channels. I asked him how many channels they had.

"Almost 200," he said. "Maybe more. It's different from back home, where we had only the two channels, 7 and 11. We have no need for antennas, either. The TV runs 24/7."

He was laughing at the look on my face. I was thinking, who needs 200 channels, and how do they get the signal to the TV? 24/7? In Lebanon, the channels only came on at 5 p.m. Boy, I had so many things to learn, and quickly.

36

THE VILLAGE IDIOT

PAUL:

The cultural differences were shocking. This society was alien to me. After years of training and fighting, being civilized was going to be hard. I was hoping I could keep it together and act relaxed and normal.

Khalil lent me a scarf. His gloves did not fit, nor did any of his coats, because he was small—an average size in the Middle East, short in North America. I kept his address and number in my thin leather jacket; he also gave me his work number.

"I think you should go out today and check out the city," he said. "The bus number is 109. Head north. It will take you near the Parliament building and a huge shopping center. Maybe you can find some gloves. It's only going to get colder."

"Colder? You're kidding, right?" I couldn't imagine anything colder than this.

He laughed, then said, "Seriously, look. The city is safe. You are going to have no trouble. If you get lost, just call me and tell me where you are. Give me the street name and number, and I will come and get you."

"Do you remember how the postman delivered letters back home, with no street names and numbers?"

"Of course I do," he said. "When I tell my friends here how we got the mail, they never believe me. Just write the name of the recipient, then the name of a school or famous building near their house, then the town, then the country. No street name, no number and postal code. People here are mystified and ask how the postman would know where to deliver the letter."

"He would be from the town," I laughed, "so of course he would know the landmark. If he did not know the recipients, he would ask the grocer or the priest. Then when he got to the home, he would tell them they had a letter, and then sit down on their steps."

Khalil started laughing so hard he almost choked on his breakfast.

"And if they don't tip him or give him a shot of *arak*? The letter stays in his bag for another day, then he will try again."

"Everybody knows why the postman weaves dangerously when riding his bike: all those shots of *arak*."

As soon as I left the house to wait for the bus in the sub-zero temperatures, I noticed a black Ford idling down the street. I might have been naïve to the ways of this society, but years of training and survival had sharpened my instincts. I waited the ten minutes for bus 109 to arrive and got on with a dollar bill in my hand. In Lebanon, I had taken the bus only once in my life, when my uncle took me to see a movie in downtown Beirut before the war.

Now, I settled at the back of the bus, proudly clutching my dollar bill and ready for the assistant to come claim it. The bus driver made eye contact with me through the mirror and told me to come forward by crooking his finger, a universal sign that I understood. He also understood that I wanted to pay since I had the dollar in my hand; he pointed to a box right beside him and motioned for me to deposit the money in the slot. I was always the top scorer in any course or military training I attended, yet I was clueless about the simplest of tasks in this cold nation.

I deposited the money and walked back to my seat. The black car was following the bus. Two people barely visible, surely they were not there to make sure I paid my bus fare: $1 was not going to change the budget of the Canadian government. I paid attention to the car, but not that anyone would notice.

The whole day was an awakening. I was flabbergasted to see some people pulling money from machines located inside the walls, with no armed guards in sight, and others getting food without leaving their cars. The list of differences between Lebanon and Canada was long, but the highlight of the day was when I saw two men arguing in the parking lot of the shopping center. I watched them shout at each other for a minute, then each one walked back to his car. No punches were thrown, no knives or weapons drawn. In Beirut, this altercation would have caused a minimum of one casualty, maybe more, if one of them had friends nearby.

Khalil had told me the city was safe and not to worry. He said this with no idea how I had gotten here or why. He was under the impression that, like thousands of young Lebanese men, I was escaping the endless war and looking for a better life and a new beginning.

I bought the warmest coat I could find. The friendly, blonde salesgirl told me it was not very fashionable but it was warm and light. She also sold me a pair of gloves and suggested I get some earmuffs, but I declined. "I think a coat and gloves are enough," I said, "and I already have a scarf that should keep me warm."

"Yes, inside the mall maybe. It is only November, it going to get colder soon."

"Here we go again about the cold," I said. "How is it possibly going to get any colder?"

"The canal will freeze and people will go skating on it, and others will play hockey."

"You are kidding me, right? They are going to play that game with the sticks right on this canal?"

"The whole city will be skating on it; people come from all over to skate. Maybe I should teach you."

"Maybe you should."

We talked for a while and I told her about the bus fare and the money coming from the wall. She told me it was called an ATM machine. We laughed hard at my naïveté. Her name was Lauren, and she was French Canadian. It quickly became clear that until I got used to the French dialect, English was easier, even with the accent.

"How long have you been here?"

"I just arrived last night," I said. "You are the first Canadian I have spoken with. Oh yeah, beside the taxi driver who went crazy on me, and the girl that sold me the bus ticket."

"What did you do to him? You seem like a polite guy."

"I am, thank you. I got into his car at the Montréal airport and handed him an address in Edmonton. That detail set him off. He threw the paper back at me and told me to get the hell out of his cab. I thought he was going to have a heart attack."

"Oh my God, you did not!" She laughed so hard, I thought *she* was having a heart attack. Tears were pouring down her cheeks. I reached inside my leather jacket and handed her the handkerchief that my mom had given me with my initials on it. I should have left it behind but I wanted something from her with me.

"This is so funny. Please let me tell my friends about it."

"They will think that I am stupid, but go ahead. I will never meet your friends anyway."

"Why don't you tell them yourself? It is a good story and it will break the ice. You can even say that you did it on purpose, if you are embarrassed."

"Are you asking me out? I might be new, but I am not stupid." I smiled while I said it. "I think you are asking me out."

"Maybe I am, maybe I am not. If I was, would you come? Tomorrow is Saturday. I get off at 5 p.m. Maybe we can go for dinner, then to a house party at my friend's house?"

I liked her. She was funny and attractive. I accepted.

"I will meet you here tomorrow at 5."

During the conversation with Lauren, I noticed a man watching us from between the clothes racks. He was a pro. He tried to be as invisible as he could, and it might have worked with an amateur, but I had spent most of my life noticing and assessing my surroundings. This was no longer a skill that I practiced; it was now instinctive and second nature to me.

I figured that if the Canadians wanted to arrest me, they would have done it at the airport, so I decided to have some fun and find out their intentions. I exited the mall's main entrance and gave my follower time to get to the car before I started walking. My friends complain that I walk so fast they needed to jog to keep up with me. However, I lost this man within minutes by doubling back and going through a corner café that had an entrance from each street. I soon got lost myself, but no way was I calling Khalil for help. Instead, I got out my map of the city and found out where I was. It was simple and very organized.

Walking back to meet the bus for route 109, I saw a

team practicing football—not soccer, which is what they call our football, but American-style football. I knew this from reading comics as a child. I spent an hour in the chilly weather, standing on a bridge overlooking the field. All of a sudden, I saw bus 109. I sprinted after it. Luckily, it stopped for an older lady who took her sweet time to board, which gave me plenty of time to catch it. Being an experienced bus user now, I made sure the driver noticed me depositing the dollar bill in the box. He asked me if I needed a transfer ticket and I took it without knowing what it was for. Crap, there were always new things.

The next day, I took extra care as I got ready for my date. I arrived at the mall an hour early. As I was getting off the bus, I noticed the black Ford again, idling with a big blond guy behind the wheel. He did not spot me. That seemed kind of strange: where was this dude's partner? I took an indirect route to Lauren's store and found him. I started watching the watcher. He waited until she was getting ready to leave, then he approached. It was clear from her reaction that they didn't know one another; he showed her his ID and started talking. She was just shaking her head. He walked with her to the bus stop, and only left her alone when she boarded. This episode took about 25 minutes.

As the agent had been talking to her, she had been looking around to see if I was going to show up. Assuming that I had stood her up, she boarded the bus. He turned to rejoin the driver, who was waiting in the car. I boarded the bus from the middle door, outside of their field of vision, and took a seat at the back. After five minutes, and once I was sure the Ford was not tailing us, I got up and took the seat right beside Lauren. At first she did not look up from her book, thinking it was another passenger, until I spoke to her. "Sorry I am late."

I knew immediately she was spooked. Whatever the

agent said had put her on her guard. This was not the same friendly girl that I met yesterday.

She cleared her throat and said, "I waited for you. I thought that you had changed your mind about tonight."

"I was late catching the bus," I said. "When I arrived, I saw you boarding this one and I got on. Are we still good for tonight?"

"I am a little tired today, maybe another day, okay?"

"Sure, no problem," I said. "I hope you feel better soon. I will get off at the next stop."

What is it about women? When they see you not pushing, they make a 180-degree reversal.

"A government agent came to see me today at work, and he asked me about you," she said finally. "Are you in some kind of trouble?"

"No, not at all. Maybe he is following up on my visa paperwork."

"How does he know that we met? And the ID he showed me was not from Immigration. It said something about security."

Back where I came from, if a girl even smelled that the intelligence network was asking questions about you, she would not even glance your way, let alone ask for clarification. But I guess over here, Lauren knew her rights and that she had not done anything wrong, so she gave me a second chance.

"I assure you, I am not in trouble. Probably because I came from that part of the world and only arrived recently, they are making sure I am not a troublemaker. Maybe he saw us talking yesterday. If you feel uncomfortable or threatened, I will leave now."

"He was only asking about you, if I planned to see you again, because we spoke for longer than usual yesterday. I told him I was just being friendly, and that I sold you some clothes. Should I have told him about tonight?"

"Tell him anything you want," I told her. "I am not hiding anything, don't worry."

This kind of calmed her down, and we started talking again. When I asked her if I should get off the bus, she said no. "We are going to a party. First, let's get something to eat."

I was hoping she was going to say *shawarma* or even *falafel*, but we ended up at a bar and grill that served burgers. After dinner, we had to stop at a liquor store, another new cultural difference. I was used to bringing a small gift to a party, not my own booze. What was the point of hosting a party if the guests had to bring snacks and liquor? I guess the key is in throwing a party, not hosting one.

At the party, she introduced me to her friends and made sure everybody knew where I came from, and that this was my second day in Canada. Most of them had not heard of the Middle East, period, let alone Lebanon.

The place was packed. I took a seat near the back door with my back against the wall. Old habits died hard. A few of Lauren's friends came over and joined us. They wanted to know about how I lived and "what it was like in Arabia," as one of them put it.

"So, you have roads and cars?"

First I had to stop myself from laughing. "No, we don't have roads," I said, very seriously. "It's all desert and sand dunes. We don't have use for cars. I saw some near the city once."

I watched the group in silence as they looked from one to another in amazement. Suddenly one of the girls exclaimed. "Yes, I know all about how you live!" she exclaimed. "I saw it in the *Black Stallion* movie."

I had seen the movie also. It was one of my favorites as a kid. "Great," I said. "Tell them the details. My English is not as good as yours, and you can describe it better."

Lauren gave me a dirty look that meant, "Don't make fun of my friends."

I shrugged my shoulders as if to say, "Let's have a little fun."

Her name was Donna. She was a stunning brunette with big green eyes that had a permanently amazed look in them, as if she was asking a question and waiting for a shocking reply. She did a great job explaining the way of life in the Middle East in the 1940s, when the story was first written. Unfortunately, Lauren noticed the banter and the flirting between us and cut her off.

"You're explaining a movie set fifty years ago, and in another country altogether, Donna. He does not live like that."

Ray, who saw himself as the cool guy, winked at me and whispered, "I think Lauren is jealous. You're joking around and giving Donna too much attention. Let's go out for a smoke."

I did not smoke and it was cold; still, I found myself agreeing and leaving with Ray. He offered me a cigarette, which I refused.

"I don't smoke," I admitted, "but I needed a break from Donna's story. It was hard to not laugh."

"Careful with Donna," Ray advised me. "Since she gets all the men, Lauren might get jealous."

"Lauren has no reason to be jealous. There is nothing between us."

"Attraction is a universal feeling," said Ray. "I am not sure how you see it. The way I see it, she is attracted to you and it shows. Take it from me, Ray the connoisseur."

The last thing I needed was a relationship. I came here with a plan. I was sure to be leaving soon. Lauren was beautiful and nice; there was no way I would lead her on just to get in the sack with her. Ray and I came back inside, and I could feel immediately that the girls had worked things out. Donna was nowhere to be seen,

Lauren had an empty spot saved for me. I sat beside her, and she snuggled her head on my shoulder.

"It is getting late," she said. "You are not going to catch the last bus."

"Maybe I should leave now—what time is the last bus?"

"You just missed it, too bad."

"I will take a taxi," I said. "I don't want to call my friend and wake him."

"If you are staying with him, maybe you should let him know that you're not coming home. He might get worried."

"I am not? Am I going to wait for the bus all night?"

That little playful back-and-forth earned me a punch on the shoulder. I could hardly feel it, but I faked it and told her that it hurt.

"Really? I felt like I hit a rock. You must be in great shape."

"I take care of myself. All these years on camels in the desert hardens you up."

"Donna made sure we knew about that," Lauren said. "Do you find her sexy?"

"Who doesn't? She is smoking hot. She is naïve, gullible, and sexy."

"Would you like me to let her know?"

"I am sure she does already," I said. "She thinks men find her sexy. But being attracted to her would take more than that, for me anyway."

"Explain yourself, strange young immigrant."

"It's hard to put into words. I like your kind more. Smart and funny."

"Are you saying I am not beautiful?"

"What I am saying is, you are more beautiful, because you have the body, the face, and also the soul and mind. You are the complete package."

"Maybe you will think I am too easy, but there are no

more buses running tonight. You are welcome to come over and stay at my place—unless you want to spend your money on a taxi."

"Can I use a phone?"

"You want to call a taxi?"

"No, I want to call my friend and tell him not to worry. He might be expecting me."

Ray was watching and smiling, having appointed himself my babysitter. With a gesture of his head, he motioned for me to go back outside with him.

"I am not sure how things work where you come from, but women here are equal in every respect to men. If you're spending the night with Lauren, you may want some protection."

"Don't you worry about my safety; I can take care of myself. You don't have to protect me."

He was inhaling smoke, then he started laughing and choking. Once the coughing stopped, he wiped the tears from his eyes and continued, "I meant, do you have a condom? Not me coming with you as protection."

"Oh no, I don't have any. Do you think I need some?"

"As I explained, if she feels like it, you might get lucky. Or spend the night on the couch, no guarantee."

He put his cigarette out and went back inside. I stayed out in the freezing air, contemplating. I wanted to stay over at her place, but in a few days or a week I might disappear. It was not fair to her. Maybe I should call a taxi and just head home.

I did not need to think very long. The black Ford drew up to the curb across the street from the house, and the headlights flashed twice. I walked over, opened the back door, got into the back seat with Mr. Watcher and his big blond buddy.

"Hello, I am going to save you the trouble of following me. Are you here to give me a ride back home?"

"You are leaving now; we will drop you off to collect

your stuff. You have ten minutes; don't tell your friend anything. Just tell him you are going to Toronto to visit with friends and that you have a ride."

While the car was pulling out from the curb, I saw Lauren looking through the window. It was the last time I saw her. Who needed protection when I had two armed men with me? It was the story of my life.

Khalil was sleeping. I left him a thank-you note: "Thanks for everything. I will be in touch soon."

We drove for about an hour heading south. Soon after we crossed a long bridge, I noticed a sign that said PRESCOTT. Another sign on the other side of the road said CANADIAN CUSTOMS. They drove a few hundred meters more and made a U-turn.

"Just get out and walk in this direction. Never come back. People like you are not welcome here."

I picked up my bag and started walking. Another black car was idling by the side of the road in the same direction I was heading. What was with all the black Fords? Why not just put a big sign on the roof that said "security"? A WELCOME TO THE USA sign was not far away. Ironic, since my original and authentic Lebanese passport was stamped, compliments of the visa services at the American embassy in Beirut, with the words "Not Allowed in the USA." Years ago, Rami and I had been sick and tired of living with the violence and decided to immigrate to any country that would give us a visa. We were not choosy. We borrowed money from friends and family members and deposited it into our accounts to show that we had savings, and for a full week we waited in the long lines and applied at the European, Australian, Canadian, and American embassies. Every single one declined us. The Americans after a two-minute interview stamped the last page of our passports with the famous "Not Allowed."

I got close to the car and tried to keep on walking.

Maybe I should have run off the road and disappeared—hindsight is 20/20. The passenger-side window slid open, and a voice told me to get in the back. As I slid in, I noticed there were no door handles in the back: it was impossible to open the doors from inside. A thick window partition separated the front from the back. We had similar cars back home, gifts from the U.S.

We entered the country without stopping at any of the kiosks. Not a word was exchanged for the almost two hours it took to get to a small private airport. We stopped beside a small private plane.

"This is where we say goodbye and good luck. Get on that plane."

"Where am I going?"

"We have no idea; our part of the delivery is completed."

Waiting for me beside the small drop ladder were two more big guys in black suits, white shirts, and power ties. There were no sunglasses to complete the outfit, as it was still dark. I climbed the few steps, took a seat at the back, and made myself comfortable. One of the men came over and sat beside me.

"You must be a big shot," he said. "We were told not to cuff you and to treat you well. You are one of the lucky ones."

"Can you tell me where we are going?"

"I can, but it will not be the truth. You still want to know?"

"It makes no difference," I said. "I will know soon enough."

"That's a good attitude."

"Is there something to eat?"

I also needed a rest. I always made it a point to eat and sleep whenever I could; you never knew when the next opportunity would come. By the time I ate and went to the washroom, the plane was starting its descent. We hopped a couple of times before we touched down. The guy who had spoken with me opened the door.

"Let's go, bud," he said.

I did not understand. "Bud what?" I asked.

"Bud what? Bud nothing—get off the plane, mister."

Another car was waiting a few meters from the steps. The back door was open. Being a fast learner, I slid inside.

The man in the passenger seat looked back toward me and said, "Welcome to The Farm."

"The farm? I always wanted to be a farmer. Ride horses and grow my own vegetables. When I was younger, I wished I could live in a zoo. My wish came true before I even grew up."

"This is not funny anymore," the man said. "I hear this lame joke every time we get a new recruit here at Camp Peary."

"'Camp Peary: where the Central Intelligence Agency trains its clandestine officers, as well as officers from other organizations specializing in clandestine activities,'" I rattled off.

Still looking at the file and ignoring me, he said. "Mossad, Deuxième Bureau, the Bundesnachrichtendienst, and now with the CIA? Very impressive. What are you, a spy scholar? You spend all your time in class and none in the field?"

I did not answer. These guys were just reading my file. I did not want to argue with them, or add to their information, so I kept my mouth shut.

"It is usually the silent types that do all the action."

No doubt he was trained in interrogations; he was trying to get more out of me. Somebody at the CIA knew something. I had delivered Ghassan to them and now they asked for me. I wondered where Ghassan was.

"We will escort you to your quarters; you can take a shower or sleep. Food is served at the mess hall. You can't walk outside without escort. Ring the bell in your room, and we will take you to your destination."

"Mess hall? I don't clean."

They laughed; they thought I was joking. I had no idea what a mess hall was.

"Am I under arrest? I need an escort everywhere but my locked cell?"

"It is not a cell. It's a small apartment, like a bachelor pad."

"A bachelor pad, heh, you should have said this at the beginning. It's all clear now." It was not clear. I had no idea what a bachelor pad was.

"Just ring the bell if you want to go out. If not, make sure to be ready by 0600 hours."

Now this one I got.

The room was simple but comfortable. The furniture consisted of one coffee table and two chairs, and a twin bed, and the washroom had all I needed: a toilet, sink, and shower. I spent the night in and out of a restless sleep. I was excited and anxious to start a whole new phase of life. The only problem was that I had no idea what it was.

I did the triple S in about twenty minutes every morning, unless I was on a mission. I was already waiting for the knock on the door when at 0600 sharp they knocked twice and unlocked the door from the outside. Two soldiers in fatigues without nametags escorted me to the mess hall. I was happy to find out what it was, because I was starving. I got some eggs and bacon, and while I was filling up a large cup of java, a man in a black suit spoke to me. "I hope you know that bacon is from pork."

"Yes, of course, and eggs from chickens, sometimes. What is your question?"

"You just answered it. I am your case officer; I will

run the debriefing and the next phase of your training. Call me Scott."

"First or last name?"

"Just call me Scott."

"OK, Scot Scott." This was a private joke; *scot* in Lebanese meant "shut up." He let me eat my breakfast while he read the paper, the sports section. I noticed he was reading an article about the same game I saw in Ottawa, with the long ball and massive men wearing armour.

"Scott, what do you call this game? Mayhem?"

"We call it football, the gridiron."

"What do you call real football? The one actually played with the foot and a normal ball."

"Oh, that one—we call it soccer, or play-acting."

"It does not make sense." I got "play-acting," though. I had been watching the game all my life and, lately, whenever there was the slightest contact, the players would go down like they had been shot, in order to draw a penalty.

"I know. Don't ask. I have no answer. Let's go, you have a doctor's appointment."

"I am not sick. I feel fine."

"It is standard procedure. We don't want you to croak while in my care."

"Croak? I thought I spoke excellent English until I got here, now I am not so sure."

"It is slang for 'die.' We have to make sure you are healthy before your surgery."

"What surgery are you talking about? Is it voluntary or involuntary?"

"Let's go for the physical, and I will explain later."

This was not your typical exam. It was a comprehensive physical exam, with laboratory tests, chest X-rays, pulmonary function testing, audiograms, full body CAT scanning, EKGs, heart stress tests, urinalysis, but (thank God) no prostate test. During the exam, the doctor told Scott, "Good, this is one less thing you have to worry about."

"He ate pork for breakfast, and I thought we had to do it." They were talking as if I was not even there.

"What are you guys talking about? Breakfast and pork: I can connect the dots. You wanted to know my religion, as Muslims do not eat pork. Read my file. But I assure you, my Muslim friends eat pork and drink more whiskey than a Scottish alcoholic. You can't be 100 percent sure from minor things like that."

"The doctor was saying you are already circumcised, so that is one thing we don't have to do."

My face hardened. "This fucking meeting, appointment, exam—call it what you like—is over until I know what is going on."

I put my clothes back on and left the exam room. Blocking my way to the outside were the two escorts. Scott came after me; I was escorted down the hall. We took seats in a small private room.

"After your training is done, you will have to look and act like a Muslim."

"I know how they look and act more than all of you put together," I said. "I grew up with them."

"I have no doubt, but they are always circumcised and we wanted to make sure you were also."

"My parents believed it was healthier and cleaner to be chopped. I remember whenever the chopper passed through the street, all the boys used to run and hide."

"The chopper?"

"An old man riding a horse or a mule, he is the circumciser. The boys who had not had the pleasure of meeting him would run and hide until he left. He used to pass by every two or three months. We would be playing and yelling and causing trouble, until one of us spotted him, and he would yell, 'Hide your dicks!' Within moments, the street would be deserted, save for those of us had been caught by him in the past."

The man did not smile. "We have to be sure that you know how to prepare and pray like a Muslim also. You will be sent undercover."

"Depends on where I am going. Don't you know that every sect washes and prays differently?"

". Do you mean the Shia wash and prepare for prayer in a different way from the Sunni?"

"Of course they do! Sending somebody to infiltrate a Shia group—if he performs his pre-prayer ritual like a Sunni, he will be compromised and discovered by any five-year-old in seconds."

"I need to make some calls."

He came back an hour later, while I was working out. I was still in the same room, doing push-ups and sit-ups. The two soldiers refused to let me out.

"Your buddy, the leader of the QJ, is now training fighters in Pakistan or Afghanistan. We are supplying them with weapons to fight the Soviets. This is getting more and more complicated by the minute."

"Let me simplify, Scott, and correct me if I am wrong, please. The jihad group that killed your Marines is now training another group that you are helping fight against the Soviets. Stop me when you think I am going off base here. The Syrians gave them up to you and told you who they are and where they went. The Iranians are your enemies, but they are the Syrians' allies. The Israelis keep important secrets from you. Saddam, who was your agent in Iraq, is now fighting the Iranians and providing weapons to the Christians to fight the Syrians. And you might use the Soviets to eliminate the Marine bombing suspect. It's very simple."

"We don't need your political analysis or lectures," said Scott. "All we need from you is to infiltrate this outfit and help us terminate this guy. You know him by sight. I heard that you are bosom buddies.”

“I feel so much better—I thought only my country was a mess. What is your plan?”

“First we need to change your appearance, create a new identity for you, and send you to prison.”

“Why all the trouble? Send me to prison right now. I need a vacation.”

“We want you to go to the same prison as Ghassan and become his trusted friend.”

“Come again, please? What genius came up with that idea?”

“Think about it,” Scott said. “Once you’re a detainee with him, we will torture you and designate you as a high-value prisoner. Soon he will start to trust you and give you contact information. Upon your escape or release, you will make your way and terminate his brother.”

“You are forgetting some small details,” I pointed out. “Ghassan knows me by sight. He will recognize my accent even from another room.”

“This is why we saw the doctor,” he said. “We want to perform some surgeries to alter your appearance. We know you are a master of many Arabic dialects. Your identity will be created to suit the background we choose.”

“Why not pay some Russian sniper to take him out? They have access to their location.”

“We don’t know where Bassam and the QJ are. We need you to find out from the brother.”

“Do you think he even knows? And that he is just going to tell me? Torture him and he will tell you all he knows.”

“We don’t torture prisoners of war. I thought you wanted to find this guy—or are you changing your colors, like your boss?”

“You just said you were going to torture me to build trust with him. Why am I so special?”

"We are going to give him the impression that we are torturing you."

"Let's go back and see the doctor, scot Scott."

"One Scott is enough. Why do you always call me twice?"

"I will tell you once this mission is over, if I ever see you again."

The resources the CIA had at its disposal were immense. They were able to listen to practically all communications around the globe, friend or foe, wired or wireless. They scanned millions daily. Creating a new identity for me, including a background that would withstand scrutiny, was child's play for them. However, they failed to understand the cultural nuances and the different mentalities of their enemies, of which they have many. They were worried about human rights and scandals, the press and public opinion, the media and the polls.

The doctors decided no major work was required to change my appearance. A couple of minor changes were enough, mostly a nose job and a minor lift of the brows. I was told to let my hair and beard grow. I complained that my beard still had some red in it, and they suggested that I color it.

I laughed at this suggestion. "I can't maintain the dark color and visit the hairdresser on a regular basis during field operations. I also can't have the color on me."

"This is temporary, while you are in jail in our custody with the terrorists."

"What happens next, when we go out in the field?"

"None of these guys will ever leave here. When you are on assignment, we will create another disguise for you."

When most people do plastic surgery, they try to improve their looks, like making their nose smaller or their skin younger. Mine was the reverse. The doctors added to my nose—now it looked more hawkish—and my jaw was squarer.

During the recovery period, Scott and I spent countless hours going over the different locations and tactics of the various groups of terrorists operating in the Middle East and Africa.

"You know what your main problem is, Scott?"

"Enlighten me, genius."

"You guys are not brutal enough," I told him. "Your jails are like five-star resorts to these guys."

"What made you such an expert?"

"These guys mostly come from refugee camps. They live in small, crowded shacks for years, and they have no sewers, no hot water, no medical care. They fight for food and most of their basic needs."

"And your point is?"

"You don't see my point? You give them three healthy meals per day, an hour's walk in the sun, free medical and dental care. I would be shocked if they ever wanted to leave."

"It is no honeymoon," he said. "After you've been in with them, get back to me. I think you will change your mind."

"They are fighting to get their basic needs. You catch them, and you give it to them."

"What do you suggest we do with them?"

"A little torture does not work; it's like a little love or a little commitment. You have to have a deterrent strategy."

"What makes you such an expert?"

"If they know for certain—not just think it, but know it for certain—that if they commit terrorist acts against you, you won't only kill them, you will kill all their families and kin and maybe their goats and chickens and burn their villages, they will think hard and long before they do it."

"Are you insane? These are criminal acts against innocent people. If we do that, we are just like them. We as a civilized nation will become terrorists ourselves."

"There you go! You're not ready to fight this war, let alone win it. That is why you need people like me."

"Like you?"

"I don't work for you. I decide if I will accept the mission and the targets, not you. If I get killed, you don't care. I am not one of you, and if I get caught you deny ever knowing about me. And when I do your dirty work, you look the other way. Your hands are clean, and your conscience is clear."

"We have to be clean. We have policies and procedures."

"No, you are like Pilate, or like an ostrich, you look the other way and wash your hands and bury your head in the sand."

"Let's prepare you to meet your new roommates."

"They are here at the camp?"

"No way, not on American soil. We are only getting you ready here with a cover. Soon you will have to fly in order to spend time with your new best friends."

"Where will I be going?"

"That I can't tell you. If I do, I will have to kill you. And you are no good to me dead."

"Not yet anyway. Very funny, scot Scott."

"Have you thought of your cover yet?"

"I need to become Ghassan's cellmate and study his habits and tendencies. When I finish, I will become him. I have a plan."

"When you go to the field, you want to be him? And you think his brother will not recognize you? You're crazy. Your plan will fail, and they will kill you before you even get close to him."

"Remember I don't work for you or any of your

allies. I am not even an asset. If I get killed you have lost nothing."

"So, pick your background and let's get to work."

"It has to be a Lebanese, a Syrian, or a Palestinian born in Lebanon; these are the only dialects I have mastered. If we go with any other Arab alias, a native will recognize the small intricacies of the dialect. They will smell a rat and they will not trust me."

"We have no Syrians in that black site. You will be the only one, perfect. You will be a Syrian intelligence officer—a high-value terrorist."

37

FROZEN

PAUL:

I was surprised to be back in Israel after only few months; I was processed and detained at Camp 1391. To be in Israel with no PLO in the camp was unusual, since their prisons were absolutely filled with Palestinians. However, this wing was reserved for foreigners. The detainees were led in blindfolded and didn't know where they were. There was no natural light and most cells were solitary. This reduced the risk of Ghassan recognizing me. I was placed in the cell next to him.

The first few months followed a pattern. I would see Ghassan on the way to and from the interrogation room. We would chat together in whispers through the bars while sitting at the edge of our cells. After a few months, he started to trust me. I was the most interrogated of all the prisoners and showed more bruises. The Israeli guards had no idea about my cover; I was treated as miserably as the rest. The interrogations were staged, and the bruises were fake, to eliminate the possibility of a leak, but the prison guards has no idea who I was.

The six months I spent at Camp 1391 were mostly a waste of time, except for the conclusion that the Israelis were no better than the Syrians—and one small piece of information. Ghassan knew only that his brother was on his way to train and graduate suicide bomber students with the help of a Saudi millionaire. We already knew that, and that the Americans were supplying them with weapons to fight the Russians. However, during a long whispering talk one night, I asked Ghassan, "If you ever get out of here, are you going to join your brother?"

"No," he said. "I paid my dues. I am going to get him to give me some money and I will spend the rest of my life enjoying spending it."

"What about the jihad? You are just going to give it up?"

"I never wanted or understood the point of it, and neither did my father. But it was fun having the power, drugs, and girls."

"So your brother was the leader?"

"If it was not for him, I would have been married with three wives and a dozen kids by now. He is not even a true jihadist."

"Yet you are going to track him down and get him to help you financially?"

"That's the plan," he said. "I wouldn't go to Pakistan or Afghanistan. They will look down on me if I drink and party. I'll get my brother to send me the money or join me on a vacation somewhere fun."

"Do you have a place in mind?"

"We talked in the past about setting up a bar in Thailand as a front for recruiting. He called it his enrolment center. Show them a good time before they died for his cause."

"This is a great idea," I said. My mind was thinking, thinking. "You will live in a fun place, with great food, and warm weather. Party and have all the girls you want as a bar owner and still help him."

"We talked about it all the time; he knew we had to move our operations to more friendly territories, but I never wanted to go with him. He promised to set me up in Thailand."

It was strange to sleep in the cell next to my enemy, not that I slept much. I would wake up frozen. Actually, it was more like paralyzed. Most nights, the nightmares would come and when they did, Bassam was standing over my bed. I would awaken, absolutely certain he was there, in the room with me. I would feel my eyeballs moving under my eyelids, but I could not open my eyes. I would stay frozen for a long time, in a state of awareness but unable to move any of my body parts while I felt the yellow eyes staring at me. I waited for the fatal blow to come but it never did. Once I collected some courage, I would start moving a finger or two until I was able to open my eyes and not find him standing there.

You would think that I hated these nightmares, but you would be wrong. I loved them. I looked forward to them. They kept me focused and scared. My fear kept me alive.

The day after my Thailand discussion with Ghassan, I checked out of Camp 1391 and boarded a flight to see my surgeon in the U.S.

Now I needed to look like Ghassan. I was sure it would not fool Yellow Eyes, but it would work on the messengers. These guys operate in small, independent cells, and we needed them to get the message to Bassam that his brother was in Pattaya, Thailand, partying his ass off and waiting for financial help.

BASSAM:

After Pakistan, the QJ moved to Afghanistan—they were told by the Saudi millionaire who they called Sheikh Osama to set up a training camp for his army. He had many soldiers and was recruiting more every day. The weather was terrible, and they lived in caves like rats; the food was not fit for pigs, but the opium was plentiful. There was no alcohol and no women to party with. They were very strict about their religion.

Bassam, sitting in a cave smoking his *argile* laced with opium, was furious and muttering. "My own guys that I brought with me are unhappy. The money I brought is also useless because there is nothing to buy with it. It is hidden away and safe, but it is equal to toilet paper right now." He sighed.

"And where is my brother?" He and Mohamed just vanished. My contacts in Lebanon have no idea where they are, the airport records show that he left the country a few months after he went home for a visit. I am not sure whether the exit records are fake or real. Why would he leave without contacting me?

"I have to find him. I will start dropping hints in the different cells, with a nice reward for the person that gets me some news about him. Ghassan would have died here."

38

TO THE LAND OF SMILES

PAUL:

I had to shave my head and grow my beard. I colored it once a week to keep it dark. I had no problem with the hair, but I hated the extra weight I had to carry with a padded belt under my clothes. Ghassan was fat, and I had to walk and move like him. It slowed me down. I could not take a chance of my cover being blown in case somebody took pictures. I started hanging out on Pattaya's Soi 16, where most of the Arab cafés and restaurants were located, smoking *argile*, playing *tawle*, and meeting people.

One of the regulars started asking questions. "Where are you from?"

"I am from Lebanon," I said. "How about you?"

"I am Egyptian, but I like the Lebanese food better. How long have you been here?"

"A couple of weeks. How about you? Do you live here full-time?"

"No, I am in and out—I come here on business."

"Here on business? Is there any other business going

on here beside the bars, hotels, and restaurants?"

He just smiled and shook his head. Then he asked me how long I was planning on staying here.

"I am waiting for my brother to join me," I said. "He is working in Afghanistan right now."

"Oh, what a coincidence. That is where my business is. What kind of business is he in?"

"I am not entirely sure. We lost contact a while back. I think he is working for a Saudi sheik?"

"I know a few Saudi businessmen over there. Give me his name—maybe I can find him and say hi for you. I am leaving soon and will be back in a couple of weeks."

I gave him Bassam's name and told him to give him my best. "If you find him, tell him to come and visit. I will wait for him here."

The next day I did not see the Egyptian. I kept my cover going. I was staying in a cheap hotel on the Soi and ate my meals in the same neighborhood. I kept my workouts to a minimum since I needed to keep the flabby look. I wore loose-fitting clothes and kept my head shaved and my beard dark. I did not visit the mosque. I played a lot of *tawle* and smoked my brains out on *argile*.

My contacts were getting worried that the plan was not working. One morning, the front desk called and asked if I would receive a guest delivering sweets. I turned the TV channel to 59, the lobby camera, recognized Scott, and gave them the go-ahead. I turned the TV on as loud as I could and opened the door.

"Scot Scott, what brings you to the Land of Smiles? Trying to get infected and start smiling for a change?"

He cracked an almost full smile, which must have felt odd. I told him to keep his voice low.

"You are still the clown." His face returned to the familiar scowl. "First, I found out what 'scot' means and I do not find it funny. Second, I don't think we are getting any closer with this operation. We might have to change plans.”

“I like it here, the weather is nice, the beach is beautiful, people smile all the time even when they don’t mean it, and the food is excellent.”

“You’re not on vacation and you’re costing us money.”

“Calm down, Scotty, or I will beam you up. I am on a very low budget. It costs less here per month than if I was in Europe for a day. Also, I am making progress.”

“Where are your weekly reports?”

“I am not writing any reports, for two reasons. One, I don’t work for you, and two, in case you missed it, this is a black operation and there will be no communication until I need an extraction.”

“Can you at least catch me up right now? I need to give my boss something.”

“This guy killed more Americans than anybody I know, he bombed your embassy and barracks. Now you are helping him and his boss Sheikh Osama train Mujahedeen. They will turn on you, believe me. He is like a growing cancer; removing him is like finding a vaccine.”

I told him about the Egyptian businessman trying to locate Bassam in Kabul. I asked Scott to check out the Egyptian—I had the impression he was being evasive. There was nothing concrete, just his body language and manners. My instincts had kept me alive so far, and I trusted them.

BASSAM:

The Egyptian friend of Sheikh Osama started asking questions about the origins of the QJ. First, Bassam was going to tell him to fuck off, that it was none of his business, until he mentioned he had met a Lebanese in Thailand who was asking about the group.

"His name is Ghassan," he said. "He looks a little older and heavier than you, Bassam, but he is Lebanese. He told me he has a brother working in Afghanistan."

"In Thailand, you say? Where in Thailand?"

"In Pattaya. The sheikh owns a medical import-export company we use to buy medications and medical equipment. The offices are in Pattaya."

"Pattaya, not Bangkok? Most companies are located there."

"Pattaya has a port, and we can ship some things in and out without detection. I don't want to bore you with the details."

"He told you his name is Ghassan? On your next trip can you take a picture of him?"

"I don't like pictures. I will not pose for one, or take one. However, I'll get a disposable camera and have a couple of guys from the office take a couple for you."

Bassam was hopeful, maybe it was true and Ghassan had stuck to the plan. If they got separated, they were to meet in Thailand.

39

HELPING THE WATCHERS

PAUL:

I could feel it: somebody was watching me. I had noticed a couple of guys following me and one ahead of me. Classic Box protocol, they were not professionals but they used classic tradecraft techniques. When I doubled back, one of them bent down to tie his shoelaces—he was wearing sandals. I almost felt sorry for him. I wanted them to follow me. I made it easy for them to snap pictures of me, though I always wore a hat, and kept a full beard, even with the surgical enhancements. I was sure that from a distance and with the poor quality of the camera, I could pass for Ghassan. Finally, I was making progress.

The Egyptian, whose name was Ayman, showed up a week after I noticed the two stooges taking my picture. He acted like I was his long-lost cousin. He gave me a hug and a slap on the shoulder and invited me to his table.

We ate falafel and hummus, drank Turkish coffee, and slowly smoked a couple of *argiles*. He took his time with small talk before he started his interrogation. "I think I found your brother," he said. "He is working with a friend of mine."

"Are you serious? What are the odds?"

"If you know where to look, as I do, nothing is impossible. Can you confirm a few facts for me? He is not sure it's really you. He said you vanished into thin air more than a year ago."

"It is a long story that I will tell him when I see him. Is he going to visit?"

"That's up to him and the sheikh. Where exactly do you come from?"

I told him the name of the town and my parents' names—that is, Ghassan's parents' names—then he asked me what school I had gone to and who was with me when I failed to show up. I answered without a second's hesitation, as I knew those facts and had most of Ghassan's life memorized. This seemed to please him immensely.

"I see you here often but I never see you at the bars picking up girls," he said.

"I have a girlfriend but she is visiting her family up north for a while."

"I will pass your regards on to your brother. Do you want to send him something with me?"

"Just give him my best and ask him to visit. I am on a budget. If he can help, tell him maybe we can buy the bar that we talked about."

I gave him that piece of information as a hook without him asking for it—a small hook but effective. Only the two brothers knew about it.

Three weeks later, Ayman came back and asked me to register a company, a bar, in Thailand using his lawyer. I would be the owner. He took my passport and information and probably made a copy of it. The money was a gift from my "brother," who would be coming for a visit soon.

"He also told me to make sure there is a private, secured room in the back, with a few couches and *argiles*."

"Tell him I understand and all will be ready."

Bassam was asking for the private room and *argiles* because he liked to smoke opium. He needed comfortable couches to sleep it off, and a back door for discreet access. He used cocaine regularly in Lebanon but switched to the more relaxing drug while in Afghanistan, the world's largest producer of opium. If you're not using opium in Afghanistan, it's like you are in the USA and have never seen a baseball game, or in Canada and never watched a hockey game. Using the stuff is the national sport. They have over one million addicts.

The sale of the bar was completed. It came with an experienced *mamasan*, who was the staff manager and recruiter, and we had over twenty young Thai girls working full-time. Lewis joined me soon after as the acting day-to-day manager while I prepared the private backroom for the royal visit. As for me, I was running a whorehouse and selling opium. These girls were mostly from dirt-poor families and were being exploited. I had become Bassam. I hated me, I hated what I was doing, but it needed to be done. I focused on the greater good, knowing I would be saving hundreds, if not thousands, of innocent lives if I could take out these men.

Ayman came back, we treated him like a king, with four girls to entertain him and keep his *argile* pipe and his whiskey glass full. To me, this was a test drive, a dress rehearsal for opening night. A few hours later, he came out of his coma and joined me at the front.

"Thanks for coming, Ayman," I said. "How was the service?"

"I am so pleased," he said. "The girls are gorgeous,

the whiskey is excellent, and the products are top quality. Your brother is going to be impressed. I will tell them. He might bring a friend for a vacation. I will let you know."

His slip of the tongue did not escape me: he said he would tell "them." The money was probably from the Saudi sheikh; I hoped Bassam did not bring him along. He was a high-value CIA asset, and I was not cleared to take him out. If he showed up, I would probably have to kill him anyway. Bassam, on the other hand, was a must for them, as payback for the bombings at the embassy and the barracks. Crazy world.

As the days flowed into nights and the nights into days, the routine got to me, but Lewis was having the time of his life: he was posing as an Iraqi enjoying every minute in the bar. He was even giving the *mamasan* a hard time about the girls' schedules and bar fine quotas. Every girl had to get a certain number of drinks purchased for her by the client and or pay the bar fine. The bar fine was the amount paid to the bar by the client when he took a girl out for a short time or a long time; this was to make up for the loss of income when she wasn't working.

"Lewis," I reminded him, "we are here on a mission. Stop being so fussy. We need the bar to be happy and working until he shows up. If we lose this *mamasan*, how are we going to start recruiting girls? I need the place to look busy. It doesn't have to be profitable."

"I can make it both. Relax—if we don't care, the staff will start wondering. It's part of the cover. I was born to run a bar."

"No, you were born to smuggle diamonds and kill terrorists—plus, this is a bordello more than a bar."

"Best kind of bar: all the clients leave happy."

"Look, just in case we receive an unexpected visit, I will make myself scarce the next few weeks. Call me only if Ayman shows up. If Bassam drops by, tell him that you will call me and I will get here quick. And don't forget your Iraqi accent. Lately, you have been mixed up."

"It's because the staff and clients don't know the difference."

"Get in the role, in case he sends somebody ahead to check us out."

I could not sleep anymore. The nightmares came and never left, even during waking hours. I stopped eating and working out. I'd waited many long years for this encounter and spent countless hours thinking about how, when, and what. I would get my revenge for all the innocent people and the fallen comrades. Would I be able to look him in the eye and kill him? I kept my CIA contact in the dark whenever possible, providing only vague details; these guys liked to run the show, and I did not want them screwing things up for me.

Yellow Eyes was mine. I made him that promise at the end of our driveway in 1975, and I would keep it. I watched the bar every hour of every day from a rented room across the street.

I was pacing the room as usual, driving myself insane with anticipation and my ADHD, which was kicked into overdrive by the tedious waiting, the hardest part of any mission. Suddenly, I spotted two figures entering the bar. The first one was tall, a giant, over six-foot-six, with a thin build and a long, black beard. He was wearing the traditional Afghan dress, a cap and loose-fitting, light linen garb designed for ease of movement, called *shalwar kameez*. The second man was dressed in jeans and shirt, and he was short but powerfully built. He did not turn around, but I did not have to see his face to recognize him. I felt him. This was the companion of my nightmares.

I called the bar. Lewis and I spoke in a prearranged code.

"The tall one keeps looking at me and smiling, maybe he is gay, or he has the drop on us, Paul. Keep your eyes open for any backup they might have brought."

"Describe the stocky one for me."

"He is asking for Ghassan and wondering why you are not here. I told him you were in Bangkok and coming back soon."

"Concentrate: what does he look like?"

"Like a typical Arab tourist. He can pass for anybody, dressed in jeans and T-shirt with the Deep Purple band logo. Except . . ."

"Except what? Does he have any distinguishing marks?"

"No, but his eyes are such a light hazel, they look almost yellow I am going to change my glass eye to this color. I think women will like it."

"Where are they now, and what are you doing?"

"Like you told me, I am serving them myself, to keep an eye on them. They are drinking Chivas 18. I've got five girls sitting with them. The tall one does not smoke. Hazel Eyes is waiting for me to bring him his *argile*."

"Spike it with the purest of pure, and get them as drunk as possible. I will sit at the bar and wait for your signal that all is ready. Get the girls out of the room—we don't want to hurt them. We've gone over this a hundred times. Are you packed?"

"Oh, yeah, for many days now. What do we do with the tall one? He was not expected."

"If he is who I think he is, we need to do everything possible not to hurt him. He's probably the one they call Sheikh Osama, and he is a special, high-value CIA asset. If we harm him, it will piss them off. The U.S. will turn on us. I don't want to pay another visit to Camp 1391."

"They want Bassam because he killed their diplomats and Marines, but we are to keep his buddy happy because he is fighting the Soviets for them? What the fuck?"

"Hang up and go to work."

40

TILL DEATH DO US PART

PAUL:

I shaved my beard and took off the padded belt I had been wearing around my waist for the last four months. It was hot and uncomfortable, and I was happy to get rid of it. I waited an hour for the party to get going and the whiskey to flow. I entered the bar wearing glasses, a baseball cap with no markings on it, jeans, and a plain black T-shirt. I changed my accent and ordered a Singha beer, a Thai brand popular with the tourists. The bartender and the *mamasan* did not give me a second glance.

Lewis came out of the back room, where Bassam and his Arab friend were partying, and winked at me with his remaining eye. I almost laughed. We joked about his winking sometimes, and I would give him a hard time, saying "Lewis, when you wink, be careful where you're walking, since you can't see anything with the only good eye closed."

I grabbed a corkscrew from the bar while the bartender was looking the other way. I did not need much of a weapon. I could do this with my hands or a pen, even with a laminated menu. I walked casually toward Lewis and together we went to the back room. His job was to keep the tall guy out of harm's way. We had agreed to do our best not to kill him unless it was necessary. Lewis was confident he could subdue him, as he was not tall but he was powerful.

To keep the girls safe, Lewis got them out of the back room. I made my way toward the closed door. I opened it slightly, started to peek inside—and froze. The giant was standing inches from me, just behind the door, smiling at me. That split second would have cost me my life if the tall guy had wanted to kill me. Instead, he smiled at me and called me by my childhood nickname, which I had not heard in a long time.

"Boulous," he said, "the corkscrew is too messy. Take this."

He handed me a garrotte wire. What was going on? Why would he want to kill his buddy? How did he know my nickname? The room spun while I stared at him. His smile became wider as recognition spread across my face. He was tall and thin, he had those almond-shaped eyes, and under the beard I could see the birthmark on his right cheek. Then he spoke in a coded language known to only two people on the planet.

"Do it, Bro," Rami said. "And then follow me through the back door."

I followed my old friend to the couch, where Bassam was in a daze, sleeping off the effects of the opium-laced *argile*. I crawled onto the cushion beside him, put my hand on his back, and shook him gently. I wiped my palms on my jeans, but his stink was on me now.

"Is that you, Ghassan, my brother?" he mumbled. "I have been looking for you for a long time."

"I have been looking for you almost my entire life." He and I had the same Lebanese accent and small town dialect, and in his state he could not differentiate between his brother's voice and mine. He just smiled and sat up with his arms spread wide.

We hugged for a few seconds, my skin burning where he touched me, and then I said, "I never got married because they say 'till death do us part.' I could not make that promise twice. I made it to you first, after you killed the cousins in our hometown in 1975, remember?"

He was looking back at me, slowly coming out of his high. As Americans say, he was having a rude awakening.

"*El Shaytan Alahmar*! I am going to kill you!" he hissed back at me.

He moved his hands to my throat to choke me. I smiled. I had spent years being choked during martial arts grappling matches, and he was not that skilled. I considered showing him how to do it right, to taunt him before I took away his last breath.

Instead, I put the garrotte around his neck. Usually the garrotte is applied from the back of the target for maximum leverage. However, we were hugging like lovers, and I wanted to see his yellow eyes one last time. I applied pressure, his eyes grew bigger, and he let go of my neck and reached for the wire. I was using a double-looped garrotte, so every time he pulled on the wire, the second loop tightened. He struggled and kicked but I wrapped my legs around him tighter. I took my time. A minute passed, my fingers started to go numb. Finally, I released the pressure as the yellow eyes turned to hazel, then to brown.

I pushed him off me.

I jammed the wire into my pocket and walked out the door.

A half block down the street, I could see the familiar, tall figure striding away from me. Glancing back, I saw Lewis a half block behind me, on his way to the U.S. embassy in Bangkok. Rami was probably on his way to the airport. I hailed a taxi and told the driver to take me across the border, to Phnom Penh. This was not like telling the driver in Montréal to take me to Edmonton. This time, I knew where I was going and I had money.

EPILOGUE

The middle-aged Thai taxi driver drove so slowly, I felt I could have outrun the car. The distance between Pattaya and the Cambodian border was about 460 kilometers as the birds fly, usually a nine-hour drive.

The driver tried to communicate with me about the fare. His English was broken and his accent incomprehensible; my Thai was not much better. He was worried that I couldn't pay him, not so late at night. His body relaxed when I handed him 10,000 bahts. But then he became too relaxed, and if he drove any slower, we would be going backward.

I needed to get out of Thailand as quickly as possible. I could not fly or take a ferry; there were no direct trains, and by tomorrow the Thai police would be looking for me. I did not trust my CIA liaison officer and so did not go to the U.S. embassy in Bangkok, as I had been instructed to do. The overnight ride suited me fine. We would make it to the border by morning and miss the long lines.

The driver figured I was going on a visa run and kept asking me if he should wait for me at the crossing to take me back to Pattaya and double his fare. Most foreigners staying in Thailand longer than the thirty days allowed on an entry permit will cross to Cambodia or Vietnam and renew their visa. I did not answer any of his questions and kept contact to a minimum. I did not want him to remember much about me when the police interrogated him.

I tried to go to sleep but my instincts did not permit me. I was sure that if I stopped watching the road, the driver would slow down even more. I did not want him falling asleep and killing us both. That would have been ironic. Frankly, I was running out of extra lives. We kept exchanging looks in the mirror.

After a couple of rest stops, we made it to the border.

Even before the driver made a full stop, five guns were drawn and directed at me. It was not the cops. These guys were plainclothes from the ISOC, the Thai Internal Security Operational Command, the equivalent of Homeland Security in the U.S. I knew instantly that my buddy Scot Scott had connections, and he wanted me back under his thumb immediately. There was no reason to play hero. I knew when to fight and when to roll with the punches. I exited the car and put my hands up. The last thing I needed was a nervous guy with a happy trigger finger.

Slowly and carefully, I turned around and assumed the required position. I was searched and patted down for weapons. The guy lingered a too long for my liking on my legs and private parts. I had dumped the garrotte I used on Yellow Eyes, so I had nothing on me beside my perfectly fake passport (courtesy of the CIA) and a large wad of cash. I said a silent goodbye to the money. I was handcuffed and pushed into the backseat of my waiting limo.

Out the window I saw the scared taxi driver pointing and talking at the same time with one of the officers. He moved his hands so much; he must have had some Lebanese in him. I asked the officer in the front seat where we were going and why I was being arrested. He stared ahead and did not answer any of my questions. Then I started to worry. Perhaps Scot Scott didn't want me back in the U.S. after all. I asked, "Are we going to the Big Tiger?"

This was better known as the Bangkok Hilton. The prison was nicknamed Big Tiger by the Thais because it "prowled and ate." The prison housed many foreign prisoners. It was a harsh place, where death row- and long-term prisoners are sent. All prisoners are required to wear leg irons for the first three months of their sentences. Death row inmates have their leg irons permanently welded on.

Again I got no answer.

I thought this guy was the silent type. Then the three Thais started talking over each other, in their language. I was having difficulty following the conversation. But I got what I wanted when I heard two words I understood: "black site."

The CIA operated many such sites throughout the world, and the prisoners were usually high-value terrorists. They had no legal rights and officially didn't exist. *Thanks, Scot Scott,* I thought. *See you in hell.* Now I was to be treated as a terrorist—after delivering the most wanted man on the CIA's hit list.

I did not blame him for his disloyalty. I would have been shocked if he had not betrayed me.

He was a CIA officer, and I was a counterterrorist operative under contract. I assumed going into this mission that once it was completed, I would be arrested—which was why I was trying to make it to Cambodia. I'd picked the wrong driver, but even the fastest driver could not outrun the telephone.

Yellow Eyes was dead. I slept, dreamless, waking rested on the hard metal cot. I stood, looking out a small prison window, jogging in place, silently planning my exit strategy. Meanwhile, the Terrorist Universities continued to breed, sprouting campuses across Europe. The CIA still needed me, they just didn't know it yet.

I bided my time. They'd be back.

ABOUT THE AUTHOR

A.E. Sawan grew up in the Bekaa Valley on the outskirts of Zahle, Lebanon during the 1975-1990 civil war. By the age of twelve, he and his family had been forced to move five times, refugees in their own country. As a young Christian Lebanese, he was detained and tortured by the Syrian army and the Palestinian Liberation Organization, the PLO.

He was recruited and became a trained counter-terrorist operative, with a talent for diffusing bombs, while working mostly behind enemy lines. He now lives in Canada.

For More News About A.E. Sawan
Signup For Our Newsletter:

http://wbp.bz/newsletter

Word-of-mouth is critical to an author's long-term success. If you appreciated this book please leave a review on the Amazon sales page:

http://wbp.bz/ghosta

Also Available From WildBlue Press

Hardened mercenaries Stan Mullens and Frank Giordano are fighting their way across the Congo jungle, having been sent to track down and kill a charismatic diamond miner, Tonde Chiora. But their victim is full of dangerous surprises, and the jungle offers more opportunities to die than to kill. Struggling to survive in the dark heart of the Congo, Stan begins to question his old loyalties – and his tenuous belief that he is still one of the good guys.

Read More: **http://wbp.bz/hdtka**

**Available from
Colin Campbell and WildBlue Press!
BEACON HILL: A RESURRECTION
MAN THRILLER.**

Former British cop Jim Grant is back in Boston, now a fully-fledged member of the Boston PD based at Jamaica Plain. Working the nightshift for fellow detective Sam Kincaid should have been an easy job but after saving a kidnapped child from a blazing house and attending a drive-by shooting in Beacon Hill it proves to be anything but. The trouble is that the wealthy target, Daniel Hunt, doesn't want to complain and Grant's bosses try and shut him down. Grant isn't one for shutting down and it doesn't take him long to discover that Hunt wasn't the intended target. After a foiled robbery and a squashed dog, the case turns personal, then the stakes really go through the roof.

http://wbp.bz/bha

See even more at:
http://wbp.bz/cf

More Crime Fiction You'll Love From WildBlue Press

HEADLOCK by BURL BARER

A paranoid recluse lures Jeff Reynolds into a complex web of deception, where delusions are deadly, life after death can be hell, and all roads lead to the McFeely Tavern.

Edgar winner Burl Barer spins a unique and wondrous mystery from the opening paragraph to the spectacular cinematic climax featuring one of the best plot twists in PI history.

wbp.bz/headlocka

SAVAGE HIGHWAY by Richard Godwin

From an internationally acclaimed author of noir thrillers comes *"the road novel from hell"* (Castle Freeman Jr., author of The Devil In The Valley). Women are disappearing on the highway, a drifter hunts the men who raped her, and a journalist discovers the law has broken down. An *"irresistible hard-boiled read that's reminiscent of old school black and white noir."* (Vincent Zandri, New York Times bestselling author).

wbp.bz/savagehighwaya

LOCKOUT by John J. Nance

The newest aviation thriller from New York Times bestselling author John J. Nance. *"A wild ride in the night sky."* (Capt. "Sully" Sullenberger, author of New York Times bestseller Sully). Whoever electronically disconnected the flight controls of Pangia Flight 10 as it streaks toward the volatile Middle East may be trying to provoke a nuclear war. With time and fuel running out, the pilots risk everything to wrest control from the electronic ghost holding them on a course to disaster. *"As good or better than any of his previous works. Hop aboard Pangia flight 10 - if you dare."* (Charles Gibson, former anchor ABC World News)

wbp.bz/lockouta